CONFOUND IT

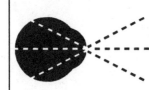

This Large Print Book carries the
Seal of Approval of N.A.V.H.

A DREAMWALKER MYSTERY

CONFOUND IT

MAGGIE TOUSSAINT

THORNDIKE PRESS
A part of Gale, a Cengage Company

Farmington Hills, Mich • San Francisco • New York • Waterville, Maine
Meriden, Conn • Mason, Ohio • Chicago

Copyright © 2018 by Maggie Toussaint.
Thorndike Press, a part of Gale, a Cengage Company.

Thorndike Press® Large Print Clean Reads.
The text of this Large Print edition is unabridged.
Other aspects of the book may vary from the original edition.
Set in 16 pt. Plantin.

LIBRARY OF CONGRESS CIP DATA ON FILE.
CATALOGUING IN PUBLICATION FOR THIS BOOK
IS AVAILABLE FROM THE LIBRARY OF CONGRESS

ISBN-13: 978-1-4328-6562-7 (hardcover alk. paper)

Published in 2019 by arrangement with Camel Press

Printed in the United States of America
1 2 3 4 5 6 7 23 22 21 20 19

To my siblings,
Cathy, Carol, Ginny, and Cliff

ACKNOWLEDGMENTS

They say it takes a village to raise a child. It may take two villages to keep a writer straight. I have been blessed with a discerning critique partner in Polly Iyer. So much of my work is sharper because she challenges me to go the extra mile. My husband Craig Toussaint is a great sounding board and brainstorming partner. Much of my network is so entrenched I tend to take it for granted. My late mom and my sisters have always encouraged me, as have childhood friends Suzanne Forsyth and Marianna Hagan. I am ever appreciative of my readers, especially those who have taken a shine to this Dreamwalker Mystery Series.

CHAPTER ONE

With her thick braids and lush figure, Sister Cipriona Marsden always turned heads. If not for her family situation, she could've graced any fashion runway. I knew who she was, of course, since Sinclair County, Georgia, is so sparsely populated. We'd never met, until a moment ago when she walked through my back door. She'd parked her clunker on the grass behind my house. I guess she didn't want her clients to see her car at a dreamwalker's house.

I had begun to welcome clients into my home, so Cipriona's phoned request for an appointment today was part of my new normal. I'd listen to her request, cross the veil to deliver the message, and return to find another satisfied client. Among other things, my special talent allows me to pass messages from the living to their deceased loved ones. I am still new to this dream-walker job, still new to embracing my extra senses, but I love helping people in this regard.

Some people call me a psychic, but I'm more comfortable with a dreamwalker label. I come from a long line of people with extrasensory abilities. Being the Dreamwalker means that locals and cops come to me when they want to contact the dead. Every request brings new challenges on both sides of the veil of life.

After greeting Cipriona, I served her iced tea and a slice of my father's homemade coconut bread. She devoured both so quickly, I gave her a second helping. As she ate, I made a mental note to send her home with several bags of fresh vegetables. Palm reading must not pay as well as dreamwalking, which routinely netted me donations of food at my back door. I welcomed the groceries since my family never charged for dreamwalker services.

"Thanks, Baxley." Cipriona blotted her lips with a napkin. "I didn't realize I was so hungry. Nerves, I guess. I've never visited a Dreamwalker before."

I'd never met a palm reader before, so we were even. Her aura pulsed in an odd way, and it wasn't pretty. Whatever was troubling this woman was affecting her entire being. Poor thing. When she came in, I sniffed the herbs in her modest sachet necklace and saw her distinctive anklet, a dime on a chain. Unusual jewelry for most folks in Sinclair County, but it worked with her gold and brown leopard-print dress.

"No reason to be nervous. I'm here to help," I said. "What can I do for you today?"

"Before I say another word, I need your assurance you won't tell a soul I came here."

"I can keep a secret." Seems like I was bound to repeat these words over and over again in my new career. Between me and my father, who'd been the County Dreamwalker before me, we must know most of the secrets in the county. The title "County Dreamwalker" was a relic from an earlier time. As far as I knew, I was the only official Dreamwalker in Georgia, though there seemed to be others around who could traverse the veil of life.

"Um-um, girl, I wish I had your striking hair. That theatrical accent would be great for my business. How'd you dye it so snowy white?"

A demon had held me over the fire, scorched my feet, and scared the living daylights out of me, along with my hair color. That was how, though Cipriona wouldn't hear it from me. "Trade secret."

She nodded in understanding. "This gig

11

must pay pretty well. You got a really nice place."

Glancing around, I tried to see my home through her eyes. The overall vibe in the kitchen ranked between well-used and vintage, but I loved living here. "I inherited this place from my grandmother. All the furniture came with the house, which was lucky, because I sold my furniture before I moved back home. It feels nice to have her things around me. I feel connected to her."

"I love my granny too." Cipriona's eyes welled with tears. She sniffed a few times. "Granny Elmira's in prison for killing my dad. That was her legacy to me. I got her trailer, though it isn't near as posh as this."

I remembered the story from the paper. Elmira shot her toxic son multiple times because she'd had enough of his aggressive, drunken behavior. The cops couldn't keep him in jail because people were so scared of him they wouldn't press charges. Rumor had it Damond killed his wife years ago, but there was no proof.

By all accounts, Damond was a terrible excuse for a human being, while Elmira had been the backbone of her church community. She'd singlehandedly raised her granddaughter. Apparently, even saints had their breaking point, because Elmira took

12

out her son with a Glock.

"This is hard for me to admit," Cipriona said. "I don't have Elmira's sight. I'm purely faking it with my palm readings, so I can't speak to spirits. My clients believe I have psychic abilities I don't possess. Anyway, Elmira is stuck in prison. I wish I could spring her, but the lawyer exhausted all the appeals. The only way to save Granny is to prove my dad murdered my mom. We need new evidence. If I can prove she did society a favor, maybe she could get out for time served. She's all the family I got left. I have to save her."

Cipriona was shaking so badly and her aura pulsing so erratically, I needed a way to calm her nerves. I'd secured all our pets, three dogs and two cats, in my daughter's bedroom as soon as Cipriona arrived. See-ing how upset the woman was, I knew our Chihuahua would help her.

I gently cleared my throat. "Excuse me just a minute."

Cipriona dabbed the tears from her face with a napkin and nodded. I dashed upstairs and extracted Elvis from the pack sleeping on my daughter's bed. He licked my face. Little Elvis was a therapy dog, and I hoped he'd work his usual magic on my current client.

When I strolled into the kitchen with him, Cipriona's face lit up. "What a cute doggie."

"His name is Elvis, and I would like you to hold him."

She took the dog and snuggled him close. Elvis rewarded her with a few licks and nestled in her arms. I watched as she cooed at the little guy, her tears drying.

"Thanks," Cipriona said. "You're good at this."

"I'm lucky to have a strong support system, but every client's needs are different. I can't promise you we'll help your granny. Even if I can find your parents on the Other Side, spirits don't always cooperate. Some of them are hostile and hold a grudge."

Cipriona didn't look up from stroking the Chihuahua. "I understand, but I have to try. I love my granny."

The woman's aura cleared with each second she held little Elvis. But something was bugging me about Cipriona, and I couldn't quite put my finger on it. "Another thing you should know is that time isn't the same over there. If I have to locate two spirits, it could go really fast or it might take all afternoon. My daughter will get home from school in an hour. If I'm still dreamwalking, will you and Elvis make her an after-school snack?""

"Sure."

I took a deep breath. "All right then. To begin, I need objects that belonged to your parents. I mentioned them to you when you booked the appointment earlier today."

"I don't have anything from my mom. She died so long ago, and we moved a lot. I brought you a pair of my dad's suspenders." With one hand still holding Elvis, she bent at the hips to retrieve them from her large purse.

The brown elastic suspenders were stretched out of shape, and the metal clasps in front had lost their gold plating. I gestured for her to place the item on the table. A cold chill coursed through me. I'd be searching for a man who had murdered his wife, a man so heinous his own mother had killed him.

"Two questions. What I should ask Damond? What's your mother's name?"

Cipriona's brief smile didn't reach her eyes. "Zaidee. Ask him why he took her from me."

"Here's the deal. I have no doubt I'll find Damond, but spirits are peculiar. Some of them speak to me, while others only show me a scene from their life. What evidence do you hope he'll reveal about your mother's

15

death? The murder weapon?"

"His meat-fisted hands are the murder weapon. He beat my mom nearly to death, then he started on me. My mom rallied to jump on his back, and then he strangled her, right in front of me."

Cipriona's aura pulsed and flashed like a thunderstorm. What a horrific scene she'd described. My heart went out to her again. "How old were you?"

"Nearly five."

"Did you tell the cops what you saw?"

She recoiled. "Hell, no. I didn't want him to kill me. He stayed away for a long time, but he came back when I was seventeen. That was bad. Bad, bad, bad."

"What happened?"

"He said I looked just like Mama and that I owed him. That she was dead because of me." Her voice trailed off to a whisper. "He climbed in my bed and tried to. . . ."

I got the message. Gritted my teeth. "Did he?"

"I screamed and screamed. Granny came running. Told him to get out of her house. He said she couldn't make him, and if she didn't watch her mouth, he'd beat the life out of her."

It was so quiet I could hear the faint tick of the wall clock, the electrical hum of the geriatric refrigerator. "Then what happened?"

"Granny shot him. In the pants. And the face."

I wanted to hug her, but I didn't want to spook her. At the same time, my sixth sense stirred again. Something was off about this account. Perhaps the father had indeed done something terrible to Cipriona, and she didn't want that to be known. No parent should betray a child like that.

I gently cleared my throat. "The things you've seen. I'm so sorry."

Cipriona shrugged. "At the time, I thought everybody had the same troubles. But that's in the past. I've got a life now, and I need to help my granny. I couldn't tell the cops what he'd done to me, not if I wanted to hold my head up in this town. Granny paid the price for my pride. Get Damond talking. See if he'll brag about other crimes, or killing my mama, so we can prove Granny did humanity a favor and that he wasn't the upstanding citizen his lawyer said."

My teeth ground together at the way her voice broke. Her last words rang true and convinced me she needed an advocate and possibly a miracle or two. "I'll try."

CHAPTER TWO

My palms tingled as I stared at the suspenders on the table. I'd made arrangements for Larissa, I'd heard the client speak the truth about her plight, but something in the air besides the musty spices around the woman's neck made me hesitate. I wished my medium friend was here instead of visiting his daughter in Florida. It would be nice to have the extrasensory backup. "Is there anything you're not telling me?"

Cipriona shrugged. Nerves. Had to be. With company coming later today, I couldn't afford to dither, so I set aside my misgivings, reached for the suspenders, and opened my senses. After crossing the veil of life so many times, I knew what to expect. The weightlessness. The feeling of falling. The unrelenting darkness. The numbing cold.

Dreamwalking was no picnic, and this journey into the afterlife proceeded as expected. Once I reached the spinning stage, I righted myself until my feet touched down again. Not my actual feet. In this other realm, I'm in spirit form only.

Gradually the fog thinned, and I found myself outside a bar. The dim light over the door illuminated a painted sign, Low Spirits Bar. There was nothing else in the murk, no wandering bad-boy spirits, no guardian angel, no nothing. Which meant Damond Marsden was inside or he wanted me to see this place.

I entered through the door, and the gloom didn't lift. "Damond?"

"Back here."

Feeling like I was blindfolded, I edged in the direction of his voice. "I came to see you."

"I don't want to be seen. Go away."

"You're spending the afterlife sulking in a bar?"

"What's it to you, lady? A man's entitled to a drink every now and then."

His voice sounded slurred, as if he'd been actually drinking. How was that possible? "My name's Baxley Powell. I'm a Dream-walker. Your daughter asked me to find you."

He muttered something I couldn't hear. I kept inching toward him, hands out-stretched. "What's that?"

"Don't trust that witch."

I stopped short at the half-truth ringing in his words. What part was truthful? The not-trusting part or the witch part? "I don't understand."

"Cipriona and my mother are thick as thieves. Always have been. Always will be."

"Why are you telling me this?" I stopped, upset with him for keeping me in the dark. "Why are we here?"

"I got nowhere else to go. Nobody wants to see me looking like this."

Irritation coated my voice. "Like what?"

A spotlight shone on Damond. I gagged at the raw flesh and bone of what was left of his face.

"I'm a freak. She did this to me."

"You don't have to look like that," I hastened to explain. "All you have to do is imagine how you looked before you got shot."

"What if I don't wanna? What if I'm sitting here waiting for her to join me in this hell? What if I want to scare the shit out of my own flesh and blood?"

I gulped, or what passed for a gulp in spirit form. "You have the power to change your appearance at will. You can look like yourself at any point in your life."

"For real?"

"I'm no afterlife expert, but that's been my experience with spirits I've contacted."

The spotlight winked on again. I braced for gruesomeness, but I saw a kaleidoscope of faces. Damond the man grinned at me, Damond the handsome young adult winked at me, Damond the teen pointed pistol fingers at me, and Damond the little boy looked like he needed a hug.

"Whoa!" I said. "You don't need to be everyone at once."

"But I like this. Why didn't anyone tell me?"

"Have you talked to anyone?"

"Nah. Two young kids tried to catch me as I arrived, but when I turned around the girl screamed until she thinned out to nothing. The guy followed her. After that I kept to myself."

"You don't have to stay in here. You can leave the bar."

"Don't wanna go anywhere. If you found me here, this is where she'll find me."

"It doesn't work that way. People like me can find you wherever you are."

"In that case, I'm gonna hop me a Harley and do a wheelie out of this dive."

"Wait! I need something from you."

"Of course you do. You're a woman."

"No need for sarcasm. Your mom's sitting

21

in prison because of shooting you. Your daughter wants to help her. She wants you to help spring your mother."

"She killed me. I won't help her."

He had a one-track mind. I had a sinking feeling I was wasting my time. But I had to try, for Cipriona's sake. "I understand that's how you see it, but if you could remember the woman who raised you, who bent over backward for you and shaped you into the man you became, perhaps you'd want to do the right thing here."

"What?"

"Because you killed your wife. Is there anything that will support that claim? Or are there other crimes you'd confess to that might help your mother get a reduced sentence?"

"Lady, I didn't kill my wife."

"Cipriona said she saw you do it. She saw you beat your wife. Cipriona said she tried to stop you but you hurt her and then killed her mother in front of her."

He settled on the adult version of himself, prior to being shot in the face. His eyes flashed demon red. "Lies."

My spirit self took a step back. "You didn't kill your wife?"

"I loved Zaidee. We was going to have us another baby."

22

"If you didn't kill your wife, who did?"

"Ask the witch."

Not this again. He was talking to me, but his answers didn't go anywhere. "I'd like to ask Zaidee. Know where I can find something that belonged to her?"

"Good question. How long've I been dead?"

"When'd you die?"

He named a year. I did the math. "Two years."

"She been gone more'n twenty. Doubt anything of hers remains."

"Her daughter."

He glared at me. "Stay away from Cipriona."

The malevolent look had me glancing down to make sure he hadn't seared a hole through my body. I seemed to be whole, so I continued, "Why?"

"She's not who she seems." With that, a motorcycle revved, and Damond scratched off.

Dang. So much for an easy case. I'd found him, but I'd gained nothing. Worse, I would have to deliver the bad news to my client.

CHAPTER THREE

I awakened in my chair, alone in my kitchen with a pair of ratty suspenders in my hand. My mouth was so dry I wished I'd left a glass of water on the table for myself. Something stirred at my cold feet. Crazy thoughts of gigantic boa constrictors filled my head. I shook them off and glanced down.

Elvis.

The little Chihuahua barked at me and raced laps around the kitchen. I glanced at the clock. A few minutes before Larissa's bus. Where was Cipriona? I called her name and got no answer.

On shaky legs, I made it to the sink for water. I drank greedily, then wiped my mouth. No jalopy in the backyard. My client had left? How odd. People who requested news from the dead always stuck around to hear what I'd seen or heard.

I reached for my phone, found the last

number that called me, and hit redial. Cipriona didn't pick up so I left a message at the beep. "I found your father, but he wasn't helpful. I'm sorry that I don't have better news for you or your granny. Please let me know what you want to do with these suspenders."

I pocketed my phone and tried to figure out why I felt so disoriented. I didn't like Damond Marsden at all and I believed Cipriona was right. Her granny had done the world a favor by taking out Damond. The air still smelled of the herbs Cipriona wore about her neck. I opened the back door to let fresh air in and then went up to release all the pets. The simple actions of walking around and doing normal things helped restore my equilibrium. I took a moment to sit on the back steps and watch the dogs romp in the yard.

My phone rang, and I didn't recognize the number. Since my cell doubled as a business phone for my landscaping and pet care services, I answered accordingly. "Pets and Plants, this is Baxley Powell."

"Mom! The school bus got stuck. Can you come get me?"

Larissa. My daughter. The urgency in her voice propelled me to my feet. "What? Are you all right?"

"Yes. I'll tell you all about it when you get here. We're just past the twisty-turny part of the road, where that new bike path is going in."

"I'll be right there."

Sure enough, the school bus was stuck in the sand. Deputies Virg and Ronnie directed traffic, and they motioned me through. I drove past the bus, did a three-point turn to reverse course, and parked my truck. Inside the bus, Larissa tugged on the bus driver's sleeve. Mrs. Rowe looked my way and nodded. My ten-year-old daughter darted along the sandy shoulder and climbed in with me.

Like me, Larissa wore a ball cap, though hers was pink and mine was green. Her long, honey-colored hair was still neatly confined in a braid down her back, while my shoulder-length locks were mostly clubbed in a ponytail. Her emerald-green eyes, so like her father's, sparkled with excitement.

"Did you see them?" Larissa asked, cuddling Elvis, whom I'd brought along for the ride.

I pulled out and headed home. "See what?"

"The fire trucks. Three of them passed the bus. That's when we got stuck, when we

26

pulled over in the fresh sand."

"I didn't see or hear any fire trucks, but I just finished a client dreamwalk. Nothing's on fire between our house and here."

"Must be a big fire somewhere. Can we go see it?"

"How long ago did they drive by?"

"About twenty minutes. I had to wait my turn to use the bus driver's phone."

Twenty minutes. I'd been dreamwalking. Did hearing the fire engines cause Cipriona to bolt?

I scanned the horizon. Nothing remarkable in the sky. "I don't see a column of smoke."

"The fire has to be nearby. If it was more than five miles past our place, the city trucks would've taken the highway instead of this state road."

Good point. Probably not a car fire if three trucks from the city had been dispatched to the county. But to merit that many trucks, it had to be a forest fire, except the sky wasn't smoky. I couldn't smell smoke either.

What did that leave? A house fire? A boat fire?

"Mom? Can we find the fire? I'm sure it would be educational."

"Ha! Trying to manipulate me, are you?"

She grinned. "Is it working?"

"I'll do you one better." I reached for the phone and hit the third number on my speed dial list. "I'll find out where the fire is, and if it's safe for us to go."

Tamika answered the dispatch line at the sheriff's office. After I asked her about the callout, she said, "No biggie. Just a house fire in the woods. Wayne sent a unit out there and determined the fire department didn't need our guys for traffic control. Good thing, since we've got two crews of deputies trying to get that school bus unstuck."

Made sense, but something nagged at me. "Should I be concerned about the fire spreading? My house is surrounded by woods. So is my parents' place."

"It's a good four miles from your home as the crow flies, a bit longer by road," Tamika said. "You and your parents should be safe. The sheriff said the doublewide is a total loss, but they have enough fire trucks out there to hold the line."

"Where is it?"

"Bartow Road. Wayne says don't go sticking your nose in the fire. He's got plans this evening."

I had plans this evening too. Two upstate deputies were coming to camp out in my yard. I'd been cleaning the yard, porch, and house for a few days now. It dawned on me I hadn't sprayed off the outside chairs by the fire pit. A thick layer of dust, pollen, and mold coated the outdoor furniture.

"Thanks for the info."

I ended the call and turned to Larissa. "We can visit the location after they've put the fire out, tomorrow or the next day. Bartow Road is so narrow, we'd be in the way today. They'll be having a time getting those fire trucks turned around. On the other hand, I forgot to hose off the chairs by the fire pit. What about some hose fun?"

Larissa's hopeful expression wavered. "Okay."

Not quite a ringing endorsement, but this was better for both of us. It would be safer. So why did I feel like a heel?

A few more miles and we were home. My best friend's trusty sedan was parked in the drive. I pulled up beside it. "Look who's here."

Larissa glanced around and pointed to the brightly colored lump on our steps. "Something's wrong with Aunt Charlotte."

CHAPTER FOUR

Her sobs reached me inside the truck. Charlotte was crying as if her heart had been ripped in two. What had happened? We rushed to her side.

"Charlotte, what's the matter?" I asked.

She lifted her head and stretched out her arms toward me. Larissa glommed onto Charlotte as well. "I can't do it," my friend managed between sobs.

Tears dotted the inside of Charlotte's glasses and streamed down her cheeks. Her lower lip trembled, a narrow ribbon of pink in a wan face.

"What on earth?" I searched her face and smoothed her hair away from her brow.

Charlotte keened through her sobbing, "I'm a fraud, and he'll know."

Was this about Duncan, her new boyfriend? "Whatever has you upset, we can fix it. I promise."

She yanked off her glasses and used broad

arm gestures to underscore her words. "I lead a boring life. He'll see that I'm the small-town newspaper reporter everyone takes for granted. He'll see I'm the invisible woman around here, and it will change everything. He'll wake up from the romantic dream that I never want to end."

Definitely about Toby Duncan. I gently stroked her back. "I know you two have been talking every night. He wouldn't call you if he didn't like talking to you."

She sniffed in several ragged breaths. "I can't hide who I am here," she said. "He'll see the real me, not vacation me."

I glanced over at Elvis. He'd finished doing his business in the flowerbed and was headed our way. Seemed like Charlotte needed to hug a therapy dog right about now.

"It's okay, Aunt Charlotte," Larissa said, scooping up Elvis and handing him to her honorary aunt as if she'd read my mind. "He likes you. You like him. The attraction goes both ways."

Charlotte set her glasses beside her on the steps and buried her face in the dog's short fur. Elvis slinked around and licked Charlotte's wet face. "I'm a hot mess. I tried cleaning my house, but it's no use. There's too much stuff to put away, and I can't part

31

with anything. What people say about me is right, Baxley. I am a hoarder." Her voice sounded less desperate, more resigned.

"It doesn't matter, Char. You are who you are. If Duncan doesn't appreciate you, he doesn't deserve your time and attention."

"Easy for you to say." Charlotte yanked off her glasses and wiped her face on her magenta sleeve. "You've always had guys chasing you. I've never been so lucky. Duncan may be the only man who ever shows an interest. If I blow this, I lose my chance at being a couple. I lose my chance of having kids. I should leave town and not answer my phone all weekend."

She shrugged us off and lumbered to her feet. "That's what I'll do. You tell Duncan I got called out of town on an assignment."

I tugged on her arm. "Sit down. I'll do no such thing. You have every right to a relationship and a family. If this guy doesn't work out, you'll easily attract another. There's plenty more where he came from."

"I don't want anyone else." Charlotte plucked an invisible piece of lint from her royal-blue shorts. Though it was September, the temperature registered in the eighties. "I want Duncan."

"Then stay and fight for him. Don't let fear make you stupid. That's not your style.

Treat this weekend like a story you've been chasing for a while. Be yourself. That's what's important."

"I'm embarrassed for him to see where I live. Can I stay here?"

"You're welcome to stay."

"Great. I could tell him I'm having some work done on my place."

Her sudden gaiety struck a false note. Duncan was a cop. If he was any good, he had a nose for the truth. Poor Charlotte. I wanted her to be happy. "Better not to lie."

"I'll figure something out."

"Do you need to zip home and get your things?"

"Nope. I have a bag in the car." She managed a shaky smile. "I was pretty sure you'd talk me off the ledge. If not, I was heading over to St. Simons to hole up at the beach until the guys left."

We hauled Charlotte's gear inside and moved her car. We'd just started hosing the furniture when a horn beeped.

They were here.

CHAPTER FIVE

Before the truck pulling the RV came to a complete stop, Toby Duncan leapt out of the passenger side and bounded toward Charlotte. Though their romance had a supernatural start a few weeks ago, it seemed to be a real thing.

I deposited the chair I'd been carrying next to the others Charlotte was hosing down. My friend turned and gasped when she heard him call her name, soaking me with the hose in the process. I shrieked like a girl, but I retreated to give them privacy. What a romantic guy! Duncan swept Charlotte into an embrace worthy of the big screen.

The hose fell to the ground, so I turned off the valve at the side of the house. Joy and happiness radiated in waves from the reunited couple, making me glow by virtue of proximity. Charlotte was finally getting her shot at love. Lucky duck. The screen door behind me banged open, and Larissa streamed out with all three dogs.

Sam Mayes stepped out of his truck, lifted his dark glasses. He looked good in my yard. A silly thought for sure, but he definitely seemed at ease. We were both five feet six, but he was built warrior-solid while I tended to look lanky. His Native American heritage showed in his high cheekbones and strong nose. As was his custom, he'd worn his long hair tied back in a low ponytail.

Our gazes locked, and the air around me became supercharged with electricity. Even at this distance, I felt his virtual hug. It enfolded me like a cozy blanket straight out of the dryer. Shamelessly, I relished the sensation of such exquisite caring and basked in the heat of his desire.

Then my daughter careened into Mayes, and he tore his gaze from mine and engaged her in conversation. We'd met and parted as friends, Mayes and I, but everyone knew he wanted more. He'd promised he wouldn't push, that I could set the pace and terms for our relationship.

Instantly, the memory of the virtual kiss we'd shared under a waterfall flashed into my thoughts. Maybe it was the wet clothes that triggered the memory. Maybe Mayes was thinking about it. Maybe it was me.

Life with Sam Mayes would be sensual and rich in ways I'd never experienced. At times, he could read my thoughts, and if I allowed myself, I could tap into his. But I still saw myself as married, even though the military had declared my husband dead.

I couldn't.

I shouldn't.

"Mom!" Larissa shouted.

I snapped out of my reverie to find Mayes standing before me, a question in his glittering, dark-brown eyes. As I drank in the sight of his chiseled body, I extended my hand in greeting.

He took it and drew me into a bear hug. Despite my best intentions to keep our relationship platonic, I was caught off guard by the emotions swirling through me. A gulping sob escaped. I'd missed seeing him. Holding him. Sensing him.

"Shh," he said, stroking my head and back. "I've got you."

And he did.

I held on for a few more precious moments, indulging my need for physical touch. Heat built, and moisture steamed from my clothes.

"Love the wet T-shirt look, Powell," he murmured in my ear. "Very sexy."

Restraint surfaced, and I pulled away to

gather myself. "Welcome to the Georgia coast."

"Thanks. I love the scenery." He bent down to calm the dogs clamoring for his attention, petting Maddy the black lab, Muffin the Shih-Poo, and Elvis the Chihuahua. He surprised me by picking up Elvis. Darn if the little dog didn't nestle under the man's chin and moan contentedly.

Larissa tugged on Mayes' arm. "Are you a dog whisperer like my mom?"

"No one's like your mom," Mayes answered, standing. "But this little guy is one of us. He seemed concerned about something, so I offered him comfort."

"He does seem more relaxed now," I added, wishing I'd scrubbed the wry note from my voice.

Mayes mouthed a silent question. "Jealous?"

I glared at him. Nothing good could come of examining my gut reaction to his presence. I needed to set some boundaries and make sure he realized this was a friendship, not a courtship visit. Holding hands and sneaking off like Duncan and Charlotte just had wasn't in our near future.

"Let's get the camper slotted behind the greenhouse so the driveway's free for vehicles to come and go," I said. "Y'all want to see the local highlights this evening, or would you rather take it easy?"

Mayes rolled his neck and handed Elvis to my daughter. "I'd just a-soon relax after that long drive. This is a sweet place you've got here, Powell. Feels good."

"Wait till you visit Mama Lacey and Pap's place in the woods," Larissa said as she accepted the Chihuahua from him.

"I'm sure it's nice, but this place has everything I'm looking for." He pointed at the greenhouse. "Show me where you want the camper. I'd hate to run over any of your beautiful plants."

He thought my plants were beautiful? My eyes went a little misty. "If you don't mind, Larissa will show you the area while I finish hosing the chairs. We'll figure out supper next."

"Oh." He hesitated. "I brought plenty of steaks for the grill. I hope that's all right. I forgot to ask if you ate steaks."

"We do, and thanks."

As we got our visitors settled, my thoughts went haywire. Mayes was here. Larissa liked him. The dogs approved. Elvis adored him. There had to be a downside. Oh, yeah. I was married.

After a delicious home-cooked dinner,

Mayes and I relaxed at the campfire. Duncan and Charlotte left to check out her place, a huge step for her. I suspected, given that they couldn't keep their hands off each other, they'd spend the night over there.

As twilight deepened, Larissa and the dogs went inside to watch her favorite TV program. So she said. I had a feeling she was matchmaking.

"You working a case now?" Mayes asked.

"It's been quiet here. No murders, no petty theft. I had a routine dreamwalk today for a client concerned about her granny in prison. What about you?"

"No open cases on my plate right now either, though Dr. B's after me to form a cold case team of people like us."

Dr. B was Dr. Gail Bergeron, the state archaeologist, and I'd worked with her on several cases. She'd been calling me as well. Though she meant well, her arrogant and demanding nature made dealing with her a series of skirmishes. I'd ignored her calls. "How many of us are there?"

"You and I are the only ones I know of in law enforcement. My sheriff tried working with several psychics over the years, but it never worked out. Old-fashioned police work solved those cases, not charlatans."

"Given her negative experience, it's a

wonder your boss wanted my help on the energetic vampire case."

A slow smile filled his face. "As I said earlier, you're in a league of your own."

I blushed at the compliment, hoping the heat of the fire would hide the evidence of my discomfiture. "It's not like I sought this vocation out. You make my abilities sound focused and professional. I'm neither, and except for the last six months of my life, I've blocked my paranormal senses. If the dreamwalker job hadn't been literally killing my dad, I wouldn't have accepted the responsibility."

"But you did. Accept it."

"Yeah. So?"

"That took guts." The fire crackled for a bit. Lightning bugs danced at the edge of the woods. "You don't seem like a novice. You seem very tuned in to your extra senses."

"I've been figuring stuff out, but I had help from my parents and friends."

Another silence settled around us, an easy one. A full belly. Good company. Starry skies overhead. I could get used to this.

We made plans for the next day, plans that included a boat ride with my dad to the barrier islands and a picnic lunch. Dinner would be a gathering at my folks' place.

The dawn call I received changed everything.

CHAPTER SIX

Sheriff Wayne Thompson did a double-take when he picked me up for the new case. My mom had collected Larissa ten minutes ago, and Charlotte and Duncan had yet to surface. They must still be at her place.

Good for her.

Good for them.

Wayne and Mayes sized each other up like sumo wrestlers looking for a takedown opportunity. Wayne still carried the lean shape of his football quarterback days, and he had a few inches of height on Mayes. Turned out, the men had mutual acquaintances, and in less than five minutes they were yucking it up like old friends. Wayne even called Mayes' boss to get him assigned here for the case.

Mayes told Wayne he wasn't letting me out of his sight. I would've been annoyed if he'd said anything else. Mission accomplished, and the three of us rode in Wayne's

Jeep to the scene. Surprise, surprise, a body had been discovered in the ashes of yesterday's house fire.

"The trailer is a rental, according to the property records," Wayne explained on the way. "I've got a call in to the landlord, but so far he hasn't returned my calls."

Charlotte would be sorry to have missed this call-out. As a newspaper reporter, she lived for breaking news. If her rival reporter at the newspaper got the story, she'd be ticked. I shot her a quick text message about the fatality, but she didn't respond. She and Duncan must be totally wrapped up in each other.

"What caused the fire?" I asked.

Wayne met my gaze in his rearview mirror. "Fire chief said the place was a meth lab."

"Shouldn't your guys have known about the cook site?"

"Meth labs are a universal problem. We have so much territory to patrol in Sinclair County, so many foreclosed homes that could be drug labs, not to mention occupied homes where people are cooking, that we could work nothing but the meth angle for weeks and still not eliminate the problem."

Beside me, Mayes cleared his throat. "We're seeing a lot of shake-and-bake labs

43

in north Georgia. Earlier this week a deputy stopped a couple walking down Main Street. They were acting strangely, so he asked them a few questions. They got twitchier by the second. Fortunately, he'd already called for backup. Both the guy and his daughter had portable meth labs in their backpacks made from plastic soda bottles. The little girl was making drugs in her kiddy-character knapsack. Hard to believe."

"I hate that," I said as we zoomed past orderly acres of pine timber. "What kind of lowlife turns their kid into a walking meth lab?"

"A dumb one," Mayes said. "Especially since it turned out poorly for the dad and the kid. Another case of someone not thinking things through."

Meth labs used dangerous chemicals. Flammable ones. How could this be a good idea for us to investigate? "Is it safe to go inside?"

"The house will be cleared before any of us are allowed inside," Mayes said. "Hazmat has been out there since daybreak. And we're doing everything by the book in this one. Because of the drugs and the fatality, the Georgia Bureau of Investigation has been notified."

I hadn't worked any cases with the GBI,

and truthfully, I wasn't looking forward to it. Wayne and his deputies always moaned and groaned about the state big shots.

"Got a name for your GBI point of contact?" Mayes asked.

"Burnell Escoe. He's new to the region. You know him?"

"Don't recognize the name. But I could ask around if you like."

"No need. We have to work with him. If he's got issues, we'll learn them soon enough."

"Is he already at the scene?" I asked.

"Coming down a little after lunch. That's why we're documenting everything and playing by the rules. I do not need the GBI breathing down my neck. I've already had this talk with my guys at the station. You two, be mindful of what you say and do around this guy. Any problems with him and you come to me. Understood?"

I nodded. After a while, so did Mayes.

The coroner's van and a cluster of other emergency vehicles were already on site when we arrived at Bartow Road. My dad waved a greeting as he zipped on his official coroner coveralls, alongside his helper, Bubba Paxton. Deputies Virg and Ronnie rolled out crime scene tape along the property frontage, but they stopped when the sheriff waved them over. In their spiffy Class A khaki uniforms, these men resembled competent cops. I knew otherwise, but these good ole boys came with the job.

As they approached, I noted the hub of activity over at the Hazmat side of things. A row of containers occupied a plastic drop cloth on the ground. Two people wearing white head-to-toe protective suits exited the building and headed for the tarp. They carried empty soda bottles.

I introduced Mayes to everyone. My dad hugged him. Everyone else did the manly head bob of acknowledgment.

"We've got to do things in order, Tab," Wayne cautioned my father. "Don't remove the body until we clear the scene. We can't get inside until Hazmat clears it. Speaking of which, everyone, gather 'round. Meth labs have their own protocol. All of us will wear Hazmat suits to enter the building as a precaution."

Bubba Paxton groaned out loud. "That suit is as hot as summer pavement."

The fire chief broke away from the Hazmat unit and strode toward us. Harvey Foster was about ten years my senior. His tall, lean physique gave him an advantage over the other men present, every one of them shorter. He wore ash-coated yellow

46

boots, a white Tyvek suit, and a respirator around his neck.

"My cousin, the arson investigator, has been assisting me and the Hazmat team today," Foster said. "Not that I suspect arson, but I wanted a second set of eyes out here. Gene and I combed the site looking for the ignition source. A mobile home this old, we felt sure it would be the wiring, but the incomplete burning had us puzzled."

"And . . . ?" the sheriff prompted when Foster ran out of words.

"That's when we found the body. It's charred pretty badly in places, but we think it's an adult female, given the clothing. I should add, based on the contents of the closets, it appears a female and a male lived here. Possibly a mother and son from the clothing sizes."

My stomach clenched. I'd never seen a burnt corpse before, and I wasn't looking forward to having that image etched in my mind. Worse, what if it was the son who'd died? I shuddered.

Mayes wrapped an arm around my shoulder. Instinctively, I edged closer to his warmth.

The sheriff shot an annoyed glance our way before glaring at the fire chief. "Anybody besides Hazmat and fire been inside?"

"Nope."

"Is it safe for my people to enter the house?"

"We didn't find any pockets of fire or hot embers and cleared the place for Hazmat. They brought out the last of the container from the meth lab just now and gave the all clear. It's safe, but your people should still exercise extreme caution."

"You've got photos of the lab?" Wayne asked.

"We do. You'll have full access to our findings and reports, and we'd like the same courtesy from you. Plus, we'd appreciate you not moving anything but the body. We have yet to determine the cause of the fire."

"Gotcha covered." Wayne turned from the fire chief. "Virg and Ronnie, you guys go next door and find out who lived here."

"Hold up," Ronnie said. "I already know. The Pig Woman."

Wayne shook his head. "What?"

"The Pig Woman. Jerk next door must've filed half a dozen complaints about her blasted pigs."

"The woman with the pot bellied pigs?"

"That's the one."

"What's her name?"

"Mandy Patterson."

Wayne studied the ground a moment. "It's

48

coming back to me now. Mandy's pigs turned up their noses at their pig-chow dinners, escaped under the fence, and got into the dog-food bag on the neighbor's back porch. The guy nearly had an aneurism telling you about it, right?"

"Yep. Good ole Ricky Dixon. He's wound tight, that's for sure. If his wife wasn't bedridden, he'd be a permanent bachelor because no woman would put up with his sh—, uh, stuff."

"Head over there anyway. I want a statement from him about what he may have heard or seen. I want to know where those pigs are. Take Powell with you so I know if he's lying."

He was sending me away from the scene? I didn't want him to think I couldn't do my job. I pushed away from Mayes' protective arm. "I can do it," I said. "I needed a moment to prepare for seeing the charred body."

Wayne snorted. "Sometimes I forget you're a chick, Powell, but I can read you like a fast-food menu. This is the best use of your time. Dixon is important. He's either a witness or a suspect, and I need your take on what he says."

His words didn't ring quite true. My spine stiffened. "I said I can do it."

49

"Sure you can, but Mayes is a cop. He's seen burn victims before. He'll assist me because he wants in on the case. With the fire department's approval, I'll collect one or two personal items belonging to the victim, and you can go inside the place once we remove the corpse. Right now, I need you next door with my guys."

Crap. I was being sent away on the "B" team. Simultaneously, Mayes had been promoted from spectator to "A" team. Good ole boy networks never died.

Though my pride smarted, I couldn't deny I was glad to be granted a respite on the viewing. Wayne was doing me a favor, so I should hush and be gracious about it.

"Virg, let's get that statement stat," the sheriff said.

"Roger that, boss man." Virg cocked his head at me. "You ready?"

I nodded and gathered my thoughts. I might not like being sent away, but I would do my assignment. As a police consultant, I needed to let my abilities be tasked however the sheriff deemed fit. Didn't matter about the temporary demotion, I'd do my job. I would get justice for this victim.

"If this guy doesn't cooperate, I'll light him up with my Taser," Virg announced as we trudged down the dirt road to the neighbor's home.

Ronnie laughed, an affable giggle with a sinister twist. "Go git 'em, Virg."

Having been on the wrong end of Virg's Taser before, I didn't wish that experience on anyone. "You will not. The object is to gather information, not have this man sue the sheriff's office. If he won't talk to you, I want a crack at him."

"No way he's gonna talk to you. I'm telling you. This man's crazier than a sprayed roach."

CHAPTER SEVEN

"Shuddup!" A male voice bellowed at the chorus of barking hounds that heralded our arrival at the concrete-block home. The noise level didn't abate until one dog yelped. Had he kicked his pet? I'd never met Ricky Dixon before, but I disliked him already, even if he was caring for his bed-ridden wife. If his animals looked mangy or malnourished, I was siccing Animal Control on him.

Nature was reclaiming the concrete-block house, from the thick carpet of leaves and Spanish moss on the roof, to the vines and swamp funk creeping up the sides. A porta-ble air conditioner droned in the nearest window. An array of old semi tires and ropes dotted the front yard in a semi-circular pat-tern. They looked like dog tie-ups to me. Not a water bowl in sight.

Another strike against this man.

The door creaked open and a slight, wiry

man stopped in the threshold. Four hounds crowded around beside him, all glowing with canine health. "You. What you want?" Dixon snarled, accenting his question with a belch.

Ricky Dixon's missing teeth didn't bother me, but I wasn't crazy about the early morning beer breath or the long greasy hair. Good hygiene and sobriety were important in my book. Fortunately, the smell of his breath quickly dissipated in a mouthwatering aroma of roasting meat that wafted out the door.

"We want to talk with you about your neighbor, Ms. Patterson," Virg said. "Did you call and report the fire?"

"I don't know nuttin' 'bout no fire, and I ain't gotta talk to you." Dixon puffed up his bantam-sized chest. "I got rights."

"No one's accusing you of anything," Ronnie said. "We want to know if you saw anything unusual yesterday, or if you noticed something different next door yesterday. We're asking nice-like for your cooperation."

Dixon took another pull from his beer. "I noticed that woman didn't come outside yesterday and holler for her pigs. That's what I noticed."

"When's the last time you saw Ms. Patterson and her son?" Virg asked.

"You need to arrest that no-count son of hers. Doodle's in and out of there at all hours of the night. When he cranks up that car, the exhaust backfires loud 'nuf to rouse the dead. I've called y'all about his disturbing the peace, but he's long gone when your deputy gets here."

Virg made notes on his pad of paper. "You see Doodle Patterson yesterday or last night?"

"I never look over there when I drive by. Bad for my blood pressure. I ain't seen that boy in months, but I hear his god-awful music all the time. It ain't music at all, just a lot of angry talking and thumping bass. It oughta be a crime to call that crap music. But that ain't the worst of it. All that junk in the yard. They's all the time hauling in more things to fix in that front yard. Ruining my property value, that's what they're doing. That boy is a bad seed, I tell ya. I don't want no truck with him or his kind that come around when his mom goes off with her slacker boyfriend."

I glanced around Dixon's weed-infested yard. Since I was a landscaper, I considered myself a pro in this field. It would take a solid week of pruning to turn this place into a welcoming area. Dixon couldn't be too concerned about property values, not with

54

the state of his yard.

"What kind of people?" Virg prompted when Dixon ran out of steam.

"Those skanky friends of his, that's what. The beanpole girls don't hardly wear any clothes a'tall. The guys look rough. Sooner you haul him off to prison, the better."

"What about Ms. Patterson?" Virg asked. "When did you last see her?"

"I dunno, man. I usually hear her over dere, calling those danged pigs. 'Soooooey, Sooey, Sooey.' Now she's got this three-legged goat what comes over and bugs me. Cain't you write her a citation or somethin'?"

Virg leaned in close. "Speaking of her pigs, any idea where they are?"

The scrawny man edged backward. "Them people are whacked out. Seriously messed up."

"How so?" Ronnie said.

Dixon shot an exasperated glance over at Ronnie. "Anybody that'd bawl over a missing pig is a loon in my book."

He'd sidestepped the question about the pigs' location. We needed that answer. "What happened to the pigs?" I asked.

Dixon shrugged. "Don't know. Cain't say. Don't care."

This was getting us nowhere. I edged

between Virg and Ronnie. "I don't believe you."

"Why'd I lie?" Dixon said. "I hate pigs, unless they's the eatin' kind."

He spoke the truth about wanting to eat the pigs. What was going on here? "Did you do something to the pigs?"

"What's it to ya, lady?"

"Answer me."

"Nah." He chugged more beer. Burped again. "Don't think I will."

"You must've seen something," I said, softening my voice and reaching out to pat his arm.

He lunged away from me, stepping on a hound. The dog yelped and scurried away. "Yowsers," Dixon said. "No touching."

Dang. I thought I'd been so smooth. I retracted my hand and jammed it in my crystal-filled pocket. The energy from the crystals counterbalanced the negative juju steamrolling off this angry man.

"Hold the bus." Dixon waggled a finger in my direction. "I know who you are. The psycho what helps the cops."

Ronnie's giggle got nixed by his partner's glare.

"Mrs. Powell is a police consultant," Virg stated with authority. "She's a psychic."

"Big whup. Take Ms. Goody Woo-Woo

56

Shoes next door and let her do her circus act over dere. Ain't got nothing else to say."

"So you didn't see or hear nothing and you don't know anything about Ms. Patterson's pigs," Virg confirmed.

"Persackly. Y'all go on about your bidness."

Virg dug in his pocket and withdrew a crumpled card. "Here's my number if you remember something later."

The man took the card, read it, and tossed it on the floor. "Don't know nuttin' about the fire or no loud noise either."

Virg had already turned to walk down the wooden steps, but he stopped. "Loud noise?"

"Don't know nuttin' about that. Woke up me and the missus, 'sall." With that, he slammed the door in our faces.

"She-ite," Ronnie said as we trudged up the dirt road to the burnt trailer. "We got diddly. The sheriff's gonna be pissed."

"We got plenty," I said. "The son's name is Doodle. The pigs are missing. A three-legged goat is missing. A loud bang occurred at the same time as the fire. And Ricky Dixon hates his neighbors."

"We knew that last part afore we even went next door," Virg said. "What's your Spidey sense tell you?"

"Dixon told us the truth, but he's got secrets."

"What's wrong with your foot?" Ronnie asked.

I hadn't realized anything was wrong with my foot, but sure enough, I wasn't putting all my weight on my left foot. "Must be something in my boot," I said. "There's a sharp pain in my heel."

"Uh-oh," Ronnie said, his rounded face squeezed in a scowl. "Somebody's done put the root on you."

"Don't be ridiculous," I said. "There's no such thing as putting the root on anyone."

"Sho 'nuf is," Ronnie said. "Get yourself some of your mama's herbs to wear around your neck."

Herbs around the neck. I knew something about that, only I couldn't call it to mind because I was focused on this case. Dixon's secrets may or may not be relevant to his neighbor's death. The place was a meth lab. What parent raised a child in a meth lab, for goodness sake?

"You believe in hoodoo, Ronnie?" Virg asked.

"I believe in taking precautions. You should too."

Once again, the cops closed ranks, walking ahead of me. I limped along, unable to

58

step on my left heel. Virg had said hoodoo, but I was sure he meant voodoo. I couldn't put any credence in his remarks, but danged if I could dismiss them either. Until I knew more about what we were facing with this case, I'd keep my eyes and ears open.

CHAPTER EIGHT

Back at the Patterson home, the activity level had dropped from beehive frantic to good ole boy coffee klatch. All the Hazmat and fire people had their suits half peeled off. Most sat inside their air-conditioned vehicles drinking bottles of water. The sheriff, my father, Bubba Paxton, and Mayes were nowhere in sight.

"Get your sweatbox suit on," Virg said. "I'm sure the sheriff will want you inside."

"What about you?" I asked, eyeing the open boxes of Hazmat apparel under the nearest tree. From what I'd seen of the people suited up, these suits came in XL and XXL. I'd be swimming in one, that's for sure.

"Me and Ronnie is on crowd control, plus I gotta write up Screw Loose's statement."

No stray people were watching the scene, but that didn't mean a carload of folks wouldn't drive by at any time. I understood the need for outside guys, but since I'd been excluded from the indoor team earlier, I was less certain about my odds of getting inside.

I sat beside the tree, unlaced my boot, and checked out my left heel. No rocks in my shoe, nothing poking in my skin. Hmm. Was there a chance Ronnie had called it with voodoo? I'd ask around to find out if we had local practitioners, but only if the pain in my heel persisted. I assumed I'd stepped wrong and bruised my heel.

Duct tape proved to be a necessary accessory to my protective gear. I taped the size XL suit to my rubber boots and gloves. Before I donned the respirator and the hoodie, I crossed the yard to stand beside the coroner's gurney parked at the concrete-block stairs.

"We're back, and I've suited up. May I come inside?" I hollered through the doorway.

I heard movement inside, then someone appeared at the door, carrying a crate of bagged evidence and a camera. Wayne placed the crate in the doorway, removed his respirator, and nodded at me. "Just give us a sec in here. What'd you find out next door?"

"Mandy Patterson and her son Doodle live here. Mr. Dixon mostly ignored them except when the pot bellied pigs became an issue. He doesn't care for the son at all. Loud music and lousy taste in friends were the reasons he gave."

"Virg writing it up?"

"He is."

"Good deal." He glanced over his shoulder and then grabbed the crate and moved toward me. "Here they come."

My father, Bubba Paxton, and Mayes walked out, carrying a black body bag. They laid it on the gurney, and as one, pulled their hoodies down, yanked off the respirators, and unzipped the suits. All three men were slick with sweat. Though it was late September, the temperature today was easily mid-eighties.

"What'd y'all find out?" I asked, noticing a trickle of moisture already running down my spine.

The men glanced at Wayne. "Our vic is a woman, most likely Mandy Patterson," Wayne said. "We'll need a medical examiner to give cause of death, but it appears there are no other obvious signs of trauma."

"The fire killed her? Why didn't she run out the door?"

"Until the ME completes the autopsy, we won't know."

Virg and Ronnie ambled over. "Them pigs

62

are missing," Virg said. "And they's a three-legged goat, too, someplace 'round here."

Wayne nodded and tried to hide a smile, but couldn't. "I'm gonna take Powell through the place and then we'll turn it back over to the firemen. Virg, you're staying on crowd control. Ronnie, you're on critter patrol. If Burnell Escoe from the GBI arrives, get him outfitted and point him in my direction."

Virg and Ronnie jostled their way back to the cruiser.

I turned to Mayes. "What about you?"

Mayes pointed to the cluster of emergency vehicles. "I want to talk with the fire guys. I may be able to expedite their sample processing with my upstate connections."

"They'd appreciate that," I said.

"We got what we came for," my father said, "so we'll head out. See you at dinner, Baxley."

"I could use a shower," Bubba Paxton said as they walked away. "I'm soaked to the bone."

Dad and Bubba maneuvered the gurney over roots and around odd bits of trailer in the yard. "You can get a shower at our place," my father said.

"And then there were two," I said when it was just the sheriff and me. "What's your take on the inside?"

"One room is mostly gone. I assume that's where the fire started, probably the meth lab. We found the vic in the bathtub."

"In water?"

"Not really. My guess is she was showering when the fire broke out. That would explain her lack of clothes. One wall collapsed over the tub, which saved her from a complete burn, but she lost a lot to the fire."

"Will I see her?"

"Not like that, if I have anything to say about it. I gathered some of her belongings for you to do your touch test, so we should be good. I want you to see the layout before we leave. Step where I step. We know the floor is solid in certain places."

I felt giddy at not having to see the burnt woman's body. "No sign of the son inside?"

"Nope. No pigs or goats either."

My foot twinged again, and I drew in a quick breath.

"Something wrong?"

"Foot's got a mind of its own today." A bird called *purty, purty, purty* in the distance. I shifted most of my weight to my right foot. "You thinking arson or accident?"

"It could go either way."

"If arson, I should examine the doors and windows."

"Not much left of them. We get inside and you see something you want, call it to my attention. I'll bag and tag it. Any questions?"

"I'm good." We sealed our protective gear, and I followed him up the concrete-block steps. With a respirator on, my loud breathing sounded like Darth Vader's. I remembered the sheriff's instructions to walk in his footsteps, so I watched his boots stir clouds of ash and debris. My heel still bothered me, so I walked on the tiptoes of my left foot.

We stepped over a wire conduit and some PVC pipes. Wayne halted and made a sweeping arm gesture. I couldn't understand his garbled speech, so I raised my gaze and saw the roof was totally gone. Blue sky domed above us, and the sun brightened the drab interior.

God, it was hot in these suits. My shirt was soaked through. Judging by the charred appliances, the sink, and couch springs, this seemed to be a combination kitchen and living room. I could tell nothing about the people who lived here.

Just yesterday, the lady of the house stood at this sink washing her dishes. She'd gone about her chores like it was any other day. But it wasn't. What a difference a day made.

A large bead of sweat rolled into my eye, blurring my vision. Wayne said something else to me, but the sound was far away. The room before me swirled in a circle and then took shape. White cabinets, white appliances, blue countertops. A woman in a faded floral robe puttered around the kitchen, tidying this, wiping that. Freshly brewed coffee perfumed the air, making my stomach rumble.

She walked to the living room, adjusted the superhero throw pillows on the couch, and squared up the magazines on the gleaming wooden coffee table. The top magazine had a familiar yellow border around the edge of the cover. The woman stood, rubbing her lower back, her amber eyes dull with pain.

Uh-oh. I recognized that move. Her back hurt, or her kidneys, or she might have cramps. Either way, if it were me, I'd head to the shower for some relief. My thoughts gelled. That's just what Mandy Patterson did, right before she died. I was being shown her last minutes on earth. A dreamwalk.

"Mandy? Can you hear me?" I asked.

No response. It was as if she didn't see me at all. The vision was a loop from her past, a sequence of events she wanted me to see.

Purposefully, I glanced around the room, hoping for some clue as to what had happened. My overwhelming sense was that of tidiness. There were no rumpled clothes in laundry baskets waiting to be folded. No dishes were stacked in the sink; no bills and catalogs cluttered the counter.

With a sigh, the woman ambled down the hall, turning left at the first doorway. The bathroom. Mandy closed the door, turned on the shower, and disrobed. As the water warmed, she sat on the side of the tub and chewed her fingernails. There didn't seem to be much in the way of nails on any finger, but she gnawed on her index finger just the same.

What was going through her head? All I could hear was the sound of my breathing and the flowing water. If she had any last thoughts, she wasn't sharing them with me. Finally, the water temperature suited her, and she climbed in, drawing the white shower curtain closed behind her. The spray pounded on Mandy's lower back, and her eyes closed. Been there, done that. What wasn't I seeing? Her bath products were bargain brands, same as in my shower. Her skin was flawless. There were no piercings, no tattoos. She looked to be about five feet four, and maybe a hundred twenty pounds or so. Her hair was closely cropped, giving her a stylish, no-nonsense look.

The only touch of femininity I observed in her entire home was the floral robe. Everything else seemed utilitarian, as if frills had no place in her life. How did she come to be so rigidly disciplined, so compulsively neat?

I tried to reach her again. "Mandy? I'm Baxley Powell, the Dreamwalker. Can you tell me what happened to you?"

The vision flickered, like the end of a movie reel. A loud explosion sounded, knocking Mandy down. She fell and stared at me with sightless eyes. Flaming pieces of the ceiling and roof landed on her. I hovered closer, desperate for even a hint of what caused the explosion.

A rattling from her chest had me reaching for her hand. Though she had already passed on, her death felt like it was occurring right this minute. "It's okay, Mandy," I said. "Death's not so bad. Just let go."

Her fingers tightened around mine as the fire roared around us. Two words came out on her last sigh. "Tell them."

CHAPTER NINE

Wayne tugged on my arm, and I came back to full consciousness. I'd had a vision without holding anything of the victim's in my hand. Being in her house was all it took for me to see Mandy Patterson. How was that possible?

The sheriff's respirator face plate hovered right in front of mine. He said something again, garbled through the protective clothing, and I assumed he asked me if I was okay. I nodded my head, which put him at ease.

We trekked into two other tiny rooms. Each held a metal bed frame and lots of wall and ceiling debris. The hall ended abruptly as if a dinosaur had munched off the end of the mobile home. From the mini-crater in the adjacent soil, I judged this might have been ground zero for the explosion that caused the fire. Metal creaked and ash stirred as we walked, but no more ghostly visions waylaid me. Wayne pointed out the bathroom. Curious, I went off script, not following his footsteps, to venture into the room. A small sink and a toilet were on one side, the three-quarter-length tub on the other. All were charred with soot and dusted with ash. Sunlight flooded the entire space.

Mandy Patterson died here. She'd shown me that final scene for a reason. What was important about this room? Did she expect me to notice something here after the fire? Not likely. The ceramic fixtures survived, but the fire took care of the walls and any personal items.

The showerhead pipe was still in place, as were the water control knobs. I wanted to touch the blackened tub, and if not the tub, then one of those knobs. I pointed to them and stated my request as clearly as I could, given the respirator I wore.

Wayne shook his head and pointed to the door. I got the message. He wanted me out of there. I followed his arm gestures and headed outside because I was hot, tired, and thirsty. He kept a gloved hand on my shoulder the entire way. Guess he didn't want me to make another detour.

Once we reached the decon station, Wayne ripped his full face respirator off and whirled me around. "What part of follow-in-my-footsteps didn't you understand? What did you think you were doing in there?"

His face looked red and angry. I fumbled to pull my respirator off, getting it caught in the hoodie part of my suit. Mayes came to my rescue and untangled the hoodie and the respirator. "Thanks," I told him.

I unzipped my suit and felt some of the humidity inside escape. My clothes were plastered to my skin, my hair, a soppy mess. How did astronauts do this for weeks and months at a time? I accepted a bottle of water from Mayes and took a long swig. Then I turned to Wayne, who was still steaming like a bull in the ring.

"I was doing my job."

He leaned into my personal space. "Your job is to follow my lead. It's too hot to be trapped in these suits for one of your dreamwalks. I wanted you to see the floor-plan and to get a feel for the place. That's it. My guys can haul whatever pieces we need to the office, and you can examine them in the air conditioning."

Reading between the lines, I realized he'd intended to sit in the air conditioning while I worked. "For your information, I saw something in there." Once the words escaped my lips, I winced. Wayne did not need to know that my abilities had expanded. I was better off letting him believe I had only one paranormal gear. Wayne had already blabbed about my dreamwalking to all his sheriff buddies. Letting him know anything extra about me was the equivalent of telling gossip central.

My words had the effect of a bucket of ice water thrown on his temper. As if he were an alchemist, his anger transformed into a different element. His eyes narrowed into a laser-like tractor beam. "Tell me."

"I'll tell you because I'm a team player, not because you asked me so nicely." I drained the rest of the water bottle, then wiggled out of the suit. If I ever needed to drop five pounds in ten minutes, this was the way to go.

"Powell, you're trying my patience."

"Don't you want to wait to get back to the air conditioning for a report, Sheriff?" I asked in a saccharine-sweet tone.

"I want answers."

"Then let me give them to you. Mandy died in that tub. She was taking a shower when the explosion happened. In that instant, she was surprised and frightened and worried."

"She told you this?"

"I saw it. I saw her last moments. Heard

the roar. Saw her face for the millisecond before the ceiling fell on her, and her skin caught fire."

Wayne's features morphed into his stony cop face, the one where I couldn't read his expression, the one he turned on his criminal suspects. I didn't like it at all.

I sensed Mayes hovering at my elbow, waiting to leap to my rescue. While I appreciated the gesture, I could handle Wayne.

"You were supposed to wait," Wayne said.

"You think I control when the dreams come? Think again."

Silence rang around us. Not a trace of air moved back here in these pine woods. It felt cloying and itchy and uncomfortable. I was too hot. I was freezing. The world started to spin. I tried to brace my legs, but they refused to cooperate. I might as well have been trying to balance on a pine cone.

Strong arms closed around me, and the daylight winked out.

CHAPTER TEN

A cool cloth caressed my brow. The air was easier to breathe. I felt cradled and cherished. I floated into consciousness reluctantly, burrowing into the strong arms that held me. He smelled nice, like home and woods and safety. Another gentle stroke from the crown of my head down my neck. Oh, it felt so good to be held. A murmur of contentment welled in my throat.

"She awake?" a man said.

I knew that voice. Wayne.

"Getting there," another man whispered.

The right man. Mayes. I fought the rising tide of wakefulness, knowing everything would change when I opened my eyes. I savored the tender touches he gave me, each one a beautiful memory to store forever, as I drifted through a wonderful lucid dream.

"What's wrong with her?" Wayne asked.

"Dehydration and denial."

"The first I get, but the second?"

"Complicated."

"Don't mess with my Dreamwalker."

His arms tightened around me, sending a jolt of his irritation and more through every nerve ending. My breath caught as I careened back to reality.

"She's not yours," Mayes said simply.

"Not yours either," the sheriff countered. "She's married."

The vista beyond my eyelids brightened considerably. I became aware of an engine running. The sheriff's Jeep. Of cool air brushing against my skin, filling my lungs. Air conditioning. Of being a steamy mess. Of my personal body odor. That did it.

My eyes flickered open. Just as I'd thought. Mayes held me in the backseat of the sheriff's Jeep.

"Morning," Mayes said.

"Morning." I pushed against him, trying to rise, but his steely arms didn't give an inch. "I'm okay."

"Yes, you are."

Belatedly, it occurred to me that Mayes had been using my close proximity to transfer his energy into me. He'd taught me how to do that during our last case at Stony Creek Lake. We shared similar paranormal skill sets, and even though he claimed I was the stronger of the two of us, I had a feeling he didn't have a clue as to his true potential.

I gazed up into his brown eyes. "Did you. . . ."

He stroked my hair again. "I did."

No wonder my entire body hummed. I'd been super charged. I felt strong enough to leap pine trees in a single bound. What had that energy transfer cost Mayes? "And you?"

"Okay."

"Y'all talking in code?" the sheriff asked. "What's going on back there?"

My irritation at Wayne hadn't mellowed. "Stick a pin in it. I'm fine, thanks to Mayes."

"Can you work?"

"I can, though I don't much care for your demanding attitude."

"I wouldn't have an attitude if you hadn't scared me half to death. You were supposed to wait until we got back to the station to do your woo-woo thing. You're not a fainter. No one ever faints around me unless they're pregnant. Unless that's it. You preggers, Powell? This guy knock you up? Because it sure as hell doesn't look like your relationship is as platonic as you led me to believe."

Feminine intuition told me Mayes would love to be the father of my next child, and that irritated the heck out of Wayne. I didn't need male posturing. Fortunately, Mayes held his peace.

This time when I pushed away from Mayes, he let me go. "Knock it off," I told Wayne. "We're in this together. I want justice for Mandy as much as you do."

"Don't go getting sappy on me, Powell," the sheriff said. "The woman lived in a meth lab. She was no innocent."

"So? She wasn't sloppy about how she lived. Everything in her house was shipshape when I saw it. Nothing out of place. I refuse to believe that she killed herself."

"Making meth isn't a good career path, even for a neat freak. It's dangerous."

"So is driving a car. Will you bother to find out what happened to her, or will she become another statistic?"

"She'll get the attention she deserves. What else did you learn about her?"

"I relayed everything I know about the vision. Why she shared her final moments is a mystery to me. I wasn't trying to get a reading, and as you saw, I wasn't touching anything."

"You been holding out on me?"

I raised my hands in surrender mode. "Absolutely not. This was a first. I can't say as I recommend it either. Very disorienting."

"Not as disorienting as death." Wayne craned his neck around at some sound.

Mayes followed suit. "What is that racket?"

I gazed over my shoulder and saw a rooster tail of dust and a compact car speeding our way. *Oh, joy.* Who would it be? The GBI guy? A friend of the deceased? A relative? A drug customer? Or maybe the killer himself.

CHAPTER ELEVEN

"Where's my mom?" the teenager shouted from behind his open door, engine still running, music cranking and thumping in our ears. He wore his dark hair in a close-to-the-scalp cut, and his jeans and T-shirt looked rumpled. His boxy feet were bare. Could this be Mandy's son?

No one had mentioned a dad living here, just a mother and son. This young man looked to be the right age for the son.

We piled out of Wayne's vehicle. The firemen edged closer, and the testosterone content in the air shot up to about two hundred proof.

I must be a thrill junkie as well, because adrenaline flooded my body. Instinctively, I dropped into a ready stance, with slightly flexed knees and a lower center of gravity. My fingers curled into my palms.

"Who are you people?" the boy yelled again, wide-eyed. "This is private property.

Get out of here, or I'm calling the cops."

Wayne stepped forward. "I am the cops. Sheriff Wayne Thompson. Why don't you turn off the car and come over here to talk to me?"

"You don't look like a cop," the boy said.

Wayne turned to Mayes and spoke softly. "Get Powell to safety. We can't see his hands. He could have a gun."

Mayes scooped me up in his arms again and moved behind Wayne's Jeep. *Crap.* A moment later, Mayes had his weapon drawn. Waves of tension radiated from him, enveloping me. *Double crap.* Due to our energy sharing and close proximity, I felt what he felt.

Fear for my safety. Protectiveness. Focus. Self-control. Responsibility.

Despite his instructions to keep down, I lifted my head to see what was going on.

"But we do," Virg said, stepping out of the shadows with Ronnie, both in their Class A khaki uniforms. "Do what the man says, boy, and it'll go easier for you."

I noticed Virg had pulled a weapon. *Please let it be the Taser and not his handgun.*

"I don't know you people," the boy yelled, his voice edged with fear.

A chunky fireman stepped forward. "You know me, Doodle. Jerome Green. You work

80

at the animal shelter with my wife."

The boy took a step toward the man. "Mr. Green? Is that you? What's going on here? Where's my mom?"

"You need to talk to Sheriff Thompson, son."

As Wayne and Virg approached the boy — Wayne openhanded, Virg with both hands around a weapon — even I saw the boy's hands were empty. I stood and thanked the high heavens no one would get killed today. Beside me, Mayes secured his weapon.

His hand clamped on my shoulder. "Stay back. As a precaution, until they pat him down."

I answered back in the same low tone. "He's a kid, a scared kid."

The superior look Mayes shot me made heat rise to my face. Kids stole guns all the time. Kids shot people. I knew that, but I also had a daughter. If Larissa ever found herself in this situation, I hoped she'd be treated with common courtesy and respect. I hoped cops would never approach her with weapons drawn.

My left heel twinged again. An arc of pain shot up my leg. I let out a small gasp and braced my hands on the Jeep. What was wrong with me?

Up close, Doodle Patterson was shorter

than I thought and antsier. He protested being searched, but the cops did it anyway. Protested again when he was told he was going to the police station. Ronnie had the honor of driving Doodle's pimped-out ride to the cop shop.

Soon, Wayne, Doodle, and I sat in Interview Room Two. Mayes and Virg watched from behind the two-way mirror. The red dot in the corner showed the camera was recording the session. It should've felt like business as usual, but it didn't. More like a volcano poised to erupt.

Though I wasn't sure if those were my feelings or if I was still connected emotionally to Mayes, I ignored the personal vibes and focused on Doodle Patterson. He was all of sixteen, going on thirty-five. Another kid who'd seen too much, too soon. Didn't everyone deserve a normal childhood? What must this kid have seen, living in a meth lab?

"Where were you last night?" Wayne asked.

The boy shook his head. "Nah-uh. You said you'd tell me about my mom. Where is she? Did you lock her up? Is she here? Is that why you brought me to the station?"

"I ask the questions," Wayne said in a stern tone. "Tell me, or I'll track the GPS coordinates of your phone."

"No way can you hicks do that. You don't have the budget for any of that high-tech crap."

I held my breath. Wayne was sensitive about his budget, and he despised criticism of any kind. This kid must have a death wish.

"We can track your movements, believe you me," Wayne said through gritted teeth. "How'd you like to wait in a holding cell while we ascertain your whereabouts during and before the fire? Since you think we're hicks, it may take us a day or two. I live to lock up punks like you."

The boy paled. His hands came up in surrender mode. "No bars. No jail, I mean. I can't be locked up. I have rights."

"Then tell me. Where were you last night?"

Doodle shrugged and slouched in his seat, his eyes narrowed and calculating. "I stayed with a friend. Big hairy deal."

"Which friend?"

"Why all the questions?" The teen bounced in his seat. "You think I torched our place? Why would I do that? All my stuff was in there. This is sick, man."

My emotions took a nosedive. Poor Doodle. Everything he owned was gone. His mother was dead. Unless he had extended family, he was alone in the world.

The sheriff steepled his hands together on the table. "The only thing *sick* here is the lack of straight answers I'm getting from you. Unless you give me information I can verify, you will become my guest."

"All right, all right. Lovey's house. That's where I was. Mom was riding me about my homework, and I couldn't take it. So I split. Didn't mean to stay all night. We were . . . talking. Afterward, I fell asleep. Didn't wake up till morning. Can I go now?"

Wayne glanced at me, eyebrows raised. I gave a slight nod of my head to indicate Doodle was telling the truth.

"I need Lovey's real name and address."

The kid froze. "Can't. Her mom doesn't know I slept over. I'll get her in trouble."

"You'll be in trouble if her story doesn't match yours."

The boy swore. He turned away from us, and when he turned back, his eyes glittered. "LaTanya. Her name is LaTanya Tuttle. There, are you happy? Can I go?"

Wayne nodded at the mirror. I knew that meant Virg and Mayes would be verifying Doodle's alibi with the Trotter girl. "Not just yet. Where are the pigs?"

The teen's face flushed to a lurid shade of

crimson. "That SOB next door threatened to eat them. Our pets. I told him I'd eat his dogs if he so much as touched our pigs. He pulled a gun on me. He's the one who should be arrested."

"Were you on his property?"

"So what if I was?" Doodle sighed as if the weight of the world lay on his shoulders and hung his head. "Petunia got loose again. Our back door doesn't latch right. She's smart and knows how to open the door. She can open cabinets and other stuff too."

"Why does she go next door? Why not run free in the woods?"

"She's not that kind of pig. And she loves dog food. It's like piggy catnip for her. Once she discovered where Old Man Dixon kept the bag, she went for it every time she saw daylight. I bought him a new bag, but that wasn't good enough. He said he'd shoot her the next time she went over there. Shoot her and eat her."

The raw edge in his voice rang true. I wanted to wring Ricky Dixon's neck myself. There was no call to say such things to a kid.

"Where's Petunia now?"

"Two days ago, I hid her and Patches at the shelter. They're staying in the feral cat enclosure. They don't like being caged, but

Petunia is on a steady diet of her favorite dog food now. She's happier than I thought."

"And the goat?"

Tears flowed. "Someone shot my goat. For reals."

"On your property?"

"I found Cotton Tail in the woods with a bullet hole in her head. Someone walked up to her and put the gun to her forehead. She didn't even know to be scared."

"You have an idea who did it?"

"Sure. That bastard next door. Cotton Tail liked to walk on his cars. I didn't see the big deal, but Dixon really wigged out about it. I told him I'd make it right, but then I found her dead. I want to kill him for hurting her. That's why I took our pigs away. To save them."

The boy's aura pulsed wildly during this last bit. Some of it was a lie. Bummer. I had mixed emotions about the kid now.

After an awkward round of silence, Wayne asked, "You know anyone who'd want to hurt your mom?"

"What?"

Wayne repeated the question.

"I want to see my mom right now. I answered your questions. Where's my mom? Is she in another room?" He hollered her name, twice.

"She can't hear you." Wayne made a simmer-down gesture with his hand. "We know about the meth lab, Doodle."

The kid's lips clamped shut. If looks could kill, we'd be deep-fried hush puppies by now.

Wayne tried several more questions, but apparently Doodle had exhausted his supply of answers. I knew the sheriff expected an insight or reading from me, but Doodle's answers confused my truth-detecting sense. When I reached across the table, Doodle jerked away, leaping out of his chair and backpedaling with his hands in the air. "Don't touch me. I don't want anyone messing with my mojo."

I crossed my arms, hiding my tingling palms underneath the barrier. Why was I suddenly the Wicked Witch of the West? Was someone spreading lies and misinformation about me? I wasn't vindictive, and I wouldn't harm anyone, not even a defiant teen.

The sheriff directed Doodle back to his seat and then broke the news of his mother's death. Tears streamed down the teen's face. To give Doodle privacy, we stepped into the hallway. "What'll happen to him now?" I asked.

"Foster care if no relative claims him," Wayne said. "There's no dad in the picture."

"Isn't he too old for foster care?"

"Nah. You'd be surprised by the number of kids in the sixteen-to-twenty-year-old range who are in the system."

I digested that for a moment. I couldn't imagine getting told I had to stay with strangers at that age. This kid had some rough days ahead. "He lied to us, but I couldn't get a clear read on which statements were false."

"Figured. I'll give him a day or so to stew about the fire and his mom, then I'll come at him again." Wayne sized me up. "Go to the doc in the box for your foot, Powell."

"Is that an order?"

He shrugged. "Take it however you like. I'm fresh out of sugarcoating."

CHAPTER TWELVE

"I see nothing wrong with your foot." Dr. Teal scowled at me over the top of her turquoise-framed readers. She'd poked, prodded, and X-rayed my foot. She'd had me walk around the exam room. Up until this moment, I'd found her friendly, attentive, and compassionate. "Is something else going on in your life?"

"Not that I know of, but I'm not making this up," I said. The paper on the exam table crinkled as I shifted in my seat. "The pain started this morning."

"Be that as it may, your stride is fine now. Nothing's broken, inflamed, or wounded. None of the symptoms you described are evident."

Was she calling me a liar? "I didn't imagine the pain. It's real."

The efficient doctor continued checking things off on her tablet screen. "Someone who does police consulting work like you should expect emotional fallout."

I glanced over at Mayes, who'd accompanied me to the exam room. "The pain comes and goes. I'm not having any pain right now, but when it hurts, the sensation is like I've stepped on a nail."

A printer whirred. Dr. Teal grabbed the sheet it ejected and handed it to me. "Go see a podiatrist for insole fittings if this continues."

I stomped out of the office. "I don't make things up."

Mayes cracked a rare smile as he settled into the driver's seat of my truck for the twenty-minute journey back to Sinclair County. "She said see a podiatrist, not psychiatrist."

"Same difference. I don't need a shrink or a foot doctor. Something abnormal is going on with my foot." I buckled my seatbelt on autopilot, wanting to yowl in frustration. We'd wasted an hour and a half to find out nothing was wrong. I needed a do-over button for this morning. "Would you mind swinging by my place on the way back to the office? I'd like to freshen up."

"We can do that."

The miles rolled by in blessed silence. I gazed at the roadside scenery as it changed from shops and plazas to forested tracks of homes. My thoughts veered back to Mandy Patterson's charred husk of a trailer. Gone, and for what? That's what we needed to figure out.

The memory of Mandy's final moments surfaced in my head. The flames. The noise. The falling ceiling. I gasped and gripped the armrest.

Mayes shot me a worried look. "Want to talk about it?"

I unclenched my fists. "I think Mandy was dead before her skin fried. A big chunk of ceiling fell on her, and then she blacked out." I glanced at Mayes again. So somber, so in control of himself. "Sorry, this isn't the coastal vacation you thought you were getting."

On the straightaway, he smoothly passed a pickup pulling a boat trailer. "I wanted to see the area, meet some of the people, and hang out with you. This is happening exactly as I envisioned it."

"But we're wrapped up in a case."

"Cases happen. Fact of the matter is I'm glad we have a case. Gives us another chance to work together again."

Some of my tension ebbed away. Mayes didn't hold me responsible for his personal entertainment. My allegedly dead husband, Roland, wouldn't have been so generous.

But Mayes wasn't my anything. He was a different man, with different expectations. Including romantic aspirations. Best not to think about that.

The warrior in Mayes shone through, even in something as simple as driving a vehicle. His confident bearing spoke volumes about who and what he was.

"Did you have a dreamwalk when you went inside the trailer?" I asked.

"Didn't happen for me. You have a lot more practice in talking to the dead than I do."

A strangled laugh caught in my throat. I coughed to cover the rude sound. Then I figured, what the hay? *I don't want to pretend with this guy. I want him to know the real me.* "Strange thing to say. I've only been doing this for a couple of months. I was under the impression that you'd been spirit walking for most of your life."

"Not the same thing. My quests have been for knowledge and wisdom from tribal elders."

Why was he downplaying his abilities? "Seems like the same thing to me. Are you ashamed of what you do?"

"No." He barked that out, then grimaced. "Sorry. I want to be honest with you, but it's second nature to conceal my abilities."

"Why?"

"Because. . . ."

"You sound like a teenager. Because why?"

"Because my job in law enforcement isn't suitable for a holy man. If my tribe members knew the scope of my abilities, they would make me the holy man."

"Your tribe members know. Several of them helped us when we went up against that psychic vampire at Stony Creek Lake."

"Those are men I trust with my secret. And you. You're part of my secret. Don't out me to the tribe, okay?"

"I won't. But my guess is they know already, and you're fooling yourself. There's a certain power in your aura."

He managed a wry grin. "Not many energy readers in my tribe."

"It would only take one."

That wiped the smile off his face. "Oh."

"You're different from the mainstream, Mayes. Just as I'm different."

"But we're not the same. I'm at level one with this stuff, and you're off the charts."

"I don't believe you, and according to you, I'm the expert here."

He glowered at me. We were making progress. "Denial may give you peace of mind, but you're fooling yourself."

Mayes started to say something and

93

stopped. I imagined the gears in his head turning around this information, trying to make sense of it. I'd seen the respect his friends accorded him. He was already their holy man, whether he acknowledged it or not.

We crossed the county line and had another five miles of bridges and low country before we reached our county seat, Marion.

"I do not bear the sign," Mayes said.

His words confused me. "What?"

"The sign of power. You bear it."

I still didn't understand. "Come again?"

"Every holy man I've ever known had snow-white hair. Like yours."

"Oh, that." I pointed to my head. "I didn't have this before I accepted what I could do. Once I owned up to my abilities, some of my hair turned."

"Then when your pal on the Other Side nearly cooked you over a fire, the rest went white."

"It's more than that. Words have power. You are a man divided, Mayes."

"I love my job."

Lord, he was hardheaded. "I don't get why you can't be a tribal leader and a sheriff's deputy."

"The holy man has certain responsibilities

to the tribe, to the nation. Those are absolute."

"It's a new day. Figure out how to have both."

In the acute silence that followed, my phone buzzed. Charlotte. About time she surfaced. I clicked to answer the call. "Hey."

"I don't know where you are, but you should get out here right now."

I sat up straighter. "Where are you? At your place?"

"At the sheriff's office. All hell is breaking loose. The GBI is here. The cousin's here."

"Are you talking about the Mandy Patterson case?"

"I am indeed. Tamika brought me up to speed. Guess she felt sorry for me. Anyway, this woman is raising Cain because they won't release Doodle to her. I got some video with my cell. Maybe my boss will put it on the newspaper's website."

"Who's the cousin?"

"June Hendrix."

The name was as explosive as TNT. June crusaded all over town for this, that, and the other. Rumor had it she fought dogs, which made me hate her even though we'd never met. She'd been kicked out of several charities for misappropriation of funds, though she'd never been charged. June believed the world owed her. She was trouble.

We crested the last bridge. "We'll be there in five minutes."

CHAPTER THIRTEEN

Though I had a key and permission to use the staff entrance, I asked Mayes to park in front of the law-enforcement center. Charlotte made a beeline for us as soon as we turned into the visitor parking lot. Duncan followed her down the sidewalk at a more leisurely pace, hands in his pockets. His gaze was firmly locked on Charlotte, as if she hung the moon.

Charlotte glowed. I'd never seen her so happy. She flung herself in my arms, and we would have fallen if Mayes hadn't momentarily steadied my shoulders. "Are you okay?" I asked.

"Never better." She rebounded and straightened her crooked glasses. Even the freckles on her face had an added luster.

"I was worried about you," I whispered. "About . . . you know."

"*You know* is numero uno with me," she whispered back. "I feel like I've awakened from a long sleep."

The image of Charlotte in a Sleeping Beauty gown flashed in my head. I bit back a smile. "So, it was okay? You're not sore or anything?"

"The earth definitely moved, but I can't talk about that now." She flapped a wrist in front of me, bubbling with excitement. "I nearly missed the big case because I was crossing virginity off my bucket list. I have to hit the ground running on the story to scoop Bernard. Think I've already got the basics covered. What do you think of this angle: 'Meth dealer dies in blaze'? Oh, and don't speak to Bernard. He's out here trolling, but he can't have my story."

I reeled at her rapid-fire words, and Mayes caught me again. With both of the men listening avidly to every word we spoke, I took the hint to avoid all talk about Charlotte's bucket list, though I had a million questions for her about the Big Night.

The case. We were here because Mandy Patterson's cousin had surfaced. "Where's June Hendrix?"

"They took her inside, but not before I got an exclusive interview with her. Eat my dust, Bernard." At that she glanced up and muttered, "Speak of the devil."

Bernard Rivers, her rival reporter at the

newspaper, approached swiftly. "Ms. Powell, may I have a quote from you about the meth lab explosion?"

The longer I took to answer, the more agitated Bernard became. He tapped his slim reporter notepad in the palm of his hand. The repetitive motion and the desperation rolling off Charlotte's nemesis seemed out of proportion with current events. Was something else going on here? Something besides professional rivalry?

"No comment," I said, though it was plain to see his approach to the case was much more levelheaded than Charlotte's. Too bad these reporters couldn't collaborate.

"Ms. Powell, I have equal rights to any information you share with Charlotte."

Duncan's chest swelled, and I had the strong sense he might swat Bernard out of the way. I understood his protective impulse. Charlotte finally had everything going for her. She deserved personal and professional happiness.

My eye twitched, and I faked rubbing it until the muscle spasm stopped a few minutes later. "I'm not a police spokesperson, Bernard. I can't help you or Charlotte with case quotes. You know the drill. Go through proper channels for the official statement."

Bernard's expression turned sullen. "It's not fair that Charlotte gets insider information from you and I don't."

"She's my source, moron," Charlotte said. "Back off."

"This is highly inappropriate. I'm filing a complaint," Bernard groused, moving toward Charlotte. When Duncan blocked Bernard's access to her, the smaller man turned and marched back to the lobby.

Bernard reminded me of a playground bully. He had the swagger and bluster, along with the bragging rights for the territory, but Charlotte's rising star at the newspaper unnerved him. "He could get you in trouble, Char," I said. "He's the kind of guy to grind through the official complaint red tape and get you fired."

"Bernard's hot air." Charlotte's eyes flashed defiance, and her chin rose. "I'm not afraid of him."

"You should be," I said. "He won't give up."

"I can take care of him," Duncan said, leaning in. "Just say the word."

"No one's taking care of anyone." I eyed the lobby window where Bernard stood staring at us. Putting Charlotte and Duncan in that small space with Bernard would be like igniting a powder keg. Not a good idea.

"For goodness' sake, both of you, play nice. Why don't y'all head out and grab some lunch?"

Duncan's eyes warmed. "I could eat."

I rewarded him with a bright smile. If only Charlotte were so easy to redirect.

"What if I miss something?" Charlotte asked.

"There's nothing to miss. It's early days in this investigation. We don't even know if there's foul play or if Mandy's death was accidental. Do yourself a favor and enjoy the rest of the weekend with Duncan."

"But I need this story."

"You need to make sure your *guest* is having a good time."

That did it. Charlotte got a wide-eyed, startled look and chewed her bottom lip. She seemed to be weighing her desire to be top dog at the paper against having a personal life.

Duncan stroked her arm, and Charlotte shifted her attention to him. His eyebrow lifted in silent question. A tremulous smile came over Charlotte's lips, and she laced her fingers through Duncan's. "All right. Lunch it is. Will y'all join us?"

I glanced up at Mayes. "No reason for you to skip a meal. I need to sit in on this interview and meet Mr. GBI. Why don't you join them?"

Mayes took his time answering. "I'll wait to eat with you."

Looked like I had a shadow. "Suit yourself."

After seeing Charlotte and Duncan off, I strolled around to the staff entrance, Mayes matching my pace. Inside, we hurried to the observation room to catch the remainder of the June Hendrix interview.

June Hendrix, a petite woman with a few extra pounds, had thinning brown hair and a pale mole on her face. From the moment I saw the way she carried herself, the tilt of her head, and the shrewdness in her eyes, I knew we were in for a rocky ride. She was shaking her finger at the sheriff and another dark-haired man, exhorting them to call Child Protective Services right this minute.

I'd never met the extra man in the interview room, but seeing as how he was sitting on the sheriff's side of the table, I concluded this was the GBI guy. I elbowed Mayes. "You know him?"

Mayes shook his head.

Judging only by their postures, the new guy seemed more rigid. Did this mean he would be a by-the-book kind of person? If so, that might leave me out in the cold for this case. More than ever, I wanted to see this one through.

"Calm down. We'll get Doodle's custody issue straightened out in due time," Wayne said. "Meanwhile, what can you tell me about Mandy?"

June's animated face clouded. "She's got an arrest record, that's what. She had no business taking chances while she was raising her boy."

"You knew what went on at her place?" Wayne asked.

"I knew she cooked."

"Cooking methamphetamine is illegal."

"I tried talking sense into her, but she was as hardheaded as they come."

The new guy leaned over and whispered in Wayne's ear. Wayne nodded and settled back in his seat, giving June his gunslinger stare. "Who'd she work for?"

June shrugged and cast an anxious glance at the window where we watched. "Nobody."

Interesting. The first crack in her cool. Who did she think was back here? Or was she looking up here to keep from looking at Mr. GBI? She'd told the truth so far, but she seemed overly militant. Why? Who was she afraid of?

"I doubt that," Wayne said. "Where'd she get her supplies?"

"There are ways to get anything. You gotta know the right people."

"Mandy had contacts in the drug world?"

"Mandy had a brain. She figured it out. Now I'm her only relative, and I gotta pick up the pieces of our family. Doodle comes home with me today, and I want it on record that I'm his legal guardian."

The sheriff busied himself glancing at papers in his folder, ignoring the dark-haired man to his left. Finally, he gazed at June. "How will you support him?"

"My money comes in each month. And I'll get more if I have him."

"Your government subsidy?"

Her dark-brown eyes flashed with annoyance. "It's my money. In my bank account."

"I wasn't aware you worked."

"I don't have to take this crap from you or the GBI suit staring at me." June leaned forward and slapped the table with her palm. "Where's my nephew?"

"Where were you last night?" Wayne smoothly countered.

June erupted from her seat like a waterspout, whirling and angry. "What the hell is wrong with you? You think I had something to do with Mandy's death? No way. Uh-uh. You're not gonna pin this on me."

"You didn't answer the question. Where

104

were you last night?"

"At home."

"Alone?"

"No, I was having an orgy. The mayor and the entire county commission were there, along with six of your deputies. Satisfied?"

Wayne said nothing, giving her his patented death glare.

Standing next to me in the observation room, Mayes laughed. "This guy is good."

I stiffened. "Whatever you do, don't tell Wayne. His ego is already bigger than three states."

In the interview room, Wayne pulled out his phone, checked the display, gathered his papers, and gestured to the other man to rise. He turned to June before they left. "Sit tight."

June paced the room for a moment before she walked over to the mirrored observation window and glared at us. Her lip quivered, and she returned to the table and sat as ordered.

I opened the door and caught Wayne's eye as he passed. He shook his head and mouthed, "Wait." He strode down the corridor to his office, the other man at his side. The man's eyes swept over us as they passed, but there was no flicker of interest. It was as if we didn't exist. Now he was sequestering himself with Wayne. What did that mean? Would we be kicked off the investigation?

Mayes touched my arm. "They have jurisdictional issues to iron out. It's always that way when an outside agency gets involved in a case."

"Maybe. Seems weird that Wayne wouldn't introduce us."

"He will. Later. Like I said, they have to sort out priorities for solving the cases. There's Mandy's death and the meth lab business. Mr. GBI will care the most about the meth lab."

"Seems like a person's life should count more."

"Taking out the meth lab supply chain will help a lot of people."

"I'm sure your thinking is correct, but things are weird here. Wayne's never treated me like he didn't want to be around me."

"It may not be you. Wayne objects to my presence."

I gazed at him. "Try not to take it personally."

"But I do. Take it personally." He laced his fingers with mine, sending tingles up my arm. "I've made no secret of the fact that I'm interested in you. But he wants you."

"Not going to happen." At Mayes' crestfallen look, I winced. "I mean, I'm not interested in Wayne."

"Are you interested in me?"

I tried to turn away, but his fingers held me fast. "Bax?"

Out of nowhere, tears sprang in my eyes. "It's complicated. I'm complicated."

"I can do complicated. That doesn't scare me."

"It should."

He raised our joined fingers to his lips. A thrill of passion surged up my arm. For a long moment, I let the forbidden pleasure run amuck through my entire body. "I'm not free," I managed. "Besides, it couldn't work. We live too far apart."

"We're not far apart now. I'm standing right here, loving you, wanting you. Do you see me?"

"This isn't the time for this conversation."

With his other hand, he lifted my chin. His thumb caressed the side of my face. "Do you see me, Baxley?"

The rose tattoos on my hand and back sizzled. The marks had been put there by a powerful entity from the Other Side. That discomfort was all the warning I had.

CHAPTER FOURTEEN

One minute I stood there looking at Mayes, feeling so conflicted that I didn't know what to do, and the next, I'd wound myself around him, a vine to his fence wire. I kissed him like a woman starved for passion and backed him into the wall.

Need and want and lust sluiced through my veins. It had been so long. Too long. All I could think about was making love with Mayes. He smelled great, like woods and sea air and an exotic spice. Everything inside me clenched in anticipation.

Brazenly, I rubbed against his lean length, and sparks fired from each contact point. I grabbed at his clothing, pulled the elastic band from his shoulder-length hair, and sank my fingers into the silky stuff.

"The door," Mayes murmured between fevered kisses. "We should lock it."

Who cared about the flipping door? My libido ramped from zero to supernova in a matter of seconds. Mayes had what I needed, and I needed it right then.

Somehow, Mayes got us over to the door, locked it, then we graduated to the main event. The coupling was intense. I couldn't get enough of him, couldn't get to that edge.

Then I found the exact pace I'd been seeking, Mayes too, and thinking ceased.

Slowly it dawned on me that my arms and legs were cinched around Mayes. I was buck naked in the police station. Mayes kissed me, tenderly this time, and my emotions spiraled out of control. Again.

My tattoos stung, and that painful stimuli jarred me back to reality. I broke off the kiss, disengaged, and edged away from him.

"That didn't happen," I whispered.

He returned my level gaze, both of us naked and vulnerable. "It did."

"I don't do this sort of thing."

He laughed low in his throat. "You should. But only with me."

"No, this isn't me." I started grabbing my clothes, fumbling them on.

He walked over as if he were going to kiss me again. I blocked him with a chair. "Please. Don't touch me. Something very odd is going on here. My tattoos. They're signaling me. Rose is calling. I need to find

109

her in a dreamwalk."

Mayes reached for his clothes. "I'm confused."

"Me, too." That was the honest to God truth. My head was clearing as if I'd been in a thick fog for days. The laser-like precision in my thoughts was both welcome and scary, except I couldn't bear to turn the examination inward. I dressed in a flurry of arms and legs. "Why'd you do that?"

"For the record, you jumped me," Mayes said. "Not that I'm complaining. You can jump me anytime you like."

I rubbed my temple, as if that would ease the low-grade buzzing in my ears. "That's just it. I've never jumped anyone in my entire life. We didn't do this of our own free will. I think we had help."

"Speak for yourself. I've been wanting to make love to you ever since I first saw you. I hope you have the same urge again. Soon."

The raw emotion in his eyes worried me. I didn't need ESP to know the tryst had been more than sex for him. "I need to talk to Rose. Can you keep an eye out for trouble?"

Mayes laughed and zipped his pants. "What would trouble look like? A sexy nymph with designs on my body? I hope trouble gets her act together and jumps me again. Trust me, I will definitely be on the lookout for trouble."

"I'm ignoring you." I scooched down the wall in the far corner of the room and turned my thoughts to dreams and my supernatural mentor, Rose. She'd bailed me out of tight scrapes, but Rose never did anything for free. She'd gotten her hooks into me when Daddy crossed the crystalline bridge on the Other Side and couldn't return. Rose found him for me, to the tune of one hour of my life. Another time, she'd transported me and Gentle Dove, my mom's best friend, to the ER, when it was a life or death situation. She'd required another hour of my life when my ghost dog trapped me in the transition zone.

Cha-ching. Rose now owned three hours of my life. Far as I knew, she hadn't collected on the debt, and the last time we'd met, she had been on a power trip. She'd nearly roasted me like a rotisserie chicken.

According to Rose, she was an angel undercover in the demon world. She'd shown me her wings, so I believed her story. But lately, I sensed Rose had a private agenda.

I called her name as I searched for her in the murk of the Other Side. Rose didn't respond, but I seemed to be walking in a structured dreamscape that resembled a corridor of hotel doors. Should I start knocking on doors? Did I want to see the others Rose had compartmentalized? Did I want to know what any of them were doing?

No.

I didn't want to keep walking either. I had lots to do today. "Rose? I'm here. Where are you? Show yourself."

A door opened to my left. I entered. A cluttered bordello met my eye. Luscious scarlet swaths draped a king-size four-poster bed. Soft pillows crowned the bed, but the main draw, the centerpiece impossible to miss, was the barely decent tattooed woman lounging on the mattress.

"Feeling better?" Rose purred, stretching languidly.

Her smugness said it all. She'd instigated that sexual encounter. My hands fisted at my sides. "You can't do that," I yelled. "You can't mess with people's emotions like that."

"I can, and I did. You've been unusually tense and uptight. The exercise did you good. There's a different air about you now."

"It's an air of desperation. Mayes expects me to be his girlfriend now, but I'm married. My husband is still out there, somewhere. My husband whom I love and have never, ever cheated on."

Rose examined her black-tipped finger-nails. "Until today."

"Not fair. You have to take this back, to make this right."

Rose levitated off the bed. "I don't take orders from you. Besides, I did you a favor. I could've had him service us and blanked both your memories."

"Getting laid isn't part of our deal."

"Our deal is you owe me three hours of your life."

"You used some of that time today."

"That? I don't think so. I have something else I need you for."

"A deal's a deal."

"Listen to me, you ingrate. I'm calling the shots here. . . ."

Rose broke off as a loud claxon tone drove me to my knees. I clamped my hands over my ears, knowing that this was a dream and that I couldn't lower the sound. Abruptly, it ceased, and Rose looked petulant.

In the blink of an eye, she stood beside me, dressed demurely in a simple white gown. Not one of her tattoos showed on her skin. The cluttered boudoir gave way to the unrelenting grayness of the dreamscape.

"You will be credited fifteen minutes off your debt, though that's extremely generous on my part. Your guy's got good stamina, but he lacked finesse in his three-minute effort."

"It was more than three minutes," I heard myself yell. Seeing Rose's smirk, I realized I'd fallen into her trap once more.

I swallowed the growl in my throat, quickly trying to connect the dots. Rose had a boss. The boss sanctioned her. I should be grateful. I bowed my head momentarily. "Thank you for that concession. Will you also let Mayes know it was you instead of me?"

"No. This is your mess now."

"But, but. . . ."

Rose raised her hands in mock surrender. "I gave at the office."

I closed my mouth. Rose began to fade. "Wait! I need to ask you about something else. Two somethings, actually. My case —"

"Can't talk about the case. I just got reamed out by my boss. You gotta do more discovery work for yourself. You already know how to find Mandy Patterson."

I cursed under my breath. It would take twice as long to close cases with me fumbling around up here. "Okay. Moving on, I've been having fleeting pains here and there. The doctor says I'm fine. Could it be voodoo? Is that possible?"

"Anything's possible. Haven't you figured

that out yet?"

"But why would I be a target? What did I ever do to them?"

Rose crossed her arms and gazed down her nose at me. "Indeed."

"That's it? You can't tell me who is behind this?"

"Nope. Discovery. That's your job."

"This sucks."

"You could always get laid again." Rose laughed hysterically as she faded from sight.

CHAPTER FIFTEEN

My head bobbed as I came back to my normal senses. The small observation room zoomed into focus, cold and impersonal. Everything in here, from walls to the table and chairs, was a shade of gray. I would forevermore associate the plain room with the emotional combustion of what Mayes and I did here.

Not quite consensual sex.

Cold seeped from the tiled floor and numbed me like an epidural. I clambered to my feet, feeling as wobbly-kneed as a new foal. Mayes watched me like a hungry predator. A chill shivered down my spine that had nothing to do with temperature and everything to do with sensual abandon. My pulse skittered. Oh, it would be easy to have a torrid affair with this man.

The sex had been amazing, but it was more than acrobatics and physical release on my end too. Mayes was a Dreamwalker.

116

He knew the things I dealt with on a daily basis and wasn't freaked out. He had a good job. He respected and knew my family. He treated me with respect. Even now, after I'd waved a big red flag to stop any further intimacy, after I'd denied responsibility for my actions, he still wanted me.

I hesitated. How could I explain and keep my pride and respect without shredding his? I didn't like cleaning up Rose's mess, especially since she'd usurped my free will to get her jollies. I'd known what I was doing during her takeover, but I couldn't stop myself.

Dear God. I still owed her two hours and forty-five minutes of my life. Would she use me to satisfy her baser urges?

"Did you find her? You weren't gone very long," Mayes said.

The tang of our sexual encounter lingered in the air. Great. While I'd been trying to get Rose to square things for me, Mayes had been immersed in this pheromone-laced atmosphere.

"I found her."

"And . . . ?"

I stared at my hands, willing each finger to move independently. I was in control of my body, not Rose. "And she orchestrated what happened here."

"Prove it."

My ears heated. It was hard to meet his fierce gaze, but I dug deep. "I can't. She refuses to come here and apologize. I'm sorry you got caught up in her mischief. Truly sorry. I wish she'd left well enough alone, but she didn't." I swallowed thickly and forced the rest out. "I'm attracted to you, Sam Mayes, but I made a commitment to my husband. Until I know what happened to him, until I know where he is, I can't move forward in a relationship with you or anyone. I'm being totally honest with you."

His face clouded. Would he conclude I was making excuses? Was he hoping Rose would pay us another visit — say, this evening when everyone else went to sleep?

It stunned me to realize I wanted that too. That one taste of this man would never be enough. We hadn't known each other very long, and I'd never been to his house or met his family. But still. The tangible, incendiary, and wonderfully X-rated chemistry between us made me realize how empty my life had been. How lonely I'd been.

The reality of sexual attraction clashed with the responsibility I had to my family. Never would I have acted on the attraction, not while there was a chance Roland was still out there. When I made a commitment, I stuck with it.

My eyes misted. Stuck. That's exactly how I felt. Trapped in an Other World-like dimension of reality, unable to move forward or back. I would honor my vows, and if that cost me Mayes, I had to live with that. A deep sigh shook my entire body as I resigned myself to my duty.

"Where are we?" Mayes asked.

"What?" We were at the sheriff's office. He knew that.

"Us, Bax. I'm talking about *us*. You look miserable, and that was never my intent in visiting you. We were friends. Now we're . . . I don't know, prickly, awkward even."

"Any chance you'd forget what happened earlier?"

"Not a chance in hell."

Though his words were alarming, the cheesy smile on his face was contagious. I laughed. "It was worth a shot."

"Friends?"

"Friends." I glanced around. The room next door was dark. Questions about the case rattled around in my head, but my stomach growled. The sheriff would let me know when he needed me. "Apparently, I'm hungry."

"About time." He opened the door and motioned me through it. "And after we eat, I'll catch you up."

During lunch at the barbecue joint, Mayes asked about the history of Native Americans on the coast. I shared what I knew of the Guale Indians who'd been here when the Europeans arrived in the 1700s. "You should talk to Running Bear tonight at my parents' house. He lives and breathes this stuff."

"He's familiar with their totems?" Mayes asked.

"I believe so. He is a deeply spiritual man and my father's best friend. He's very interested in meeting you. Will y'all exchange a secret handshake or something?"

Dishes clanked as a waitress cleared a nearby table. I instinctively held my breath in the frigid silence. Inwardly, I cursed my glib remark. An apology was on the tip of my tongue when he answered, "Or something."

The flat tone of his voice told me I'd hurt him. "I'm sorry. I wasn't knocking your culture or anything. I was thinking you and Running Bear were both powerful spirit-walkers and holy men for your people. That you would have so much in common that you would recognize each other in some special way."

His expression cleared. "Apology accepted."

"I don't know what it's like to walk in your shoes, but I know what it feels like to be different. I didn't intend to be negative."

He regarded me steadily. "God willing, you will never know what it's like to grow up in another man's world, to be subject to his rules, to be told where to live and what to think. My people have barely clung to their traditions. Generations' worth of history is lost every day as we assimilate into the white man's world. The elders pressure me to step forward and lead the tribe, but I'm being assimilated too. This job, it suits me. You. You suit me. I am a man at war with myself."

I'd hit a nerve all right. I sucked air through my teeth. "I'm an idiot. That's the only explanation that makes any sense."

His hand covered mine. "You're not an idiot. I look like a tough guy, but my heritage is my Achilles heel. Your remark shouldn't have bothered me. But it did. And because of the mind-blowing sex we shared, you felt my distress. And I feel your distress at upsetting me. So, we're even."

The sounds of the busy restaurant faded.

Mind-blowing sex? Euphoria flitted through me. He'd enjoyed it as much as I had, but I couldn't handle the guilt that came with adultery. I'd hoped he wouldn't bring up the encounter, especially in a public place, but he was good at pushing my buttons.

"I don't know about 'even,' but I promise to pay closer attention to what I mean to say."

"You're all right, Powell." With that, he deftly snagged the check from the waitress and paid in cash.

I waved a twenty at him. "Wait. We should split that."

"Not happening."

This wasn't a date, but I could see paying the bill was important to him. "I'll get it next time."

He didn't respond, going all inscrutable on me. I could do inscrutable too. I thrust on my dark glasses.

We headed to the sheriff's office, and I turned my focus to the case. I needed to find Mandy Patterson's spirit, to learn what caused the explosion that took her life, and the best way to do that was to touch her things. If the arson investigator had found the source of the fire, even better.

"So, June stormed out of the interview and dragged Doodle with her?" I asked as

Mayes slowed to turn onto the state highway. He'd only been here a day, but he already had a good grasp of the basics of getting around Marion.

"Doodle balked, but the sheriff said it was either his aunt or Child Protective Services for Doodle. The kid's face turned white."

"He doesn't get along with his aunt?"

"She views him as a meal ticket, and he knows it. There's no love lost between that pair."

"How odd." Just then my elbow twinged. I winced.

Mayes noticed my sea change immediately. He scanned the vicinity and slowed the truck. "What is it?"

"Sharp pain in the elbow. Feels like someone jabbed me with a knife. Same point-source throbbing I felt in my heel before. This isn't natural." The pain intensified. I couldn't breathe for a moment.

Mayes pulled over onto the shoulder and unhooked his seatbelt. His hand rested lightly on my arm. The pain subsided.

"How'd you do that?" I asked.

"We did it."

"How?"

"There seem to be some lingering side effects from . . . before."

"The mind-blowing sex?"

He gave me a sensual smile. "Yes."

"Do tell."

"I'd rather show you."

"No." I batted him playfully, dislodging his hand. Pain throbbed in my elbow. I moved his hand back to my elbow and the pain receded. "How is this possible? Your touch is like taking an aspirin."

"It's more than that. Slip into your extra senses and look at my aura."

"Hmm." I did as he suggested, not sure I liked the fact that his touch took away my pain. His aura had transformed. The dark, emerald-green cloak of power he wore so naturally was shot through with bright blue. My aura was bright blue. The colors were still distinct, yet integrated. "Weird."

"Not weird. Fantastic. Our energy fields merge when we touch. Keep watching mine as I remove my hand."

Sure enough, the blue in his aura winked out as soon as he released me. He touched me again, and the blue returned. "Your blue aura changes to turquoise when I touch you. You see it, don't you?"

"I can't see my energy field. You know that."

"But you know it's blue, right?"

"Yes."

"Our connection is enhanced, not just in

this world, but my guess is in the next world as well."

"What does it mean? Will it stay this way?"

He gently massaged my elbow, soothing the hurt exactly at the nexus of pain. "I don't have answers. This is a first for me."

"Are you in my head too?"

"A little. Pain penetrates through the virtual firewall you always have up."

"How do you know about that?"

"I just do, same as I know the pain is gone from the spiritual attack."

He removed his hand, and it was true. The pain wasn't there anymore. "Does this link work both ways?"

He shrugged. "Try to see what I'm thinking."

I took his hand and focused the same as I would when I sent a telepathic message to my father or daughter. The image of my face caught up in sensual bliss flashed in my head. "Not fair."

He grinned. "Mind-blowing sex. I can't stop thinking about it."

I let go of him and the image faded. "Now what? How will we find out who's attacking me?"

"Seeing as how the onset is new, I believe it's related to the case."

"Who is it? Why are they doing this?"

"Given the timing of the attack, I believe it's someone involved in the case. You know any voodoo priestesses?"

"No." An image of a cloth sachet flashed in my head, followed by the scent of herbs. "Maybe."

"And . . . ?"

"And I shouldn't make an accusation because I lack proof. I'm thinking of Cipriona Marsden, my dreamwalking client yesterday. She's a palm reader and her granny's in prison for murdering her father."

"We should pay her a visit."

"Agreed, soon as we have a spare moment. I have something of hers. It gives me an excuse to see her again."

"Good." He buckled his seatbelt and eased the truck onto the highway. "Getting back to our blended auras. We should try a dreamwalk together to see if we have more firepower."

"Then we need to visit the evidence room."

"Headed there now."

CHAPTER SIXTEEN

We burst in on Mr. GBI, Burnell Escoe, and the sheriff in the evidence room. I covered the awkwardness of our intrusion by introducing myself and Mayes.

"Nice to meet you, but you're not needed here." Escoe had rolled up the sleeves of his starched dress shirt and taken off his suit coat. The long examination table before him was full of boxes. "I've taken point on this investigation, and I'm playing this one by the book. We need solid connections between the evidence and the suspects. No loosey-goosey stuff."

I glanced over at Mayes. His grim expression mirrored the sheriff's. "So we're off the case?"

Wayne gave a terse nod, squared his shoulders. The Sinclair County Sheriff's badge on his belt caught the light and glinted. "The focus has shifted from the cause of the Patterson woman's death to

ID'ing her distributor and finding her boss."

His words riled me. "You don't care what happened to Mandy?"

"She isn't our top priority, but you may follow up on something else for me. You ready for a new assignment?"

"Sure." I infused my voice with cheer despite the anger churning in my gut. "What do you need?"

"Swing by the animal shelter and check on those abandoned animals. The ones in our backburner case."

"The shelter?" The words were out of my mouth before I connected the dots. According to Doodle, his pot bellied pigs were stashed at the animal shelter. Was Wayne doing an end-run around Mr. Perfect?

"Yeah. You're good with animals. Take a good look around the pet pokey. Maybe you'll notice something the others have missed."

"They weren't present at the time of the incident," I reminded him.

I didn't miss the disbelief or the sneer from Burnell Escoe. He couldn't wait to be rid of me and my loosey-goosey ways. I couldn't wait to prove him wrong.

"I wouldn't have a consultant on my staff that couldn't take orders," Escoe said.

"Do it," Wayne said. "Something's due to

break on that other case soon."

His sharp tone aggravated me, but his eyes told a different story. He seemed to be laughing silently. At me or Escoe?

"Yes, sir."

CHAPTER SEVENTEEN

Mayes was still laughing when we returned to my truck. "Not funny," I said, holding my hand out for the keys after he opened the driver's door. "I can't help it if I'm good with animals."

"I never thought of you as a pig whisperer, that's all. Your boss is too funny."

We clicked our seatbelts and rolled out of the lot. "He's a riot, all right."

Mayes studied me across the console. "You two have a history, don't you?"

He seemed to be holding his breath. My answer mattered to him, a lot. I went for casual, unwilling to reveal the layers of my history with Wayne. "I've known him for a long time, if that's what you mean. Why?"

"He knows about us."

Gravel crunched under my tires as we entered the access lane to the animal shelter. I didn't want Wayne to know I'd had sex with Mayes in the Observation Room. My gut clenched. "He couldn't possibly."

"He does. The knowledge blazed in his eyes just now in the evidence room. For someone who's in the slow lane career-wise, he's good at reading people."

I didn't want the sheriff knowing our private business. Best to steer the conversation in another direction. "Don't underestimate Wayne. He used to lull his opponents into complacency on the football field, then he'd strike with touchdown passes. He has a talent for reading situations and strategizing."

"Were you two together then?" Mayes asked.

The chained gate across the road halted our forward motion. Floyd's sign, OUT ON AN ANIMAL CALL, hung beside the lock. I could maneuver around this physical roadblock, but I wasn't sure I could work around this question. Best to quit hedging or Mayes would think I was hiding something.

I sighed. "We've never been *together,* and we never will be. He's not competition, if that's what you're worried about. He views me as a departmental asset. That's the disconnect you're feeling."

His face clouded. "Not buying it, but as long as Wayne doesn't try to drive a wedge between us, I'm happy with the status quo."

My scalp felt tight, as if my head might blow off. Was Mayes calling me a liar? Was he calling my morals into question? Suddenly, the situation overwhelmed me. Brooding men. Dead people. Sex. God, just thinking about having sex at the police station had my hand shaking. Rose and her bright ideas could go jump off a sand dune. My fingers coiled into a fist. "Wouldn't want you to be unhappy."

His gaze narrowed. "What's with the attitude?"

"I can't quite get my equilibrium around you, and it irritates me to be off-balance."

He grinned. "Great sex does that."

"Knock it off. I mean it."

My voice sounded sharper than I'd intended. Mayes clammed up, and I felt awful, like I'd kicked a puppy. My emotions were bouncing all over the place. I had to do better. I genuinely liked Mayes. Even though I was annoyed with him, I preferred his company to anyone else's. He grounded me, except when he didn't.

Like now.

"I apologize," I began slowly. "Sex keeps creeping into our conversation. Are you doing that on purpose to keep me off guard?"

"Not my intent, but look at it from my

132

perspective. The woman of my dreams fulfilled my fantasies today. That experience tops everything in my personal highlight reel."

Woman of his dreams? I'd never been that to anyone, not even Roland. Though my husband said he put me first, the military was his first love. I'd been an accessory. Odd, I'd never realized that until this minute, until I experienced what it felt like to have a guy put you first.

"You're not tricking me into another discussion of sex." I cut the motor and opened my door. "Think pigs. Big, hairy, grunting pigs. Think of them stomping on Escoe's head."

He followed me down the fence line. "I thought these were those cute little piglet-looking pigs."

"They get big."

"How big?" he asked.

"Big enough that you can't believe people keep them in their homes."

"Big enough to eat."

We edged through the narrow opening between the fence post and a tree; then it was smooth sailing to the shelter. However, our goal was the fenced pump-house structure beyond the shelter, directly ahead of us.

"People who own these pigs would shoot you for even thinking that," I said. "To them, these animals rank the same as other people's pets."

"Duly noted."

Mayes caught my hand and clasped my fingers in his. The world slid more clearly into place. The hue of daylight softened. My worries eased, until I realized Mayes had caused the mood change. "How'd you do that? How is this synchronicity possible?"

He gave my hand a gentle squeeze, assuring me he knew I'd registered the change in scenery, inside and out. "Feels good, doesn't it? Like coming home."

He'd spoken out loud, but in truth, he could've said it in my head. I'd felt his thoughts along the virtual border I'd erected in my mind. It was petty of me to keep him out, but I needed that space to be private.

But *coming home.* That described the rightness of it. I nodded. "Good description."

His thumb rubbed over the back of my hand, and the remaining tension eased from my body. I could get used to feeling treasured. I *so* could get used to it. If only I had some idea about my husband's true circumstances. . . .

Best not to worry over a matter I couldn't resolve. Best to stick to concrete questions I could answer, like the fate of these pot bellied pigs.

This area was designed so neutered cats could come and go on the property at will. The external feeding station created a safe haven to re-home feral cats that were unwelcome where they'd been trapped.

I didn't see any sign of Petunia or Patches. Instead, I saw a pig-sized bowed-out section of fence wire around the cat house. I called both their names a few times as I scanned the vicinity. Nothing moved in any direction across the lawn.

"Jail break," Mayes said. "They're long gone."

I eyed the back of the shelter. Petunia loved dog food. The feral cat shelter had no food or water right now. With her keen nose, Petunia would smell the shelter's dog food.

"Not necessarily. Let's check the shelter." I studied the dog runs and the exercise yard behind the main building as we approached. No dogs outside. No grunting pigs on the grounds either. No breaks in the chain-link fence, though the gate was open. "Well, well, well."

We entered the gate and latched it behind us. Inside the shelter, dogs barked at our

135

approach. A few darted out in their runs to yap at us. Cats perched atop cages on the back porch, watching us intently. I felt a wave of cold on my leg. Oliver, my ghost-dog companion. He wanted me to know he was present.

"Oliver?" Mayes asked.

"Yes. You feel him too?"

"I do." With his other hand, Mayes pointed to the back door. It gaped open. "Smart pig."

"Doodle said the pigs could get out of their trailer. Guess one of them figured out how to work a doorknob with its snout. They must be inside somewhere. I never thought I'd say this, but I wish Virg was here with his stun gun. I have a feeling this pig won't let us get between her and her dog-food stash."

"I'll protect you," Mayes said.

I glared at him. "No shooting the pigs. We're not eating them."

We walked through a laundry area in the back, then a big cleaning station. "Quarantine wing's off to the right; the main kennel's to the left. The cattery is directly ahead. Bulk food storage is in the admin area between the cattery and the quarantine wing."

"Sounds like you've been here a time or two."

"I've leash-trained some dogs to give them a better chance of adoption. I haven't been out here in a while. Just too busy with police work to even keep my Pets and Plants business going full blast." We rounded a corner. I heard grunts. "We found them."

Big trashcan bins of dog food lay on their sides, and pellets of dog food littered the floor. Two fat pigs — one mostly black, the other speckled — lay on the heap.

The animals looked up warily. I didn't trust the militant gleam in the dark pig's eyes. I tried calling her name. "Petunia. Come here." Nothing. I tried the other pig's name. "Patches. Come." Nothing. I approached slowly, still tethered to Mayes by our joined hands. The frequency and pitch of pig grunts went through the roof. We retreated, and the noise level dropped.

Both pigs wore body harnesses that would accommodate a leash clip. To move these chow hounds, I needed to get these hulks leashed up and escorted to the backyard. "Go to the wash area and grab two leashes, please," I said to Mayes.

When he departed, the noise level dropped to nothing. Hmm. Were they responding to human interference or to Mayes in particular? I circled around until I stood opposite the door. Mayes returned, and the pigs squealed like banshees.

"They don't like you very much," I observed.

"I've hunted many of their brethren," he said, tossing me a leash. "Maybe they sense I'm a predator."

I clipped a leash on Patches. He barely spared me a glance. Mayes had his complete attention. "We need to move the pigs outside to the exercise yard. They'll get sick if they keep eating this dog food. Too bad we don't have Doodle's phone number. We could let him know what's going on."

"His contact information is probably listed in the office, since he volunteers here," Mayes said. "I'll find it once we relocate the pigs."

"Good idea." Leash in hand, I reached for Petunia's harness and plunged headlong into a dreamwalk.

CHAPTER EIGHTEEN

The familiar dreamwalking sensation of tumbling through a dark void eased slowly. I became aware of my inky surroundings and the continued presence of Oliver, the black Great Dane who'd befriended me on a spirit walk a few months ago. I knelt to pet my favorite ghost dog. He licked my face and barked happily.

"You need to find a spirit over here," I told him. "Someone who loves animals and has plenty of time for you."

I straightened and noticed a glow to my left. Oliver and I headed toward the faint light. The mist thinned, and long shadows stretched before me. At first glance, they appeared to be writhing, but then I realized the sense of movement was a byproduct of a whirling ceiling fan suspended beneath a weak light.

Reassured, I took another step forward. "Hello? Anybody here?"

The tableau filled in before my eyes. Tabletops bore glassware, tubing, cold-tablet packages, and boxy equipment I didn't recognize. Jugs of paint thinner, gasoline, and drain cleaner lined the base-boards, alongside discarded packaging. Pinpricks of light showed through a wall. I studied the oddity closer, realizing the light came from edges of cardboard taped over a window. A flat-screen monitor with a picture of a yard dominated one wall. The image flickered, and another outdoor vantage point displayed on the screen. Security cameras?

There was an odor. My nose wrinkled at the acrid scent. Sulfury, like eggs gone bad. A figure wearing a respirator over a bandana-covered head moved around the room doing repetitive tasks. I'd never set foot inside a meth lab, but I had a sinking feeling that's where I'd landed. Even though I was here in spirit form and this wasn't real time, merely a memory this spirit wanted me to see, I instinctively covered my nose with the hem of my T-shirt and re-treated to the doorway.

The spirit wore pink gloves, same as the heavy-duty ones I cleaned with at home. I'd purchased the pink color because I was tired of the sameness of the yellow ones.

"Mandy?" I asked. "Is that you? Is this your lab?"

The person continued her tasks.

Drat. The downside of static dreamwalks was the lack of interaction. I wanted answers so that I could get justice for Mandy. I didn't like the guesswork of figuring out why this scene mattered to her.

Since I'd accessed this dream through touching Petunia the pig, this had to be Mandy's lab. Though her house had been orderly, this room would never win her a homemaker-of-the-year award. Too dark, too cluttered, too dangerous.

Why would she turn her house into a meth lab? Why would she put her life and her son's at risk? If he'd been home during the explosion, he'd be dead too.

A noise sounded. Thumping, on the door. The masked figure glanced at the monitor and saw a vehicle approaching. She hurried to the door, stepped across the threshold, and turned to triple-lock the door behind her. She removed her respirator, bandana, and gloves. Her blonde hair and her face matched Mandy Patterson's driver's-license photo.

At the sound of grunting, I glanced down at Mandy's feet. A smaller version of Petunia wagged her tail happily. Mandy made cooing sounds and told Petunia she was the best pig ever. Petunia was a watch pig? Had she sensed the school bus coming down the road?

Mandy hurried to her front stoop and waved at the bus driver. A young boy sprinted off the bus and raced toward her. She knelt and gathered him in a big hug.

"You're all stinky again," the boy said, hugging her and Petunia, "and wet."

"Don't worry about it, hon. I'll shower in a bit. Come inside and tell me about your day at school. Did your teacher like your essay?"

"She did! She used my story about why I want to go to the moon as an example for the whole class. She said I had real potential. What's 'potential,' Mom?"

Mandy handed Doodle a juice box and some pretzels. "It means you're smart. That you can make something of yourself."

"Like what?"

"Like anything." Mandy filled a glass of water for herself from the tap and sat down at the table with her son. "You could be an astronaut, a doctor, a lawyer, anything."

"What if I just want to be a little boy?"

"You can be that too, but when you get older, you could go to college and learn about everything. I've been putting money aside for you, saving toward that goal. One day you'll live in a big white house."

"With a picket fence and lots of grass and flowers, like Joe Joe's house in town?"

"That's right."

"And kids won't make fun of my shoes anymore?"

Mandy's head snapped back as if she'd been punched. "Is someone bothering you at school, Doodle?"

He glanced down. "The mean boys. They say I'm poor. They call me names."

"What names?"

"Bustard. They say I'm a bad name 'cause I got no daddy. One boy calls me Nappy. Why don't they like my curly hair, Mom?"

Mandy blanched and leaned forward. "Did you tell your teacher about the name-calling?"

"No. That makes it worse. Last time I told on them for pushing me on the playground, they dunked my head in the toilet."

"Why didn't you tell me? What are their names? Is that Hutto boy behind this? He's bad news, I know that for a fact because his daddy is a miserable excuse for a person."

"I thought you liked Mr. Hutto."

"I worked with him once. I don't like him."

"Why don't you work with people you like?"

"You'll understand one day. Adults work to pay bills and to set money aside, for important things like college."

"You're going to college?"

"No, silly. You are. You're the one with potential. I'm just a mom."

The scene blurred. I fought the fade, wanting to see more, wanting to know more about Mandy Patterson, but she'd finished with me and returned me to my world. I came to my senses, a hand on Petunia's portly flesh. The pig eyed me uneasily, as if she knew something weird had happened.

"Welcome back," Mayes said from the doorway.

I blinked at the brightness of the room. After the shadowy world of the Other Side, illumination of any kind was blinding. My mouth was dry. No sign of Oliver.

"Was I gone long?" I asked.

"Five minutes, tops."

"Felt like longer."

"I have a water bottle for you. I'd hand it to you, but the pigs don't like me."

"Keep the bottle for now. I've got to move these pigs outside." Figuring Petunia was the ring leader, I led her, and sure enough, Patches followed, fat bellies on both pigs

144

swinging with every grunting step.

After the pigs were outdoors, and we locked the back door, I grabbed a broom to corral the spilled food. Mayes stopped me. "Leave it. Write a note to the Animal Control officer and let's get going."

"It won't take long to clean up the mess."

"Yeah, but there are probably rules for sanitizing the room. The food may all have to be thrown out. You don't want to get mired in Doodle's mistake."

"How so?"

"He shouldn't have stashed the pigs here. This place is for dogs and cats."

I stored the broom in the closet. "We don't have a pig rescue shelter."

"Not our problem. Prioritize. Finding homes for these pigs isn't as important as learning what happened to Ms. Patterson. What'd you see, by the way?"

"I saw an afternoon scene from early in Doodle's life. He rode the school bus home, and his mom was cooking meth. She stopped to welcome him home. Apparently she considered him a child prodigy, but he was being bullied at school."

"Anything stand out in the dreamwalk?" Mayes asked as we walked to the truck.

"The meth room resembled a science lab trashed by teenagers. Not neat or tidy. I didn't understand what she was doing at first, but it was the room where the explosion occurred. Anyway, she told Doodle she was putting aside money for his college."

"She's been cooking for a long time?"

I squeezed through the opening between the fence and tree. Mayes followed, and then we edged along the fence line to my truck. The afternoon sun felt good on my face.

"That's my take on it," I said. "Doodle seemed younger than Larissa, so maybe five or six years."

"Seems like your sheriff should've known about her operation."

"He didn't."

"Hmm. Must mean she didn't sell locally. Her anonymity could be because she supplied product for another region. That would make her a powerful asset and a secret weapon for a drug cartel."

"She had security cameras in her yard. I saw the feed in the dreamwalk."

"Too bad we can't access those vids. She would most likely have pics of the arsonist."

"Not a chance, not unless the feed went offsite, and then, how would we find it?"

Mayes went silent for a moment. "We should check the woods bordering her trailer for cameras. There's a chance the files remain on the camera itself."

My feet dragged to a halt. I met his gaze over the hood of my truck. "You think the images survived the blaze?"

Mayes shrugged. "None of us thought about cameras this morning. You saw the feed, right?"

"I did."

"Then you can show me where the cameras were pointed. I'll backtrack from there."

"Sounds good."

"If that doesn't pan out, our best shot is to find that money. Given Mandy's lack of detection by local law enforcement, I suspect she cranked out a lot of meth. That kid must be flipping rich. No telling how much money is in his college fund by now."

"We should flag Mandy's bank accounts and make sure that June doesn't get her greedy paws on his college fund."

"I'm sure your sheriff will hit the banks on Monday. Banks are closed over the weekend."

"Right. The weekend." Today was still Saturday. I had another day with Mayes and then he'd drive home on Monday. This weekend was zipping by at warp speed.

Mayes withdrew a slip of paper from his pocket. "I copied the kid's cell number from the office. Let's see if he'll meet with us."

"You're full of good ideas."

CHAPTER NINETEEN

Doodle met us at the hamburger joint. "I got nothing to say to you people."

"You came," Mayes said, gesturing for the kid to sit with us. "Might as well hear us out."

The teen reached behind him, grabbed a chair, and reversed it to sit down. Guess he didn't care to sit beside either one of us in the booth. He was also closest to the door. Smart kid.

"We know your mom cooked meth, Doodle," I said. "We also know why she did it. For you. For college."

His brown eyes blazed, but he said nothing. Anger radiated in waves from this young man. How could I reach him?

"We want to learn the circumstances surrounding her death," I continued. "We want you to have peace of mind so you can move on."

"My mom is dead. Nothing can fix that."

At last! He was talking. "She visited me in a dream. You were in it too. And you were talking about a Mr. Hutto."

Doodle blasted out a string of cuss words. I was surprised my ears didn't blister from his fury. When he paused for a breath, I asked, "You didn't like Hutto?"

"No matter what she did, he yelled at her. He worked with her for a day, then Derenne moved in. He was worse than Hutto because he yelled and beat my mom. I should've killed him while he was sleeping. Now he's killed my mom, and I have to stay with Aunt June. This blows chunks."

I connected the dots. "Derenne was your mom's business partner?"

"Not hardly. He was her boss and land-lord. He made sure she did what he wanted."

"How'd he do that?"

"Said he'd make me an orphan if she quit. Said she was his personal property. Like he owned her. I hate him."

"What's Derenne's full name?"

He reared back, eyes round. "Learned my lesson about bullies years ago. My lips are sealed."

Mayes shifted in his seat like he was getting ready to say something. I shot him a sharp look. "Bullies can be stopped, but

150

they have to be exposed. They live on people's fears."

"You don't understand. This guy's a hunter. He's always boasting about his kills. He will kill me, and no one will care. I'm a nobody."

"You're a somebody. I'd notice if you were killed, Doodle."

"Doesn't matter. If he finds out I talked to you, I'll be dead."

"You can't spend your whole life looking over your shoulder. We need to bring this man in for questioning."

"Find him some other way. I gotta go."

Quicker than the blink of an eye, Mayes blocked the boy's exit. "Stay. Just a moment longer."

Doodle shrank toward me. "Why?"

"We want to help you, but you have to help us first."

The boy froze as a group of people entered the building. He let out a long sigh when they took no notice of him.

He sat, but I knew I didn't have long. "Where did your mother bank?"

"She didn't have a bank account."

"How did she pay her bills?"

"In cash or money orders."

"How old is Petunia?"

"She's nine."

"Was she always a watch pig?"

Doodle nearly cracked a smile. "Yeah. She always knew when a vehicle was coming."

"She'd thump her head on the door of the lab?"

He blinked. "How'd you know that?"

"I just do."

"That's wrong. I gotta go."

He rose, and so did I. "Wait. Your pigs are in trouble. They busted out of the pen you had them in and broke into the shelter. We moved them to the exercise yard. You might want to check on them before you do anything else."

"What?" His hands shook, and his face paled. "I gotta save them. They're all the family I have left."

Mayes and I watched him flee. "That went well," I said.

"Good line of questioning." Mayes smiled at me. "We now know she cooked for Derenne for six to eight years. Where'd the money go?"

"If she didn't have a bank account, maybe she hid the money on her property."

"Or she laundered it to create Doodle's college fund," Mayes said. "I know someone who's pretty good with computers. He could search investment companies using Doodle's Social Security number."

"Won't that upset Mr. GBI's apple cart?"

"It's a lead. If it pans out, I'll let the sheriff know. Escoe is being shortsighted by dismissing your helpfulness. If he thinks he'll find a buyer's name in all that rubble from the fire, he's mistaken. Mandy was a survivor. Had to be or the job would've eaten her alive before now."

My pride still smarted from the GBI agent cutting me out of the picture. "Why is Wayne going along with him?"

"Is he? Wayne sent us to check on the pigs. You had a dreamwalk. We now know Mandy's trucker boyfriend was her landlord, boss, and enforcer. That's a lead Wayne can use."

"I guess."

"We're still on the case. Just doing it on the QT. It's a matter of perspective. Wayne knows you have value. He'll bring you back in due time."

"How do you know?"

"It's what I would do."

A group of teens walked by, laughing and talking. Mayes' words lifted my spirits. I wasn't off the case. I was working undercover. I liked that, a lot.

"Getting back to the case, if Mandy didn't use a bank, then she probably didn't use a lockbox to store her money or her important papers."

"Probably not. We'll keep pondering the money angle. Meanwhile, we have two leads to show for our efforts. Better yet, the drug-supply-chain lead may get Escoe out of here sooner. If Derenne's the distributor, I can't run his name without attracting the wrong kind of notice."

"We'll tell the sheriff and let him take the heat. Imagine how happy he'll be to learn I speak pig very well."

"And we'll continue to think about where Mandy stashed her cash. If we find it, we may solve the case without Escoe. Wouldn't that beat all?"

I smiled big. "It would."

CHAPTER TWENTY

After leaving the sheriff a voicemail message on his cell with our findings, we stopped at my house to grab several grocery bags of fresh veggies. This edible bounty came as a fringe benefit of being the Dreamwalker. Bags of food showed up on my porch several times a week, same as they had at my parents' house when my dad was the Dreamwalker.

The amount of donated food exceeded my needs, so I paid it forward by sharing with the community food bank. This batch of mostly sweet potatoes, kale, tomatoes, onions, and fresh peaches would certainly add to the fare at tonight's cookout at my parents' place in the woods.

Out of the blue, worry crowded in. My family leaned toward counterculture instead of mainstream. Mayes seemed determined to mainstream himself. Would he consider our lifestyle backward?

"What?" Mayes said as we carried the bags to my truck.

"Do you know what you are getting yourself into tonight? Most people avoid Mom and Dad unless they need help or sanctuary. Folks consider them to be burned-out hippies. Fair warning: very odd characters turn up at their place."

"I'm not one to be swayed by public opinion. Besides, I've already met your parents, and they're good people. I respect them, and their unique abilities. You're blessed to have them in your life."

As we stowed the food, I savored Mayes' words. Mom and Dad were givers, and I was proud of them. "What about your folks? You don't talk about your family much."

He frowned. "My parents expect me to embrace the old ways, to follow tradition, and to take my place in tribal leadership. Yet, they drive new cars and watch movies on their flat-screen TV."

His observation filled me with sympathy as I eased the truck out of the driveway and steered to my parents' house. "I'm sorry."

"They put no pressure on my brother or my sister to be wholly Cherokee. Just me. How fair is that?"

"Fair?" Words long swallowed boiled in my craw and then erupted. "There's no such thing. Let me tell you what I think about 'fair.' It took two years to straighten out the red tape surrounding Roland's death benefits; meanwhile, I had to support us. I love my folks, but I couldn't move in with them. The world is not fair. Never has been. Never will be."

Lines on the road slipped by in a hurry. The sky looked the same as it had earlier except now I felt icky. Why had I blurted that out? Mayes didn't need to know my money troubles. Worse, he'd finally opened up about his family and I'd told him to suck it up. It was so quiet in the truck I could hear the faint ringing in my ears.

Several miles rolled by, and I couldn't stand this awkward vibe. "I'm sorry. I don't know what came over me. I meant to show you I understood having the deck stacked against you, but once I opened those emotional floodgates, more came out than I intended. I can't discuss my problems with anyone. Not my parents, not Charlotte, not my daughter."

"I'm a good listener," Mayes said.

My eyes misted with tears. A sob escaped.

"I'm also very interested in your safety," Mayes said. "Pull over in front of that house."

The old McCauley place. I eased into

their weed-choked driveway. When I shifted the gear lever into park, Mayes unhooked our seatbelts and drew me into his arms. I let myself go, ignoring the wisdom of holding him at arm's length. He offered comfort, and I welcomed it.

After a few minutes, my tears subsided. My head felt stuffy, but my heart felt lighter than it had in a long time. "Thank you," I managed.

His arms tightened around me, and I realized he'd been softly chanting this whole time. Though the words sounded foreign to my ears, their effect soothed me. I stilled again, letting the moment happen.

The chant wound down in its own time, and an easy silence followed. "That was lovely," I murmured into his damp shirt.

He caressed my hair, splayed his palm across my back. Neither of us moved for a while, then I glanced up, not knowing what to expect. He touched his forehead to mine and released me.

I wasn't entirely ready to be released, but I felt stronger, as if the load that had bent my shoulders for years was gone. "What was that song?" I asked.

His face glowed. "A Cherokee healing melody. It is generations old, handed down orally among my people."

"What do the words mean?"

"It is about healing, tuning your inner light, and opening to possibilities."

I bowed my head to him, moved that he had shared so much of himself with me. It had felt so intimate, so personal. "I am thankful. You're full of surprises." And tenderness.

Another easy silence followed. "I have much respect for you, Dreamwalker."

"I'm humbled by your words. Truthfully, I'm a rookie on the paranormal level. But you, in contrast, you are a powerful holy man, whether you acknowledge it or not."

He lifted my chin and regarded me steadily. "The healing chant was for you alone. I do not do this for others."

"You should. Your family is right about your talents."

"My elders . . . they seek another path for me. A path I do not want."

His frank words opened another festering wound in my pride. "Do you think I wanted to be the Dreamwalker? This job was killing my dad, but if I didn't take it, the power and responsibility would shift to my daughter. That wasn't happening."

"You were born to be a Dreamwalker."

"You are a holy man."

We stared at each other for a moment and

then I burst out laughing. His expression tightened into a mask, so I hugged him until his tension eased. "Sorry. We're fighting about the oddest thing, about what makes us who we are."

"But not *what* we are."

An odd distinction. "If you say so."

Without further incident, we drove to my parents' cottage in the woods. I recognized the parked vehicles as those of Running Bear, Gentle Dove, and Bubba Paxton. They were my father's dreamwalking friends, and I'd inherited his paranormal support team when I became the Dreamwalker.

Mayes stood beside my truck for a moment, his hands raised to the east. Not knowing if this was another cultural moment, I froze. Would he burst into song? Would his words once again arrow straight into my heart?

Instead, he turned to me with a face as radiant as sunrise. "This place. It's special. It speaks to me."

"My grandparents nearly had a stroke when my dad decided to build here instead of at the waterfront. Dad held fast, and we've all benefited from his choice. The energy here is right. That's the best way I can describe it."

"The Great Spirit is pleased with him."

"You get that from your communion with nature just now?"

He gave me an odd look. "I've known it from the start. Your father is a good man."

Why was he testy with me again? "Great. Let's introduce you to everyone and get these vegetables to the kitchen."

"Mom!" Larissa called.

I turned to greet my daughter, but a terrible rending pain in my gut drove me to my knees. As I collapsed, I heard Mayes cry out and drop to the ground as well. The world faded to black.

CHAPTER TWENTY-ONE

I revived on the living room floor of my parents' cottage. For once, the drone of the weather channel Mom always watched had been silenced. The terrible pain in my gut had eased, but the uncomfortable pressure remained. My hand immediately went to my belly, dislodging several gemstones. Pain stabbed, harsh and ugly, taking my breath away.

"Be still, hon." Mom's soft voice soothed as she reapplied the gemstones. I opened my extra senses and viewed the scene from outside my body. Mayes and I lay side by side on a quilt in the center of the floor. Running Bear was chanting and splashing something over us while Mom, Dad, Larissa, Gentle Dove, and Bubba Paxton sat cross-legged around us. All the dogs were present. Elvis the Chihuahua nestled at my side.

Mayes joined me in the dream state.

"What happened to us?" he asked.

"The pain. It came back, this time in my belly. I passed out. Did it happen to you too?"

"Aah." He nodded sagely, as if the knowledge of the universe belonged to him.

When he didn't elaborate, my temper flared. "I hate it when you do that. Please tell me."

He watched me closely. "We are bound."

"How is that possible?" I edged away from him, watching the tableau below from across the room. "We have similar traits and interests, but bound? That's an odd word choice."

He shrugged.

I fumed silently. We weren't bound after energy sharing here and at the mountain, which suggested the Rose-orchestrated intimacy was the possible binding force. *Bound* sounded permanent, as in forever and ever, amen. Were we psychically fused together? Was that possible?

If so, I'd paid a helluva price for Rose getting her jollies. My anger welled and billowed like thunderheads. Were free will and freedom of thought figments of my imagination? This was my life. I should be in charge of my thoughts and actions. I resented being someone else's puppet. Or some*thing*

163

else's puppet. Was an entity from beyond doing this to me . . . and to Mayes?

An urge to let go flitted into my thoughts. I ignored it, but the tension in my body and mind eased a bit. I wanted to let go, but trust was in short supply. "What's Running Bear doing?"

Mayes edged closer. "Purifying us."

I couldn't quite wrap my head around his words, especially now that I was silently repeating the chant. "Are we dirty?"

He hesitated before reaching out with his virtual hand. "It is a ritual cleansing. To remove the harm from us. Allow him to finish. He is helping."

If that would get me back awake and thinking my own thoughts, fine. I accepted his hand and his help. The chant washed over me and through me until I couldn't tell where I began or ended. Light warmed the chill from my body, and as I yielded the last bit of resistance, I felt part of something bigger.

"There you are," Mom said.

I felt the pressure of her hand on mine and surged awake from the best sleep I'd ever had. Contentment and happiness pulsed through my body, along with a sense of satiation. My flesh and bones were lighter, cleaner. I felt whole, as if I'd had a tune-up.

A timeline of events flooded my thoughts. My collapse. Running Bear. The purification ceremony. I struggled to sit in the candlelit living room. The group had disbanded, and only my mom remained with me. "Did I die?"

"Not in the traditional sense," Mom said.

"I feel different. What happened?"

"You've been keeping secrets from us."

Air huffed from my lungs at the reproach in her voice. "And you and Dad haven't kept things from me?"

A frown lined her face. "We were protecting you."

"I get that, but your choice to reel out dreamwalker information a little at a time has left me fumbling in the dark. Dreamwalking is more complicated than I was led to believe."

My father joined us, sitting cross-legged beside me. "Experience is the best way of learning, but you should've told us of your indenture."

I glanced at the tattoo on my hand. Was it my imagination or did it glow brighter than ever? "How'd you find out about Rose?"

"You told us, during the purification."

Several cracks appeared in my good mood.

"That's not fair. My deal with Rose is a private matter."

"Not according to Mayes." Dad gentled his tone. "We are all bound, daughter."

The walls of my Zen-like state toppled. "I'm starting to hate that word. Mayes says I'm bound to him, and now you're using that word too. I don't regret the choices I've made. You and Gentle Dove wouldn't be alive if I hadn't asked Rose for help."

Gentle Dove and Running Bear slipped in, sat beside my father. "For which we are all grateful."

The candles on the nearby coffee table flickered at their arrival. I remembered my manners. "Thank you, Running Bear, for whatever you just did. The pain in my belly is gone."

"The voodoo priestess can't harm you now," he replied.

My thoughts raced. The pains I'd felt in my foot, my arm, and my belly. I'd suspected voodoo after Mayes managed to stop the elbow pain earlier today. We'd planned to visit Cipriona Marsden, to see if she was doing this to me, but the day had gotten away from us.

I gazed at Running Bear, feeling the love and caring radiating from him and the others in the room. They wanted to help. I nearly sobbed with relief. I didn't have to carry this burden alone anymore. I trusted and believed Running Bear. If he said there was a voodoo priestess, it was the truth.

"Who is she?" I asked.

"Only you will know," Running Bear said.

"Oh?" I wasn't certain of Cipriona's involvement, merely suspected it.

Gentle Dove cleared her throat softly. "She visited you recently and stole something of yours."

"I haven't noticed anything missing." Something popped into my head. "Except for maybe a hank of hair that's shorter than the others. But maybe I did that myself. I can't remember. Besides, other than Charlotte and family, I don't have company at home, only dreamwalking clients."

Silent expectation lapped around me. I'd had three dreamwalking clients this week, but only one session had felt disjointed. Sure seemed like all avenues of inquiry were leading to Cipriona. "A client left while I was dreamwalking for her the other day. Cipriona Marsden, the palm reader."

"Hmm. Her grandmother dabbled in the black arts," Mom said. "Could be."

"I don't get it," I said, thinking aloud. "I was only vaguely aware of Cipriona until yesterday, when she asked for help in trying to free her granny. Why would she target me?"

"Could be a competition thing," Dad said. "People who visit you wouldn't need a palm reader."

"Or it could be another reason," Mayes said. He entered the house and sat beside me. "This could be about our homicide case."

Though he didn't take my hand, it felt like he did. His masculine energy enfolded me, and it felt good. "It's true that Cipriona came to see me the day Mandy Patterson died, but nothing about this meth lab case leads to her. I agree with my father. Professional jealousy seems more likely." My thoughts veered in another direction. "Thanks to Charlotte and the newspaper, everyone in town knows I've helped the sheriff with cases. I suppose the palm reader could've established an alibi visiting me, but since my thoughts were elsewhere, I can't verify how long she stayed at my house. When I called her afterward, she didn't answer. So far she hasn't returned my call or answered my question about what to do with her father's suspenders."

"This palm-reader woman sounds like a strong candidate for your voodoo priestess," Mayes said. "I'll ask Wayne to lean on her."

Alarms clanged in my head. If the sheriff "leaned" on my dreamwalker clients, word would get around, which would not be good. "Hold up. We have no evidence. This is conjecture. You know better than to make a leap like that."

Mayes shrugged. "Officially, I'm still detailed to Wayne for this case. I could lean on her myself. She hurt you. I take issue with her behavior."

I knew my sheriff. Even though he arranged for Mayes to be one of his guys temporarily, Wayne was top dog. He'd view Mayes taking the initiative as outright mutiny. No telling what Mr. GBI would think. "You're right about taking this to the sheriff." His face lit up, and I plunged forward with the rest of it. "Let Wayne handle the interview."

"You'll want to find the answer, of course," my father said, "but she can't hurt you that way anymore. Running Bear's purification made you whole again. Whatever she did to get past your spiritual defenses in the past, she can no longer gain access."

"Really?" He nodded, and I felt lighter in my heart. "The first two times were bad, but that last attack was off-the-scale worse. Voodoo must be very powerful."

"We were fortunate," Mayes said.

Being knocked out by overwhelming pain seemed the opposite, but I wanted to see where this was going. "How so?"

"Because we were surrounded by your dreamwalking support team. As a collective, they knew what to do. If you'd been alone, the result could've been much different."

I glanced across the room at Running Bear. "Thank you." My heart swelled with love as I gazed at each dear face. They were so selfless, so caring. It humbled me. "I am so very thankful for all of you, for your community of kindred spirits."

"It is our way, and it will be your way," Mom said. "Your grandmother had a team of helpers that we learned from, and now you are starting to attract kindred spirits."

With a start, I realized she was right. My medium friend Stinger was like-minded. And Elvis, our Chihuahua therapy dog. And Mayes. Couldn't forget him. And Oliver my ghost dog. My helpers came in all shapes and forms.

"I can't say enough to thank you. I couldn't do this job without you all. I wish I didn't keep finding trouble and being laid low."

"It's the nature of the work," my father said. "And you're doing splendidly. My mom had a saying that I frequently used to help reshape my frame of reference. 'Each day is a new beginning.' I took those words to heart. Each day brings the chance for healing and wholeness for each of us and those we can help."

Healing. Once I'd accepted my spiritual gifts for what they were, I'd stopped being a woman divided. While I'd been helping the living and the dead, I'd been helping myself by stretching and growing. Emotion choked my throat.

"Thank you," I managed.

Outside, a car door slammed. Someone was here? I hadn't heard anyone drive up. The serenity of the room shattered at the loud noise. My pulse kicked into overdrive.

"Ms. Powell! You out here?" a male voice shouted.

CHAPTER TWENTY-TWO

Mayes bolted out the door as I scrambled to my feet. Mom, Dad, and I followed him into the night. Under starry skies, twin headlights illuminated the lawn. The air vibrated with grunts and squeals.

Doodle Patterson stood next to Mayes. The teen could barely contain himself as he wrung his hands. "You gotta let me leave my pigs here. I got nowhere else to put them. You gotta help me."

"I don't have to do anything," Mayes said. "I'm not the property owner here. Tab and Lacey Nesbitt live here. Appeal to them for mercy. How'd you find this place?"

"Asked a buddy of mine when I couldn't find Ms. Powell at home. Aunt June won't let me keep them at her place, and the dog-pound guy said they couldn't stay there after the damage they caused. I've got to pay for a new lock on the shelter's back door. When I told my aunt what happened, she nearly went through the roof of her trailer."

My parents walked around to the bed of the truck and were making soft sounds to the full-grown pot bellied pigs.

I turned my attention back to Doodle. Though I believed my father's assessment of the palm reader's interest in me, this was a great opportunity to explore Mayes' theory about Cipriona. "You ever meet a woman named Cipriona Marsden?"

Doodle looked confused. "I've seen her sign on the highway like everyone else, but I've never been to see her. Why would I want my palm read? No one can see the future."

The force of his lie caught me unaware. I hadn't expected him to lie about anything tonight, since he was asking us for a favor. Now I'd pay closer attention to anything else he said.

Mayes leaned against the old truck. "What about your aunt? Has she had her palm read?"

"How would I know? Look, it's no secret we don't like each other. Aunt June only came around to our house to beg my mom for money. She never had enough, and after a while, my mom quit loaning her anything."

"How much did she borrow?"

173

Mayes' voice was deceptively soft. He'd zeroed in on that outstanding debt as a possible motive for murder. Concurrently, Aunt June moved to the top of my suspect list, and Cipriona moved to the back burner. Now that her power over me had been blocked, there was no urgency to get in touch with her.

"Over two grand," Doodle said. "My mom said we couldn't afford to support Aunt June and ourselves. She also said she wouldn't help anyone who didn't help themselves. Aunt June is a nut."

"How so?" I asked.

"Uh . . . uh. . . ." Doodle's face turned beet-red. "Well, you know how Mom made her living. Aunt June thinks I know how to cook. She's talking about renting a trailer and making me cook meth."

It took me a long moment to close my jaw. "She can't do that."

"She says she can, and if I don't cooperate, she'll turn me over to child services."

"You don't have to live with her," I said, "but that's a moot point. After what you just told us, she will lose custody of you. Wouldn't you rather live in an approved foster home?"

Fear flared in his eyes. "I'm too old. I

174

know what happens to kids like me. Foster parents want little kids. I'd run away, but I don't want to blow my chances at a decent college. Please, I beg you, don't tell anyone about her."

Everything he said was a lie.

Everything.

I was certain of it, but why would he lie to us about his situation and his aunt? Either he wanted out of Aunt June's or he didn't. His aunt didn't sound right in the head, but was that his intention? To color my judgment about June Hendrix?

Since the start of this case, I'd considered Doodle a victim. He deserved a chance to break the chains that had bound his mom into servitude.

Were those my thoughts? Or had I taken the information Mandy shared in the dreamwalks as absolute truth?

The mother in me wanted to leap to this child's defense, to rescue him, and to lock up all the irresponsible adults in his life. Except he didn't want to be rescued.

I needed to know why.

"How'll you pay for college?" I asked.

"Scholarships, and some of our rainy-day money."

The air roiled around Mayes. To keep him from speaking, I reached for his hand and squeezed it before directing my attention to the anxious teen. "Does your aunt know about that money?"

"No, and you can't tell her."

"What does she need money for?" I asked.

"Debts. She gambles. She blows her government subsidy money as soon as she gets it. We may not have any groceries for the second half of the month because she's barely got twenty bucks left. She's talking about selling this old truck of Mom's, but it runs good. I don't want to sell it. I'd rather keep the truck than my old clunker. That way at least I'd have something of my mom's."

"Has she been to the bank to be added to your mom's accounts?" I'd asked him about the bank accounts before, but I wanted to know if the answer would be the same now.

"I already told you. Mom didn't have any bank accounts. She paid for everything in cash."

That was the first thing he said that had the ring of truth, but Mandy Patterson must've had accounts somewhere to deposit the money for Doodle's college. Unless she buried the drug money in her yard. I could picture June at Mandy's burnt-out place, digging hole after hole, searching for a windfall.

"What about life insurance?" Mayes asked the young man.

"I don't know. She kept important papers in the bedroom file cabinet."

"We're headed over there tomorrow first thing. If you'd like to meet us and help us search, what time would be convenient?"

"I don't know when I can get away again. Aunt June's riding my butt about every chore that needs doing at her place, and nothing's been done in over twenty years. Plus, Derenne's back, and they can't stop yelling at each other. I hate living with them, but I can stand it for another year. I've got to find a safe haven for my pigs."

"We'll take them," my father said, walking up beside us.

You could've knocked me down with a marsh hen feather. "You will?"

"Yeah." Dad's eyes had an unfamiliar gleam in them. "Lacey always wanted to raise pigs."

She did? Funny how I never knew that. In fact, I couldn't remember the word "pig" ever mentioned at our house in conversation.

"You can't eat them!" Doodle's voice hitched as he spoke.

"We won't," Mom said. "Petunia and Patches need to feel secure again. They miss your mother."

"The sheriff can freeze your mom's assets," Dad said. "Matter of fact, technically they are frozen until her means of death is determined. It's against the law for your aunt to sell your mom's truck right now, and she could go to jail if she does. The arson investigator pinpointed the location where the fire started, but we don't know if the fire started before or after your mother passed."

"How can they figure that out?" Doodle asked, the color draining from his face.

"The medical examiner makes the call." Mayes shifted to a more active stance. He'd been relaxed a second ago but now he seemed ready to pounce. "Tell me about Todd Derenne."

"That SOB returned from a long haul an hour ago, saw our place was gone, and hightailed it over to Aunt June's to raise hell," Doodle said. "They were making so much noise the neighbors probably called the cops by now. This is the worst day of my life."

Uh-oh. Another lie. But he'd spoken so fast, I wasn't sure which sentence was a lie. Mayes shot me a warning glance. Had he heard it too? To my surprise, Mayes nodded toward the rear of Doodle's vehicle. "Let's get these pigs unloaded. You got a ramp?"

"Four thick boards."

The pigs trotted off the ramp, grunting and squealing. They ran to my mom and stayed at her side. Doodle left after receiving a promise he could visit the pigs any time.

"Call your boss," Mayes said when we had a moment alone. "Tell him about the aunt and the boyfriend arguing. Tell him about the aunt's plans for Doodle."

The shadows from the trees had merged so that Mayes' face was only lit by the flickering flames of the fire. His hard expression gave me a chill.

I shook my head. "I don't think the sheriff will help him. He's a suspect."

"This is a civil matter that involves a juvenile. If Doodle isn't safe in June Hendrix's custody, he needs alternate care."

The dots connected in my head. "And Wayne could haul them in for questioning about their domestic dispute. Gotcha." I made the call. Wayne answered on the first ring. Quickly I filled him in on what Doodle said about the new arrival, Todd Derenne.

"I'm already on my way to the trailer," Wayne said. "Dispatch notified me of the domestic disturbance. I'll meet with the units in that sector and be part of that house call."

"Just a sec." For privacy, I stepped away from the revealing glow of the fire. I leaned against the dark side of a tall pine. "You want company?"

"Keep your phone close, but I got this. If I haul Derenne in for questioning without Escoe in the room, he'll lose it. This way, I get nearly private face time with Derenne and can read his body language. If he's lying or BS'ing me, I'll call you. I need to see firsthand what his relationship is with Mandy's sister."

"You think they had something going on the side? Was Mandy's boyfriend sleeping with her sister? That's messed up."

"I've seen stranger things."

"If that's true, good old Aunt June might have another motive for murder. Jealousy. She already thinks she can step into Mandy's meth-making shoes. We've got to move that kid."

"You believe his life's in danger?"

I sighed out my frustration and shared Doodle's claims of being pressed into meth-lab service by his aunt. "He's lying about something or everything, but I don't know what. As a mom, I want to protect him, but he says he wants to live with June. It makes

180

no sense to me. Worse, I can't get a good read on him."

"He's a kid who's lived in a meth lab his entire life," Wayne reminded me. "He knows what to say and how to blend into the woodwork. A kid who's the top of his class with grades. Street smarts plus book smarts add up to a big red flag in a case like this. Doodle is no innocent."

"You're leaving him there?"

"Unless people brandish weapons or unless he demands to be removed, my hands are tied. June hasn't endangered him. You said he was lying, but he wants his aunt in his life. If Derenne or Hendrix are drunk and disorderly, I can lock them up for an overnight stay. Chances are they'll settle down soon as I show my face. Unless Doodle speeds back over here, he won't be part of the domestic violence dialogue."

"He's a kid. We should act like responsible adults and consider his welfare."

"Not buying it. People don't change. Take you, for example. You've been helping people your whole life, and you're trying to help this lying kid. I'm a cynic. Trust me, this kid knows the score. He needs to offer more than lies for me to remove him from his aunt's care."

"That's cold."
"That's life."

CHAPTER TWENTY-THREE

After the call ended, I pocketed my phone, stepped out of the woods, and glanced around my parents' yard. Everyone had reconvened around the fire pit. Mayes was in conversation with Running Bear and Gentle Dove. Dad sat by Mom, who was flanked by her new pet pigs. Feeling out of sorts after the phone call, I eased toward my mom and the pigs and sat. As I watched the flames and heard the pop and crackle of the fire, I relaxed and took a deep breath. My mom-brain kicked on. "Where's Larissa?"

"Sleeping in your old room," Mom said. "She's fine."

Good. "And Bubba Paxton. Wasn't he here?"

"Pastoral emergency with a teen from his church. He cut out right after Mayes awakened from the voodoo attack," my father said.

With Larissa and Bubba Paxton accounted for, every one of our dinner party was where they should be. I'd hoped Charlotte and Duncan would join us, but they weren't here. Across the fire, Mayes glanced at me and smiled, then he resumed his earnest conversation with Running Bear. "They seem to be getting along great," I said to my father.

Dad nodded. "They know the same people and faced similar challenges as mainstreamed Indians with tribal talent. At one large powwow, Running Bear was asked to consider a spot on the national council."

"Sounds prestigious. Did he do it?"

"Nah. Said it would take too much time from Gentle Dove, though I suspected it was because he was already helping me with cases and dealing with the aftereffects."

"But still. His peers wanted him to represent them. That's quite an honor."

"He was pleased to hold their respect, but he never regretted his decision to live life on his own terms."

"I wonder what Mayes would do if offered a similar lure. Would he choose to be mainstreamed or tribal?"

"He'll do whatever you do."

His statement sent a shiver of unease

down my spine. "I don't have any sway over him."

"He says otherwise."

I closed my eyes to gather myself. Mayes had read too much into our *togetherness* earlier today, courtesy of Rose taking over my body. My sex life wasn't something I planned to discuss with my dad. "I'm married."

"Are you?"

Dad's pointed question made me flush hot and cold. It felt as if the solid ground I sat on had turned to quicksand. He and I had been on the same wavelength about my allegedly deceased husband's unknown whereabouts the entire time. From his remark, I could see he'd changed his mind. Did he know something I didn't?

My skin prickled, and I didn't like it one bit. I felt the need to put forth my logic for Roland's state of being. "We can't find Roland among the dead. Therefore, I believe he's still alive."

Dad let my words settle before he replied. He stared resolutely into the embers. "Perhaps as the Watcher?"

Ice formed in my veins. My Watcher was private. I fought to use my voice, but it still came out ragged. "How do you know about that?"

185

"Your connection to Mayes lowered your normal firewall. Your thoughts became part of the healing circle. Those of us here now know about the entity you call the Watcher. That he's harmless, except to people who wish you harm. Is he present tonight?"

"I've only felt him when I'm at home," I said. "And he isn't there all the time. Most of the time he isn't around."

"Where is he? Or should I say, what is he?"

I didn't like where this was going. "Shouldn't we be talking about the Patterson case or why Mom is Queen of the Pigs?"

"Don't change the subject," Dad said sharply. "This is important. Have you ever seen the Watcher?"

Tears filled my eyes at the stern rebuke. "No."

"How does he contact you?"

"He doesn't. Some nights he's just there, that's all."

"How so?"

"If I open my extra senses, I can detect if anyone's in the vicinity. When I got my first dreamwalker case, I was worried someone would break in and try to harm me or Larissa. I started doing a mental perimeter check every night as I went to bed. I detected my Watcher's energy signal out there for a long time before I figured out how to reach him. I had to retune my thoughts to his frequency."

"Hmm."

My parents fell silent, and I followed their lead. I thought I'd feel better after unloading my biggest secret, but I didn't. I felt all prickly, as if I'd done something wrong.

When the silence weighed too heavily on me, I cracked. "What are you thinking?"

"This is something new. None of us have summoned a being from Beyond before."

His words added to the shards of ice in my veins. "You're saying I called the Watcher into being? That I summoned him? No way. I don't know how to do that."

"But you only detect him when you're anxious about your safety."

"Yes. One time he helped me by tying up that sleazy realtor Buster Glassman."

"Did you see him?"

"No."

"Has he manifested physically again?"

"No."

"It could've been a one-shot deal, though possibilities abound."

"The Watcher could hail from another realm, like the Little People," Running Bear said, joining the discussion.

I hadn't noticed that Running Bear and Mayes were paying attention to our conversation, but they seemed keenly interested in the Watcher. I tried to grasp the concept of Roland being trapped in another dimension and couldn't. The Little People we'd encountered in the mountain were the stuff of myths and legend, but they'd been real and powerful.

"You're sure it's a male?" Mayes asked.

"Sure."

"And he's protective of you?"

"Yes." My hackles rose. I didn't like being on this end of the barbed questions. "I've wondered if it's Roland, but I don't know. It doesn't sound like him or feel like him. But if he's done something to change, and if Roland is the Watcher, I sense he's far away. My Watcher has thought-energy most of the time he's in contact, but that's about it."

"I haven't said anything, but before I drove down here, I asked an Army buddy to look into Roland's last few months alive," Mayes said. "He was involved in a top-secret dream research program. From what my friend told me, they trained the special ops guys in extreme dreaming to better prepare for missions and debriefings. This program is highly classified. I couldn't find a trace of it anywhere."

"Extreme dreaming?" I asked. "What is that?"

"I'd never heard the term either, but it could explain how your husband might be trapped in an advanced lucid-dream state somewhere."

I gazed at the people around the fire. My people. My family. And Mayes. "Why doesn't he wake up?"

"Perhaps he can't," Mayes suggested.

"Why?"

"Injury. Research. Imprisonment."

None of those sounded hopeful. I couldn't imagine Roland — my vital, fit, and dynamic husband — trapped in a sleep-state for years. He wasn't the Sleeping Beauty type. "I don't believe you."

"Believe what you like. Other explanations about your energy manifestation venture into the realm of science fiction and time travel. This explanation makes the most sense to us."

An awful feeling squeezed my gut. "You've been talking about this? Without me?"

Mom reached across Petunia and caressed my shoulder. "We've been so concerned about you. We want to help."

"These are my private thoughts we're discussing. You're prying into my personal life. Your intentions may be good, but I'm

189

angry about this. I feel violated." I scrambled to my feet and ran for all I was worth.

My feet found the wooded path to the dock, and despite the shouts behind me, I kept going. Starlight guided me. I fought back tears. The temptation to reach out to the Watcher was strong, but I couldn't. I needed to think about this. Never in my wildest dreams had I considered that Roland might be someone's research project. Why would he agree to such a thing? Why would he put our family at risk?

CHAPTER TWENTY-FOUR

Mayes joined me at the dock. I knew he'd come. Just as he knew I knew. God, this was so circular. So incestuous. Through the healing circle, my parents and friends accessed my private thoughts. They knew about the Watcher. They knew what I knew about the case.

I gulped. They knew I'd had sex with Mayes. Heat flamed in my face. This was messed up.

"I'm sorry," Mayes said, sitting beside me.

I raised my hands, palms out. "Don't touch me."

He didn't move away, but he respected my request. He seemed to be waiting. So I lit into him. "You took something from me. My privacy."

"Not on purpose. Please, let me explain. Our mind link has always been strong. We worked the energy transfers in the mountains with your parents, so our energies were already familiar with blending. When both of us were knocked out by the voodoo, your parents and their friends linked to protect us. They created an energy barrier to block the attack. Since you were the primary victim, I was the least affected and came around first. My thoughts became their thoughts. By the time I became fully conscious and erected my own barriers, the damage was done. None of us purposefully invaded your privacy. My privacy was invaded too. How do you think it feels to have my hopes and dreams for us become group knowledge?"

His words eased the sting. I hadn't considered that his privacy had also been violated. "It's too much." I rubbed my temples, trying to ease the tension headache that was gathering speed like a tornado.

"It isn't what I wanted either. I would never embarrass you. What we have is between us. Everyone was trying to do the right thing here. Your parents and their friends weren't intentionally prying. You and I were in agony from the psychic attack. Due to their combined talents and their years of teamwork, they joined forces and made it stop. The take-home you're overlooking is that they succeeded. Whoever tried to harm you failed miserably."

I sniffed back a few tears. *Drat.* He made perfect sense. My privacy had been violated, but I'd been saved from a painful attack. My folks must think I was the most ungrateful, emotional wretch in the world.

An owl called nearby, the sound both spooky and provocative. Maybe everyone thought the worst of me. "I am thankful for their help and for your compassion. My pride will be the death of me. It was embarrassing to realize they knew about us being together and experienced it through our memories."

"My turn?" Mayes asked.

I nodded, afraid to meet his gaze.

"Whatever the reason for our intimacy earlier today, I have no regrets, because it underscored something I've known from the start. We fit. Maybe my timing is wrong because of your missing husband, but I'll wait. No pressure from me. And you know what? Both of us wanted to learn more about our talents. We wanted to know what else was out there. Today, we learned psychic attacks are real. We learned they can be blocked. From you, the rest of us discovered that protective entities like your Watcher can be summoned."

"You really believe Roland is my Watcher?"

"Makes the most sense to me." After a long moment, he spoke again. "Your power. He knew about it even if you denied it. This may not be the case, but have you ever considered he signed up to be a test subject so he could be your equal? That he wanted the ability to protect you from wherever he was stationed?"

"You're such a good person. You ascribe good motives to Roland. The sheriff swears Roland isn't — or wasn't — the man I knew. According to Wayne, Roland was a womanizer like the sheriff. I can't believe that. I refuse to believe that."

"No offense, but I wouldn't put much credence in anything Wayne says about your husband."

"Because he wants to sleep with me?" I shot him a covert look. "So do you."

"We're not the same. What has he done to look for Roland for you? What has he done to help you through this troubling time?"

"He gave me a job."

"Not entirely true. Your father had the same arrangement when he was the Dreamwalker. Wayne knew he needed you to solve crimes, so he put you on the payroll."

Everything I knew clashed with the universe of what I didn't know. "This is too much to absorb after a long day. I need to get some sleep."

"Larissa's already tucked in and sleeping at your folks' house. We could spend the night out here at your dad's cabin."

"I can't spend the night with you."

"Your parents know we were intimate. Your dad wouldn't have suggested the idea just now if he didn't approve."

Another yawn slipped out. "I'm too tired to argue. But all we're doing is sleeping. That's it. You hear me?"

"Yes, ma'am."

CHAPTER TWENTY-FIVE

My father's cabin was little more than a lean-to shelter crudely assembled by his dock. The enclosure served to keep his fishing gear out of the rain, or so I thought until Mayes' flashlight pierced the thick gloom inside. Shelves held fishing tackle and other dock supplies, but two lounger cushions situated side by side on the floor caught my attention. Mayes took a moment to shift everything around — checking for snakes, I guess — before he allowed me to sink onto the nearest one.

Sleep grabbed me hard, and I plunged into a restless dream in which I ran all night long. Morning rolled around, and I awakened cocooned in a man's arms. I felt peace and serenity, something unusual for any morning. His familiar scent sighed in and out of me. Mayes.

He nuzzled my hair, and my eyes opened to glints of daylight through the roof and walls. We'd spent the night together. Little by little, Mayes was wearing down my defenses. He'd said we were a good fit. I felt that way too, but until I had proof I was truly single, I couldn't act on any desires. I eased away from him and sat up. With the cushions occupying the whole floor, there was no place to stand.

"Good morning." His rumbling, sleep-edged voice gave me a pleasant thrill.

"Morning." I fiddled with my hair, finger-combed the tangles, and generally avoided looking at him. Sunlight glinted between the slats of wood on the shelter's sides. How late was it? "We should be getting back. Larissa will wonder where I am."

He stacked his arms under his head and grinned. "Larissa's a big girl."

"She's ten." I crawled on my hands and knees for the door.

"Guess we're headed to your parents' house," Mayes said, rising. "Give me a sec outside. I need to use the facilities."

His straight dark hair hung around his shoulders, clouding my thoughts. I remembered well the glide of its silky texture on my fingers and skin. "What? Oh. Yeah. Me too."

We'd barely finished freshening up and enjoying the high-tide vista from the dock when Charlotte and Duncan joined us. Thank goodness we'd exercised restraint this morning, or they'd have caught us in the act.

"They've got pigs," Duncan crowed, setting down the metal pail he carried. "I'd give anything to have pigs."

Charlotte grinned and handed me the pail he'd carried. "Your mom sent breakfast. Looks like you two might've worked up an appetite sleeping out here all by your lonesome."

Great. Charlotte thought I was cheating on Roland. At least she and Duncan were both unattached. They had no moral or ethical dilemmas to overcome.

I reached for the thermos and poured coffee in both cups. After handing one to Mayes and tossing him a fresh muffin, I glanced at Charlotte and encouraged her to walk farther down on the dock with me. "What are you doing awake so early?"

"Working the story. I came for a report."

"You walked all the way out here?"

"I did, and you know I hate most forms of exercise, so spill."

"I have nothing to tell. Yesterday was full of weird dreamwalks and at least three psychic attacks. But you can't report on any of those things."

She elbowed me. "Killjoy."

"I'm serious as a heart attack. Mr. GBI doesn't see the value of using psychic consultants, though the sheriff is trying to bring him around. It's a delicate situation. If you breathe a word about my dreamwalks to anyone, there'll be hell to pay. But never mind about me or the case. Tell me about you and lover boy."

Charlotte flushed crimson. She leaned in close. "He likes sex a lot. Turns out, I like it too, but every time I try to have a serious conversation with him, I end up naked. What if we don't have anything to talk about?"

"When we were in the mountains, you made a list of mutual topics of interest. Music and I can't remember what all else."

"Conversation isn't happening. Except, he talks about his mom and his hunting dogs. And now those pigs. If he didn't pour himself into making me happy, I'm not sure we'd have a future."

"You're thinking future already?"

"He's asked me to come back with them. To move in with him."

Her admission floored me. I couldn't imagine Sinclair County without Charlotte. "Are you considering it?"

"Sure. And no. I mean, I can't do that,

can I? What lovestruck fool walks away from a paying job to follow a man she just met across the state? This is the twenty-first century. Women get to have their cake and eat it too. I want a relationship and a career. I think. Oh, I don't know. This is my first serious relationship. Why should I have to make such a big decision right away?"

Before I could reply, my phone rang. Wayne. "Get over here right now," he said.

"Where are you?" I asked.

"At the office. Hurry." He clicked off.

"I've got work," I announced to Charlotte, Duncan, and Mayes. "We haven't talked about plans for today. It's Sunday. Does anyone have an interest in church? I can direct you to any of the houses of worship in the county."

"I'm coming with you," Mayes said.

"I'm with Charlotte," Duncan said.

"I want a story," Charlotte said. "I'm with Baxley."

CHAPTER TWENTY-SIX

"Did you have to bring an entire posse with you?" Wayne grumbled when Mayes and I joined him in his office. "But, baggage aside. I have good news for us. Escoe returned to Savannah this morning due to a personal matter. His mom was hospitalized after a fall. Which means he'll monitor my progress from afar. You two are back on the case."

I shared a glance with Mayes before I spoke. "I'm sorry about his mom, but I'm glad not to be sneaking around anymore. We need to find Mandy's killer."

"Agreed, which is why I called you in on a Sunday."

"What's up?" I asked, taking the high road. Mayes and I sat in Wayne's guest chairs. He'd closed the door behind us. I guessed Tamika, his administrative assistant, had informed him that Charlotte and Duncan were in the lobby.

"I locked up Todd Derenne last night for

Drunk and Disorderly Conduct. June's sporting two black eyes from his fists and won't press charges. She's already been by here this morning to find out how much his bond is. I imagine he'll be out by noon."

"And . . . ?"

"I want you to sit in on my interview with him."

"Why?"

"I plan to ask leading questions. If he talks about the case, we'll turn that information over to Escoe."

"What about Mayes?"

"I'm planting Mayes in the lobby with your friends. I want a full report on June Hendrix's conduct when she returns." He snickered. "Try to keep Charlotte from annoying her too much."

"I'll do it, on one condition," Mayes said.

"What's that?"

"Anything unusual happens with Baxley, come get me."

"I'll do what I think is prudent," Wayne said.

Mayes' chin jutted as he rose. Wayne was the taller man, but at that moment, Mayes seemed downright dangerous. I didn't want the guys to get sidetracked with macho crap. I stood and pressed my keys in Mayes' hand, closing his fingers around them.

Grateful for once for our mutual telepathy, I opened my senses to him and communicated with Mayes using mindspeak. *Wayne can't help being a jerk,* I began. *If you need access, my key to the back door of the office is on my key ring.*

He doesn't like my interference, Mayes countered. *He wants you for himself.*

I'm glad you're here, but you have to accept that Wayne is my boss.

Will you keep this link open between us?

Given how connected we are, you'll know if I'm in trouble.

I will do as he requests for now, but know this. I will come through this wall for you.

No need to hurt yourself. I'll be fine. I've sat in on interviews before.

Be careful, Walks with Ghosts.

I will.

The exchange took mere seconds, but the glare Wayne shot me spoke volumes. After Mayes left the office, Wayne turned on me. "What was that about?"

I played it cool. "What?"

"You and that Injun fella."

"Sam Mayes is a fine officer and my friend. I expect you to treat him in a courteous and professional manner. His Cherokee heritage doesn't figure into it."

"He's your boyfriend."

My boss could fish around all he liked, but I wouldn't have relationship talks with him, not ever. "My personal life isn't your concern."

Wayne turned away for a moment. "Your personal life never interfered with your work availability."

"I'm here, aren't I? You called. I came. On a weekend, no less. Let's get to that interview. I have other things planned for today."

He hurried past me to open the door. "Like what?"

"Like none of your beeswax." I scowled as I stepped past him. "Shouldn't you be home with Dottie and your boys? It is your day off."

"Crime never sleeps."

I didn't dignify that with a response. "Which interview room?"

"Two. The smallest one. I want this guy to feel like he's in a box."

I headed to the appointed room. "Is he already inside?"

"He is."

My steps halted. The protocol was for Wayne to enter the room first. "I know the drill. After you."

Wayne shook his head. "What if I asked you to conduct this interview alone?"

The fluorescent lights in the hall seemed

overly bright. "I'd say, I'm not qualified."

"This guy thinks he's a chick magnet. He'll talk to you. Lose the ball cap and hair band. I should've thought to ask you to wear a dress."

My hands remained by my sides. "I'm here to assist you in reading his emotions. I don't even know what questions to ask."

"Ask him where's he's been and why he got so drunk. Then ask him about the arrowheads in Mandy's trailer." Wayne flipped my ball cap off. "Lose the hair tie, or I'll take care of that too."

"All right already." I tugged the band free, and my stark white hair curtained down to my shoulders. "If you want a femme fatale, you should get Tamika in here. Men don't pant after me like they do Tamika."

"You've got girl parts. You'll do."

"Such flattery. You'll make my head swell."

"Derenne's cuffed and hung over, so he won't be a physical threat. Stay on this side of the table so I can study him from the observation room. Good luck."

I needed more than luck. After a deep breath, I opened the door and stepped inside the tiny room. I hated being crowded, and the man inside seemed to take up all the space and all the air.

Todd Derenne gave new angst to the

cliché of "rode hard and put up wet." He was thin and rangy, with sunken cheeks and a shaved head. I approached the small table where he lounged, feet outstretched. "Mr. Derenne? I'm a police consultant named Baxley Powell. I have some questions for you."

His midnight-blue eyes gleamed with interest. "Ain't you a ray of sunshine," Derenne said. "Come sit in my lap, sweet thang."

"This won't take long," I went on as if he hadn't spoken, sitting across the table from him. "Where were you Friday evening and Saturday morning?"

"Where I am all the time. In my rig. I had a delivery in St. Louis Friday night. Trucked it back here overnight to see my honey, only to find our place burned to the ground and my Mandy dead."

"We need to verify that delivery. May I have the destination address?"

"I got nuttin' to hide." He rattled off an address, which I wrote on the notepad I kept in my back pocket. I resisted the urge to look over my shoulder to see if Wayne got the information. "And for clarification, was Mandy your wife?"

"We weren't married by no gol-dang preacher, if that's what you mean, but we lived as man and wife for years. I loved her."

"Why not marry her?"

"I like variety. Mandy was home base, you know? Besides, with that pale skin of hers, she wasn't a looker, and she had that mewling brat around all the time. A man needs more attention than that."

I swallowed my disgust. Wayne was counting on me to squeeze answers out of this lowlife. If Mandy had pale skin, it was because she'd cooked meth for him and never had a moment to herself. "Did her death surprise you?"

"Sho' did. Between you and me, Mandy and I had a sweet business arrangement. She cooked, and I turned it into bacon, if you catch my drift."

I caught more than his stinky drift. He moved in on Mandy, made her cook for him, then he seized the meth she made and delivered it to a supplier. I guessed he tossed enough of the money crumbs her way to make it worth her while.

"Yeah, I'm gonna miss old Mandy, but the world's full of willing women. Like you. What say you and me catch lunch today when I blow this joint?"

"No. That would be totally inappropriate. Let's get back on track. The sheriff mentioned arrowheads at Mandy's place. You

207

know anything about them?"

He shrugged. "I bow hunt. I kept my gear at her place. I use arrowheads as tips. Big hairy deal."

"I thought it was your place."

"Her place, my place, it's all the same. My name's on the deed, if that's what you mean. Damn, you are one fine-lookin' woman. I bet ole Wayne is beside himself trying to bang you."

"I don't appreciate your sexist remarks. Sheriff Thompson and I have a professional arrangement. Listen, Mr. Derenne, now that you're sober, what was the fight with June Hendrix about?"

"We didn't see eye to eye."

"Was the argument about Doodle's welfare? Because June is his aunt."

"So what? She ain't no good for him. Doodle needs a man around. Someone to make him toe the line. I'm the closest thing that boy's ever had to a dad. He should be living under my roof."

"With Mandy's place burned to the ground, where will you live?"

He grinned. "June's place. She wants one of them *professional* relationships with me, which suits me fine because it lands me and Doodle in the same place. Not sure her place is big enough for all of us, but at least she put her foot down about those stinky pigs."

Interesting. Why would June live with a man who beat her face to a pulp? "Do you have any children?"

"I don't like brats."

I tapped the end of my pen on the pad. "What about brothers and sisters or parents? Any of them live around here?"

"Got me a brother up Atlanta-way, but that's it."

"His name?"

"Evan Gomez. Different dads. I don't see him much."

"You two don't get along?"

"You might say that. Old Evan is a head case. Been in and out of the looney bin." He sighed as if I'd really put him out. "We done with the foreplay yet?"

I did my best impression of one of my otherworldly mentor's crystalline smiles. "Not quite. You know Cipriona Marsden?"

"I know the family. Her granny's gonna fry soon."

"You're mistaken. She didn't receive the death penalty at sentencing. Her sentence was life without parole."

Derenne shrugged with his whole body. "Dead is dead."

"How do you know the family?"

209

"I had me some business with Damond once upon a time."

"What kind of business?"

"You sure ask a lot of nosy questions, but I reached my limit of answers. My bail bond been posted yet?"

"Mr. Derenne, we believe someone started that fire in Ms. Patterson's trailer on purpose. You have any idea who'd do that?

Gone were the flirty smiles and eye winks. His dark eyes glared at me. I shivered at the malice rolling off this man. Wouldn't want to meet him in a dark alley.

I tried one more thing. "As Ms. Patterson's boyfriend, you would've known how she handled her finances. She doesn't have a local bank account, and it's likely her personal papers burned in the fire. Do you know where she banked?"

He didn't respond, so I reached across the table to prod him. He jumped back. "I know who you are. Don't touch me unless you want me to pay *special attention* to your family."

CHAPTER TWENTY-SEVEN

Wayne herded me and Mayes into his office and closed the door. He bounded to his seat behind the desk, while Mayes and I sank into the side-by-side guest chairs. "You done good, Powell. We can investigate Derenne's alibi, vet his step-brother in Atlanta, and stake out June's trailer. Better yet, we can close this case in a few days and get the GBI out of our hair forever."

His praise rolled off me like storm water on a shiny roof. I was not in a good mood. "He threatened my family, Wayne. I don't trust him."

"Good instinct. Don't turn your back on creeps like Derenne, ever," Wayne said. "No way is he coming after you. He knows you're protected in more ways than one. The GBI was right. This case is about drug production. Someone offed Mandy to take her place in the supply chain."

I heard the word instinct, and my ears

closed. Instinct? More like common sense. My spine stiffened. I could've gone my entire life without meeting Todd Derenne. Wayne had some nerve asking me to conduct an interrogation. Now I was on this guy's radar. He could come after Larissa or my parents. How would I ever sleep again?

Before any of these angry words boiled out of my mouth, Mayes reached over and took my hand. A sense of calm washed over me. As clear as if he'd said them out loud, I heard the words, "I've got you." I managed a tight nod in his direction.

"Derenne's the missing link in the greater Warner Robbins meth ring Escoe's investigating for the GBI?" Mayes asked.

Wayne glowed. "He says so."

"Suspects lie."

"With his independent trucking career, this guy's got the means and opportunity to deliver product anywhere. We could be talking interstate drug commerce. The FBI could be looking for him. And we've got him in our hot little hands."

"I've seen these investigations stall out before," Mayes said. "Even if he is the go-between, all we have is his say-so. A good lawyer will get scum like that off every time. You need to catch him in the act, but the meth lab is gone. The cook is gone. He's currently untouchable, and you know it."

"I don't know about your north Georgia perps, but my guys are resourceful. They're used to having to make do. I wouldn't put it past this guy to pay the entire high school football team to go shake-and-bake on us."

I paled. Volatile chemicals could be in students' book bags? They could be in schools and on buses? "We have to tell someone about this possibility."

"We're telling no one," Wayne said. "Especially not Charlotte or her boy toy. Got that?"

Mayes squeezed my hand, and we nodded in unison. I don't know how I held my outrage inside. It was a miracle.

"Here's my plan. The school system has a program to match tutors with at-risk kids. Thanks to his family situation, Doodle now qualifies." Wayne waited, as if expecting me to connect the dots. The only dot I wanted to connect was my fist to his nose. This guy was willing to put an entire generation of kids at risk for a drug sting?

"I don't understand," Mayes said. "How does your plan incriminate Derenne?"

The sheriff leaned back in his chair and tapped his fingers together. "Given the way folks are going nuts over access to Doodle, I believe he helped his mom cook. That's the only thing that makes sense. So we'll keep a close eye on him too. Fortunately, I know the best tutor in the county."

Those dots were easy to connect. I'd been Wayne's tutor in high school. "Bad idea."

"What?" Mayes asked, his gaze flicking between the sheriff and me.

"Powell can tutor him, plus the kid already knows and trusts her. She can talk to him in school each day, and no one will be the wiser. It's the perfect cover."

"No," I said. "I won't do it. Whoever killed Mandy — whether it's Derenne or someone else — will come after my kid. I'm not willing to risk her safety. I don't mind talking to ghosts and spirits in the afterlife for you, or even an angel or demon or two, but I'm not inserting myself in the middle of a drug ring. No way, no how."

"We'll make sure you have protection," the sheriff added smoothly. "I'll get Sheriff Blair to detail her guy down here for another week." He grinned as if he'd had the best thought ever. "You'll be covered in more ways than one."

My face heated up, and I sputtered at his crude remark, tugging my hand free and leaping to my feet. Despicable thoughts filled my head, all of which ended with me knocking Wayne into the ozone layer.

"Forget it," I said.

"Great idea," Mayes said at the same time. "I'll do it."

Wayne nodded and turned to Mayes. "Now that that's settled, let's hear what June Hendrix's up to. What's your report from the lobby?"

I leaned over Wayne's desk. "Wait a minute. You can't brush me off like that. Don't I have any say in this?"

His gaze lowered from my face for a moment, then he flicked a wrist. "Go ahead."

Wayne was an ardent admirer of the female form. A lecher and skirt-chaser in the first degree. Was my T-shirt gapping or something? I straightened and braced my arms across my chest. "I'll agree only if Larissa has a deputy with her when she's not in school. If you have Mayes at your disposal, he can't be in two places at once. And when she goes to my parents' house, a deputy goes with her until this case is solved. I can't risk her. I won't do it."

For a moment I could've sworn Mayes and the sheriff were communicating telepathically. Wayne stared me down. "Done. We'll start the protection detail tomorrow."

"Just like that?"

"Yeah. Just like that. I'm the boss, or have you forgotten?"

My anger spilled out again. "You may be the boss of police matters, but I'm the boss of my family. I like helping you solve cases, but I don't have to do this kind of work. Keep that in mind, *boss* man."

"Jeez. Is it that time of the mo—"

"He's fine with that," Mayes interrupted, standing beside me. "I'll make sure you and Larissa are safe."

I glared at him. "How?"

"The regular way."

The regular way? What did that mean? It felt like I'd been on a roller coaster ride with this case. I wanted to get off and catch my breath, but that wasn't likely.

"I'd appreciate an update on June Hendrix," the sheriff said.

"She's tightly wired," Mayes replied. "Couldn't sit still the entire time I was in the lobby. She paced back and forth like a caged animal. She used her car as collateral for Derenne's bond. If he screws her, she'll lose her vehicle."

"He's going to screw her every which-a-way. Count on it," Wayne said.

I didn't care for his remark, but I fought the crazy tide of emotions as I sat back down. This was not like me. Why was I such a basket case today?

CHAPTER TWENTY-EIGHT

"June kept her sunglasses on most of the time, except when she needed to blot the tears from her face," Mayes said, perching on the edge of his chair beside me in Wayne's office. "Those black eyes are starting to turn colors, and her lip was split too. Derenne is one mean SOB."

"And . . . ?" Wayne asked, clearly not impressed with the June report.

"The way she talked, her very life depended on her staying on Derenne's good side."

"If he killed Mandy, that's true. If he thinks Doodle is the key to his future, then he'll keep June around because she has custody of Doodle. But if someone else killed Mandy, they'll come after June and Doodle, especially if the boy is crucial to a hidden drug empire."

"We have to protect them," I said. If Wayne started focusing on the meth-making angle, would Mandy's death go unsolved? How likely was it that her death was linked to the meth trade? Mandy's sister wanted her job, but could she be so cold?

"We'll keep an eye on Doodle, all right. Unless June orchestrated this entire situation or unless she's got leverage over Derenne, she's already living on borrowed time."

I absently twirled a bit of hair behind my ear. "That sucks."

"One more thing," Wayne asked.

"Yes?"

"That bit about the Marsden woman with Derenne. Why'd you ask about her?"

"Because I think Cipriona's got it in for me, that's why."

"Explain."

"I don't have physical proof, but I believe she tried to hurt me. My foot was in pain yesterday morning, which was her doing. She came after me twice more, but my folks and their friends stopped her."

"I can bring her in."

"Not necessary." I glanced at Mayes and then the sheriff. "We took care of it already."

"I can't let it go at that," Wayne said. "Tell me more, or I'll bring her in for questioning anyway."

"The only thing that makes sense is she

218

believes I'm her competition. In her mind, people would rather visit a Dreamwalker than a palm reader. We believe she used voodoo to cause me physical pain. The last attack took me and Mayes down late yesterday, but we were at my parents' house and they, along with Running Bear and Gentle Dove, blocked her."

"Voodoo? Get real." He sobered at the fierce expression on my face and then spat out some vintage cuss words. "Why did the crazy train unload in my county? I can't have her coming after anyone on my staff. Bad for business."

I cleared my throat. "Her grandmother is still in prison, right?"

"Yeah, nearly forgot about Elmira. She was a thorn in my side for years. Now her granddaughter is kickin' up her heels? I don't need this."

His words confirmed what the dead son had said. Cipriona Marsden was a chip off the old block. "Elmira Marsden practiced voodoo?"

Wayne glanced at the yellowed ceiling tiles overhead for a long moment. "Called herself the root doctor. After she shot her son, I went out there to arrest her. That was before I became sheriff. Her house scared the tarnation out of me, what with its dangling crystals, scary idols, and chalked markings. Good riddance, I say."

His phone chimed. He checked the message, then pocketed his phone. "That was my electronic reminder. I've got a lunch date with the new shopping-plaza owner in a few minutes. I'm meeting her at the chain restaurant out by the interstate. Seems she wants to get off on the right foot with local law enforcement."

"Who is she?" I asked. Under my lashes, I saw him preening and acting like he was king of the world. Not a good thing. His wife had put her foot down about his catting around. I'd heard she'd threatened him with taking the kids and moving to her mother's place in South Carolina if he so much as looked at another woman again. If past behavior was a yardstick, Wayne was fixing to look with more than his eyes.

"Alicia Waite is her name," Wayne said. "She's an Atlanta businesswoman seeking a venue for her personal collection of shops. I'm surprised the paper hasn't run a story on her yet."

"I'm certain they'd love to meet with her. I'll put a bug in Charlotte's ear."

"Great. I'm cutting Derenne loose in a few minutes. Go on and get out of here."

We exited from the staff entrance, but I

220

walked around to the front and waved Charlotte outdoors. She hustled to my side, Duncan trailing her. "Gotcha a story lead," I said, telling her about Alicia Waite's meeting with Wayne. "At the very least, it's a photo op. At best, you two get invited to lunch with them, and you can record the conversation, with their permission, to use in a story."

"Wow. I've been trying to reach Ms. Waite for weeks. Bernard will be beside himself that he missed this opportunity. Thanks."

Charlotte must've noticed Duncan's scowl. "Would you rather do something else?" she asked.

"I'd like to see those pigs again."

My friend's face tightened, then relaxed. "We can do both. If you'll accompany me to this business lunch, I'll hang out with you and the pigs this afternoon. But I'll have to write my stories this evening."

"Works." Duncan glanced over at Mayes. "We still leaving tomorrow?"

"I need to talk with you about that. Walk with me."

Charlotte edged closer as the men strode away. "What's going on?"

"Mayes is being detailed down here until the Patterson case closes. My guess is he's asking Duncan if he wants to stay." Charlotte's expression turned dark. "What?"

"It's major work entertaining a guest. And Duncan fills a lot of space."

"I thought you liked him," I said.

"I do. But I'm not used to being with anyone around the clock for days."

"Take your laptop with you out to my parents' place. Tell him you need some space. There'll be plenty to occupy him out there. He can talk hunting with my dad, even go fishing at the dock."

"Where are you off to?" Charlotte asked.

"Following a lead. Can't be more specific."

"Bummer. I love to follow leads."

"This is a dangerous situation, Charlotte. Mayes and I are trying to break this case open. Don't even think of following us."

"We won't." She sighed as if the world was ending. "Look, the guys are heading our way, and Duncan's beaming. I guess he plans on staying too. Oh, joy."

"Look on the bright side. At least you won't be bored."

Duncan swept Charlotte around in a circle. "Great news, babe. We're staying another week."

Charlotte made the appropriate happy noises, and Mayes and I left. "Who do you want to tackle first, the voodoo priestess or the dead meth maker?" he asked as he pulled onto the highway.

"Surprise me."

Chapter Twenty-Nine

Mayes nosed the truck off Bartow Road and onto the fringe of Mandy's yard. As he parked, I yanked the ball cap off my head, secured my white hair back with a stretchy band from my wrist, fitted the cap back on, and worked the ponytail through the back opening.

"I like your hair down," Mayes said after we stood beside the burned-out trailer.

"I've got too much to do to keep swatting my hair out of my eyes. Once we finish this case work today, I've got landscaping duties to perform. Part of my Pets and Plants business is taking care of plants in various locations, plus I've got a lot of stock right now in my greenhouse."

"How do you keep your business viable and work for the sheriff?"

"It's harder to find time for my business, but that's where my heart is, with plants and animals. I understand them better than people."

"You talk to plants?"

"Call me crazy. I do."

He gave me a kiss. "I'd call you a lot of things before I'd call you crazy."

I couldn't afford to be distracted by emotions this close to Mandy Patterson's place. Placing my palm on his chest, I gently discouraged his affection. "Not now."

"Later?"

The hopeful note in his voice twanged the guilt chord in my heart. I drew in a shaky breath. We'd clear the air about our relationship after we finished our work today. "Later."

Mayes nodded, pulled himself together, and quartered the yard. "I've worked meth-lab busts before. There are always cameras."

"Anything electronic on or in this mobile home is toast."

"Agreed. At a minimum, she would've had cameras on the doorways." He studied the trees bordering the property. "Meth cooks are notoriously paranoid. I wouldn't be surprised if there were additional cameras."

"Huh." I copied his intense gaze sweeping the trees. "You'd think we could see them."

"Paranoia, remember? Trail cams are hard to spot. I'd like to look around after you do your thing inside."

"I thought I'd do my extended perimeter check with my senses to ensure we're alone. Bartow Road dead-ends in a swamp. There's Ricky Dixon's place next door and a couple of abandoned trailers farther down. No one should ride down this road unless they're coming here or Dixon's place."

His eyebrows rose. "The extended perimeter check. Can you show me how you do that?"

"Uh. Well. Sure. Later."

"Now."

"Look, Mayes, I don't have time to explain something I do naturally. We've got a case to solve."

"We've been looking for a way to test our new connectivity. What better way than to bolster our perimeter monitor? If you do it while we're touching, I can access the probe. Chances are I can hold that focus while you dreamwalk."

He wouldn't let it go. I sighed and caved, pulling him toward a sturdy pine. "I usually do this lying down, but I have done it sitting before. One of us should lean against the tree in case we need help maintaining our upright position."

Mayes leaned against the tree and took my hand. The air hummed expectantly.

"I should lean against the tree," I said,

confused by the electricity surging up my arm.

"Come closer," Mayes said. "Sharing is easier with multiple contact points."

Knowing that to be true, I stepped into the cocoon of his arms. My extra senses shifted into overdrive without my permission. I flinched, instinctively retreating, blocking the out-of-control free flow.

"Relax," Mayes murmured, rubbing my back. "Show me how it's done."

I trusted him, so I paid attention to the extrasensory input. Our auras were melding. His dark-green energy became laced with my blue energy. Warmth and tingling vitalized my body, opening blocked channels and creating a sense of euphoria. My constant worry for Roland slid away. I was myself. I felt whole again, for the first time in years.

"This is amazing," I marveled.

"Umm," Mayes replied, then he switched to telepathy. *Use mindspeak,* Baxley. *I can hear you just fine.*

Did you retune my energy field?

We did it. I'm seeing and feeling things clearer as well. Show me what you've got, sweetheart. We're on a tight schedule, remember?

I remembered, but I also realized I might

227

have put off that relationship talk too long.
Mayes —

Not now, love. The perimeter sweep?

I growled in frustration, but I obediently
quested out, expanding my senses in an
ever-widening circle from our position. No
one in the immediate vicinity. Two lifeforms
registered at the Dixon home. Ricky Dixon
and his wife. I pushed to my normal bound-
ary range of about a mile and stopped.

*The only lifeforms nearby are two people at
the neighbor's house,* I said with mindspeak.

This is awesome, Mayes replied. *I've done
spirit questing where my essence traveled
above the earth, but now I'm fully in my body
and my senses at the same time. It's more
than adding a telescopic lens to a camera. It's
a game changer, like having a night scope on
a midnight takedown. And it's easy. Thanks
for showing me.*

*I don't do this all the time, just at night to
make sure it's safe to go to sleep.*

This is how you found your watcher?

Yes.

*We'll contact him tonight. He may already
be aware of our combined forces. Changes in
the natural energy field causes ripples.*

We disturbed the natural energy field?

*Oh yeah. I'd like to explore this further, but
shut it down so we can get our work done. I'll*

try to establish the same kind of perimeter monitor while you work.

I reined my senses in. As I did, I became aware of how closely Mayes held me, of how intimately we were nestled together. I hastily stepped away from him and blocked the mental connection.

His expression flickered and hardened. "Let's get to work."

Twisted bits of charred aluminum and metal dotted the yard, but every scrap of paper, every small personal item had been removed. My feet stopped moving as I studied how clean the yard truly was. "Wow. Wayne and Escoe will be examining evidence for months."

"Maybe," Mayes said. "But, maybe your connection with Mandy will point the team in the right direction."

"I hope so."

We walked around the exterior to where the meth lab had been. The sandy depression was pristine, as if it had been vacuumed. From this side of the trailer, I could see bits and pieces of the interior. The soot-covered bathtub was visible, along with the water pipes and the knobs.

"I'm pretty sure I can get a reading in the bathroom."

"I'm not seeing a file cabinet. I remember

Doodle saying his mother kept her personal papers in a file cabinet in her closet. The fire consumed the closet, but the file cabinet should've survived. I don't recall seeing a file cabinet in the evidence room. Wonder where it went."

"Can't help with that, but I'm ready to get started in the bathroom."

"We'll go in through the front door, like we did before. I remember where the footing is solid, so follow me."

I remembered where to step as well, but it was a small concession. Letting his command-and-control attitude pass, I followed him into the trailer. He reached for my hand, and with his touch, the sense of despair and desolation I'd vaguely sensed from this place came roaring through. Mandy had hated this trailer, this life.

"She was trapped," I said as I stepped where he stepped. "Derenne had her so cowed she could only do his bidding. The poor woman."

"This poor woman was a major drug producer for the Warner Robbins area outside of Macon. If Derenne kept her in raw material, and Mandy had no competing interests for her time, her production level could've been very high, even in this small space."

"We need answers. Did Mandy take the easy way out of a life of slavery? Would she abandon her kid at such a key time? Or was her fate determined by someone wanting her market?"

I stopped in front of the shower control. This handle was one of the last things Mandy had touched. "Time to take the plunge."

CHAPTER THIRTY

Darkness roiled and seethed around me as I transitioned to the Other Side. The customary iciness of the dreamwalk vector stretched to infinity. Futilely, I tried to orient myself, but it didn't work. Something was horribly wrong. Something was in here with me. Something that could eat me.

Stark terror bit me hard. Mentally I pinwheeled my arms backward and tried my best to change course, but I kept plunging through the inhospitable darkness.

In the past, I counted to ease the transition, as if gauging the distance of a lightning strike. By rote, I began counting. Thousand one. Thousand two. Thousand three.

Easy. I've got you.

Mayes? What? How?

Relax. You're trapped in the entry zone. Let go and exit the gateway corridor with me.

I don't understand. This isn't possible. You

were staying behind and monitoring the perimeter.

Baxley, cut the crap. My plan changed when I realized you were stuck. Mayes spoke harshly in my mind. *You're in danger. You trust me. I know you do. Finish the transition with me. Please.*

That voice in my head sounded like Mayes, but I'd been tricked by nonliving entities before. *Prove it. Show me you're my friend.*

The disembodied voice swore. We're more than friends. We're. . . . He spoke a word I didn't know, a word that sounded Cherokee in origin. I softened toward him, but then fear roared back. A cunning predator had me in his grasp. Every nuance of my spirit knew it.

Dammit. If you won't save yourself for my benefit, do it for your daughter. For Larissa.

Larissa. I couldn't leave her. The spirit was right. Nothing good would come of staying here. If I went with him, I would end up in a different realm, one where my thoughts would order as they should.

Okay, I managed. *I'll go with you.*

Let me in.

What?

Let me inside, so that our auras can mingle. I'm not whole at the moment. Surely you can come inside my spirit if you like.

Only if you invite me in.

Sounds scary. Are you a vampire?

I've never lied to you, Baxley. I don't know what all I am. My power scares me, and you are wise to be leery. Know this. I could never hurt you.

Made sense, and it wasn't like I had other options. I was sick of this long freefall. In mindspeak, I responded, *Yes, I invite you in.*

My sense of who and what I was blinked and was gone. The terror was twice as stark, more frightening than anything I'd ever experienced, but the endless tumbling ceased. Night faded to the foggy murk of the Other Side. My feet were on what passed for solid ground.

I tried to catch my virtual breath, but I wasn't me. I was me and Mayes. When I glanced at my hands, they were his hands. This wasn't right. *Let me out!*

Easy, Dreamwalker. I have you.

In the next instant, I sprang fully formed from his head. I checked my hands, my feet, my sides. Patted the hank of my virtual ponytail. I was me again. I turned to Mayes and asked, *What happened?*

You got stuck in the portal. I carried you through.

Impossible.

Very possible. We just did it.

His voice sounded so smug, so arrogant. Yet it was Mayes. I'd know that darkness he wore like a cape anywhere. *You are more than a Dreamwalker. What are you?*

I've been called many things by my people. I seem to be a combination of a holy man and a creature straight from Cherokee mythology. It's a long story, but you're in no danger from me.

And you'll share the myth with me, later.

Seems like everything with us happens later.

I don't have time to soothe your male ego. Thanks for the save. I'm grateful. But we have work to do. Let's find Mandy, see what she wants to show us, and get the heck out of here.

Works for me. Which way?

I don't know. I think of the person, touch an item they touched, and vector to them. Only this time you did the vectoring. You tell me where Mandy Patterson is.

I can do that, but only because I still have access to your thoughts.

Our surroundings began to change. Instinctively, I stepped back into Mayes.

We're in her dreamscape, Mayes said in my head. *Call her.*

Mandy? I'm here. In the ensuing silence, I recognized flasks, packages, jugs, and other

235

laboratory equipment. I knew where we were: Mandy's lab. She appeared then, suited up for cooking meth. She didn't spare us a glance because an image on the security screen caught her attention.

Mandy ripped off the mask covering her face and hurried to the door. "Doodle, come in here. Hurry."

A boy stuck his head out of a nearby room. "You said I could never go in there. You said your work was private."

"Someone's coming. No one comes here by accident. It can't be good. Hurry."

I judged Doodle to be preteen. So this was before or after Derenne came into their lives? Where were the pigs? I didn't hear or see them.

"What do you make in here, Mama?" Doodle asked, gazing around in wonder.

"I'm making your future, son. Remember that if you remember nothing else about me."

"Are you leaving me?"

"I hope not. Listen, we have to be quiet, so quiet that whoever this is thinks we aren't home."

"Did we do something wrong?"

"Not on purpose. I don't know this person, and I don't trust anyone I don't know. You shouldn't either. Not ever. Now, shh."

They sat on the floor, eyes riveted on the security camera feeds. A sports car pulled up almost to the front door, leaving ruts in the sparsely grassed sand. The female driver sat there for a long moment. She had short, chin-length straight hair and fancy sunglasses, which she ripped off and threw on the dashboard. Silver flashed as she moved her hands. Jewelry. She wore rings on both ring fingers.

The car door opened, and the woman exited gracefully, carrying a clipboard and an ink pen. She mounted the front steps and rapped crisply. "Mrs. Patterson? I'm here for the Census."

The woman stood there, staring at the door. She knocked and called out again, the silver of her rings flashing. One ring seemed elevated and more ornate than the others.

With a furtive glance around the yard, the woman tucked the clipboard under her arm and tried the knob. The locked door didn't budge. She whacked it with the clipboard, denting its pockmarked surface even more.

"Where the hell are you?" the woman muttered before returning to her sports car. She hit the gas and tore out of there, not bothering to stop at the Dixon place next door.

Curious, I thought. *Why wouldn't a census*

worker stop at every house?

The dreamscape shifted back to Mandy and Doodle. "She's gone, son. It's okay."

The boy cocked his head to one side. "What'd she want with us? What's a census?"

"Our government conducts a census every ten years to count everybody, but that woman wasn't from the census."

"Why not?"

"It's the wrong year for the census, she didn't leave a card, and she tried to break into our place."

"We should report her to the cops."

"No cops. We can't ever call the cops. You know that."

"Because of your job."

"That's right."

"Why don't you get another job? One where people don't scare you? One where we don't have to hide and be scared?"

"It's complicated."

The child lunged for Mandy and wrapped his arms around her. "I don't want a future. I'd rather have my mom."

"Hush up. You'll have a chance to break the poverty cycle because of the sacrifices I've made. You're smart as a whip, and you can make something of yourself. And you will too, or I will have wasted my life."

"If I help you with your work, will you get finished quicker?"

"I don't want you caught up in this, Doodle. You run on to your room now and read or draw more of your pretty pictures."

"Aw, Mom." The boy edged out of the room, and Mandy sunk into a rickety chair in relief. Her hands shook. Taking a closer look, I saw her coloring was off. What had spooked her?

Mandy? Can you hear me? I tried.

Go away, Mandy said. *I showed you the important stuff.*

Your son is safe, I improvised to keep her talking. *He's a good boy.*

He'd better be. I did what I could for him.

What happened in the lab, Mandy?

The scene switched back to the day of the fire. I saw a replay of the earlier scene she'd shown me, the one where she ended up in the shower. As before, the scene blacked out with the sound of the explosion.

Don't go, Mandy. Was the fire an accident?

Not an accident, she muttered as she faded from sight.

CHAPTER THIRTY-ONE

Back in the real world of Mandy's former bathroom, I awakened in Mayes' arms. His chest filled my visual field. I lifted my head and gazed at his handsome face. We were the same height, so his eyes were level with mine. In their depths, I saw many fine qualities. Compassion. Strength. Tenderness.

He seemed so familiar, and yet I barely knew anything about him. This was only the second weekend we'd ever spent together.

"How do you feel?" he asked.

"Good." I drew in a full breath and stepped away before another kiss happened. To be on the safe side, I erected my mental barrier that protected my extra senses and blocked Mayes from direct access to my thoughts. My rose tattoos were cool to the touch. My otherworld mentor was keeping her word about staying away from my dreamwalks.

Oddly, there was none of the usual fatigue I felt after a spiritual encounter. I brimmed with vitality. "Too good. You shared your energy with me, didn't you?"

He shrugged.

A conversational dead end. I was getting good at recognizing those. When Mayes didn't want to talk, he kept his own counsel. Whether that was due to his heritage, his career as a cop, or his personality, I couldn't say.

We needed to have that relationship conversation, but Mandy's fire-ravaged trailer wasn't the place to remind him we were friends and nothing more.

I glanced at the blue sky overhead, grateful for natural sunshine and balmy weather. Mandy had worked hard to provide for her son, but where were the fruits of her labors? "She told me the fire wasn't an accident. Someone started it."

"Which brings us back to our suspect list: the neighbor, the aunt, the boyfriend, or the son. We should add the voodoo woman to the list too."

"The voodoo woman? Really? It was a coincidence her visit to me occurred at the start of this case."

"Cops don't believe in coincidences. She's involved in this somehow, either for her personal gain or for another reason. Could be she has a client that wants you sidelined."

The palm reader had been starving when she visited. She seemed keen on helping her grandmother, but other than that, I didn't know much about her. Other than her attacking me with voodoo. "Someone hired Cipriona Marsden to hurt me?"

"We need to talk to her. If she acted as an agent for someone else, and that someone realizes she failed, her days could be numbered."

"I know where she lives."

"We should go there next. Anything else you want to touch in the trailer?"

"No. I'd hoped something might call my name or spontaneously occur, but this place feels empty now."

Mayes took my hand, led me out, then stopped short in the yard. "I want to check for hidden cameras."

I gazed over my shoulder at the gaping front doorway. "The fire destroyed the cams on the trailer eaves and over the door."

"But at least one camera covered the approach to Mandy's residence. Perhaps the perimeter cameras survived." We halted in the shade of a towering pine. Mayes closed his eyes for a moment. "I remember frames from three cameras that covered the front door, the back side of the trailer, and the front yard. But I also recall one road view."

There was a lot of vegetation and only two of us. "How will we find hidden cameras?"

"Assuming she bought the latest in technology, those cams would be wireless and communicating with individual receivers at her internet hub."

"What about her cellphone?"

Mayes frowned. "Oh. An app. She could've had an app on her cell. With that, she could keep track of visitors even when she wasn't home. Heck, a top system can send messages when someone approaches. Good thinking."

"Not so good if her phone burned up."

"Still worth considering. Doodle's cell may also have the app, or he may know how to access it. Better yet, the images may have been relayed to an offsite utility, like a cloud server. We need to talk with Doodle again about that possibility."

"Meanwhile, we should search for remote cameras we saw in the dreamwalk feed. The view of the front yard came from over there." I pointed in a southwesterly direction. "I'll check it out."

But when I got to the tree line and searched high and low, I found nothing. "Rats. No camera here."

Mayes had been poking around in the same general area. "Your first instinct was right. I believe that fresh gouge in the tree trunk is where a camera used to be mounted."

"We're too late, then."

"Maybe not. If I set up this security system, I would've added a backup, in case of a bust or worse."

"What's worse than a bust?" He gave me a barbed look, and my thoughts jolted. "Oh, like a fire or a homicide. You'd have wanted someone to know what happened. For justice's sake."

"Or retribution." He paced the woods, turning to check the line of sight from each stopping point. "Where are you, little camera?" he asked.

I used a stick to part the underbrush before I stepped. "How big would this secondary camera be?"

"Trail cams are about the size of a cellphone or smaller. The case is big enough to hold a few batteries, the lens, and a data storage card. It would be watertight."

"You would make an excellent bad guy."

"It's why they pay me the big bucks."

We moved branches, stepped in and out of the tree line, all to no avail. I pointed at an oak a little deeper in the woods. The remnants of a tree fort were tacked on the tree limbs and trunk. "What about up there?"

"Hmm. It's higher than we've been considering, but the line of sight fits. If the boards leading up to the platform are in good shape, I'd say it's a strong possibility."

We tromped through the underbrush. I would need a shower and a thorough tick check when we were done here. At the live oak, the weathered boards turned out to be scraps from one of those fancy composite decks. When Mayes applied his weight to the lowest rung, it held.

"I'm going up." He easily scaled the eight boards nailed to the tree trunk and sat on the platform.

"See anything?" I craned my neck to keep my eyes on him.

"The view's terrific. I have clear line of sight to the front and this end of the trailer, along with the turn in from the road. It doesn't look like this platform has been here too long. The nails still look new. This platform wasn't a kid's hideout, but it would've made a great hangout. You'd be surprised at how many people don't look up."

"The trail camera? Is it there?

He reached underneath the platform and

withdrew a small box. "Bingo." A moment later, he stood on the ground beside me, the box, a bulge in his pocket. "We need a computer, fast."

No kidding. We returned to the truck and headed to Bartow Road. A shirtless bantam rooster of man came huffing up to us, greasy hair trailing behind him.

"Help!" Ricky Dixon yelled. "She's got my gun."

CHAPTER THIRTY-TWO

"Who's got your gun?" Mayes asked, turning in his seat to block me from Dixon, the next-door neighbor.

His protective behavior annoyed me. The likelihood of Dixon carrying a concealed weapon in his sagging camo shorts were small. I climbed out of the truck and circled to Dixon. Two hundred proof fumes wafted up my nose. Dixon had either been drinking heavily or swimming in booze. A glance at his bloodshot eyes and his unsteady gait convinced me it was heavy drinking.

Mayes joined me outside the truck, doing his best to stay between me and Dixon. I grabbed his hand so he'd remain in one place.

"My wife. She got hold of my twelve gauge." Dixon gestured emphatically with his arms and paced around us, his feet leaving deep impressions in the sandy road. "Said she'd kill me if I didn't let her out of bed, so I did. Now she's done run me off, out of my own house." He swore a string of ugly words.

I heard everything he said, but it didn't quite compute. Was he for real? "You keep your wife in bed? Tied up?"

"It's for her own good. That woman's got a mean streak a mile wide. I should tape her mouth shut too because the words that come out of it are pure filth. God almighty. You gotta stop her."

So far, he'd told the truth, or at least a truth he believed. He'd been drinking both times I'd met him, and now his wife, whom I'd believed to be bedridden, was actually a prisoner in her own home? That was against the law. What other crimes had Dixon committed?

A loud blast interrupted my thoughts. It came from the Dixons' place. Mayes and I exchanged worried glances, and Dixon yowled his frustration. "She's shooting my stuff. Go arrest her. Lock her butt in jail and see how she likes that. She'll be begging to come home."

"I'll walk Mr. Dixon home." Disentangling his hand from mine, Mayes tapped his temple several times with his index finger. "Why don't you write up our investigation notes and then follow us in the truck?"

"Er, sure."

What notes? Was he protecting me again by shutting me out? I didn't like that one bit, but I had to pick my battles. Why had Mayes tapped the side of his head? It wasn't a gesture I'd ever seen him use.

In case he was signaling me, I lowered my extrasensory barriers and shot him a telepathic message. *Mayes?*

Finally. Look, I've got my hands full with this drunk. Call Wayne. Get some backup out here, ASAP. We may need a SWAT team.

Wayne's the best sharpshooter we've got. SWAT is a no-go unless we bring in outside forces, I sent him back, rapid-fire. *What should I tell the sheriff?*

Exactly what happened. We were in the area and heard a shot. Mr. Dixon flagged us down.

What about the trail cam in your pocket?

I'll give it to him when I see him. Let's focus on the immediate issue. Something odd is happening next door. We'll get back to the murder investigation soon enough.

You think the Dixons are a separate issue?

All I know for sure is the status quo changed over there. Dixon seems slimy enough that I'd be happy to arrest him for murder, but we have no proof of any wrongdoing at this point.

Dixon's wife was alleged to be bedridden. If

*she's up and armed after being forcefully
detained, she'll be royally pissed.*

*Never thought I'd say this, but ask Wayne to
send the guy with the Taser. I'd rather avoid
more gunshots, if possible.*

Will do.

Bax?

Yes?

*Will you keep the channel between us
open? That way I'll know you're safe.*

*For now, but stay out of my head unless it's
important. I'm not used to having real voices
in my head. Only dead ones.*

Of course. You won't even know I'm here.

The connection faded until it barely
registered, like a quiet engine on idle. Better than what I thought it'd be. I phoned
the sheriff and filled him in on the situation.

"Hold on a minute while I turn around,"
Wayne said. "I'm about ten minutes away
from you."

"What were you doing this far out of
town?"

"Business."

Business. Oh yeah. He'd had *lunch* with
the new outlet mall manager.

While I waited for him to come back on
the line, I rooted through my glove compart-
ment. A dental-floss container. Gum. Four

ink pens. A spare leash. Beretta. *Score!* I grabbed my handgun and watched seconds of my life tick by. Surely that was enough time for Mayes to get Dixon settled. I eased the truck toward Dixon's concrete-block house, phone snugged against my ear.

"You there?" the sheriff asked.

"Yeah."

"I notified dispatch through my onboard computer system. Virg and Ronnie are on the way."

"I don't understand the situation with Dixon and his wife."

Wayne sighed, like he'd never take another breath. "Domestic violence is about sex, control, or money. Sounds like at least the first two are possibilities in Dixon's case."

"You think he's been holding her prisoner?'

"I'll dig into Dixon's background. He could be a child molester living under a false identity, for all we know. Once we secure the weapon and the wife, I want you in that house, looking at and touching everything. Until then, you stay the hell out of the way."

"He's got hounds in there."

"I can do him one better. I've got a Dreamwalker."

CHAPTER THIRTY-THREE

I parked my truck a safe distance beyond the oak where Mayes and Ricky Dixon stood in Dixon's yard. While the men in my life were trying to protect me, I had my own dreamwalker protection plan. Both the front pockets of my jeans bulged with crystals. My moldavite necklace held a full charge. And the Beretta I'd pulled from the glove box and tucked in my waistband was none too shabby.

There was one more weapon I had in my arsenal: Oliver, the Great Dane spirit that had attached itself to me a few months ago in the swamp. I'd rescued the ghost dog from the chains it had been tangled in for nearly a century, and Oliver, in his gratitude, now followed me everywhere. Urging him to find a companion on the Other Side to follow hadn't swayed his devotion to me.

But with hunting dogs in the Dixon house, a phantom dog might come in handy. I softened my gaze slightly, engaged my other senses, and summoned Oliver. He came to me on the spiritual plane, all bouncy and tail-waggy. I lavished affection on him, petting him and cooing, and asked him to stay close. As I transitioned back to my normal senses, I felt the chill of Oliver's presence beside my legs.

Just another day at work. A crazy woman with a gun. An irate, drunken husband. A psychic with a ghost dog. And soon there'd be a half dozen cops running around here on two-hundred-proof testosterone.

Oliver and I walked over to where Mayes and Dixon stood. Both men were sweating from the heat of the day, but Oliver's ghostly chill kept me cool.

Bartow Road was a long ways from anywhere, but I heard the faint warble of a siren. Wayne would be here soon. A nod from Mayes showed he'd also heard. I could talk to him telepathically, but I'd rather not encourage too much of that. Mayes already thought we fit together like peanut butter and jelly.

Another shot rang out inside the house, and we ducked. I heard dogs barking.

"She's gonna shoot my dogs," Dixon yowled. "We've gotta get that gun."

"How much ammo you got for that twelve

gauge?" Mayes asked.

"Plenty. We cain't wait that long. My hounds are worth a fortune, I tell you. They's the best hunting dogs I ever had. If you ain't goin' after 'em, I will."

Mayes grabbed Dixon's arm. "You're not going anywhere. We're gathering information before we go inside. Tell us about your wife. What's her name?"

"I call her Tip."

"How mobile is Tip?"

"She can get around iffen she wants to. Mostly she don't wanna do nothin'. But today she woke up in a twist. Her medicine run out, and I cain't buy more until the disability check comes in."

"What kind of medicine?"

"For her head. It ain't on straight."

"How so?"

"Tip says she's someone else. Calls herself by these other names. Sometimes even changes the sound of her voice."

Dixon had told a big fat lie. It flared all around him in little shock waves. My entire body recoiled. Mayes noticed my reaction, and his eyes narrowed. We'd caught Dixon in a lie, but which statement was a lie? Was his wife ill or was something more sinister going on?

"A personality disorder?" Mayes asked.

"Somepin' like that. I forget the doctor's name for it. When her meds run out, I keep her liquored up, but she grabbed my gun after she went to the bathroom this morning. She shot off my little toe last time this happened, so I didn't wrestle her for my gun. I'm smarter than your average bear."

With each passing syllable, I liked Dixon less and less. Seeing as how I'd had reservations about him from the start, I pretty much didn't even want to look at him.

The wail of the approaching siren finally registered in Dixon's ears. He turned on me and tried to punch me, forgetting Mayes had hold of his arm. "You witch!" Dixon yelled. "You shouldn't have called the cops."

Mayes gave Dixon's arm another shake. "I *am* a cop, and you have a dangerous situation inside your home. In the interest of everyone's safety, we have to follow certain guidelines."

"I changed my mind," Dixon said, eyes wide. "Go away. She'll kill me anyway. I'm so dead. Just go away. She'll pass out sooner or later, then I'll get my gun back."

"No can do. We heard shots fired in a residence. For public-safety reasons, we must investigate, and if necessary, secure the weapon."

Dixon struggled in a frenzy of arms and

legs. "That's my shotgun. You can't have it."

Mayes held fast.

First to arrive from the sheriff's office was Virg and Ronnie's cruiser. I couldn't remember when I'd ever been so glad to see them. Virg cut the siren, but the blue lights kept flashing. Odd how that sight was now so comforting amidst all the noise of dogs barking.

Virg stepped out of the car, hand on his Taser. Ronnie dashed around the car to join his partner. "Where are we?" Virg asked Mayes.

"An armed woman inside, randomly firing off rounds from a twelve-gauge shotgun is the main complaint," Mayes said, still physically holding onto Dixon. "The complainant says she's had a lot to drink. Her name is Tip Dixon. Mr. Dixon is displaying signs of drunk and disorderly conduct."

"I'm not drunk," Dixon yelled. "She is. She's ruined my life."

Ronnie snapped a set of cuffs on Dixon, patted him down, then stashed the loudmouth in the back of their cruiser. "Now what?" Ronnie said.

"I could go in," I offered. "She might be receptive to a woman."

"No way," Mayes said. "If she's half as loco as her husband suggested, she wouldn't think twice about shooting you. I'll go in the front door while Virg and Ronnie circle around back. If we have to take her down, I'd rather subdue her with a Taser than a bullet."

"We should wait for the sheriff," Virg said.

Another shot rang out from the house, right through the roof. I hit the ground at the percussive sound, and so did my companions.

"That woman's crazy all right," Virg said, his eyes sparkling with challenge. "Let's git her."

"Glad you see it my way," Mayes said. "Got a spare vest in your car?"

"I carry the sheriff's extra vest with me."

"Perfect. I'd like to borrow it."

While amazed that Virg followed Mayes' directions, I could see that natural authority radiated from Mayes. He was born to command.

"Bax, stand behind the truck until I give the all clear. You're the second wave, as Wayne suggested previously. We need you to figure out what's going on in that house."

A protest lodged in my throat as the guys shrugged into bulletproof vests. I hoped they were shotgun-proof. Minutes later, all three cops melted away. I ignored Dixon's hollering from the cruiser and waited.

Mayes knocked on the door and asked Mrs. Dixon to show herself. I couldn't make out what she yelled back at him, but he kicked open the door. Another shotgun blast flung roof shingles in the air. Mayes called out again. Silence. Then Virg came to the door from inside. "Got her."

Mayes followed him inside. Moments later, he stood in the threshold, shotgun in his gloved hand. He waved me forward. "Your turn."

I hurried to the house. "What's the rush?"

"Lots of flammables on the back porch. We need to remove Mrs. Dixon and call the fire department. It's a wonder this place didn't ignite already. I want you to do a quick run-through, and I mean quick."

"What about the dogs?" I asked.

"Locked in a pen in the backyard. They were safe all along. Another lie from Dixon."

"We can't believe anything he told us."

Dixon's home reeked of cigarette smoke, hound dog, body odor, and stale beer. A recliner sat empty in the living room. Surrounding it were open trash bags of empty beer cans and four overflowing ashtrays.

I shuddered. "Don't see anything I want to touch."

Mayes showed me around the two-bedroom place. Besides the tiny living room, there was an even tinier kitchen, a closet-sized bathroom, and two small bedrooms. The first bedroom seemed to be a computer graveyard. A skeletally thin woman lay on the floor of the second bedroom.

Tip Dixon looked like she'd recently escaped from a concentration camp. It made my heart hurt to see her every bone outlined by flesh. Her gray hair had been cropped short, but no stylist had touched these ragged locks. Dark circles rimmed her vacant brown eyes.

I wanted to wrap her in my arms and transport her to the ER. But I wasn't willing to deal with my supernatural guide from the Other Side who could make that happen. Tip was alive. Her hand twitched after being Tasered. She wasn't at death's door from our actions, though she appeared grossly malnourished.

Tip wore a moss-green nightgown and not much else. Both her bony wrists had raw, abraded skin, as did one of her knobby ankles. She'd been physically restrained.

I gasped. "My God. The rumors are true. She's a prisoner in her own home. Her husband is a monster."

CHAPTER THIRTY-FOUR

Mayes guided me from the bedroom into the narrow hall. "Dixon's story isn't clear. We know he's a liar. By all accounts, he's a grumpy old guy complaining about everything. He doesn't get along with his neighbors, and he has an abusive relationship with his wife."

" 'Abusive' seems too light a word for her starvation and two black eyes. Isn't Tip's emaciated condition enough to send him away for life?"

"Not always. Judges tend to be lenient about domestic abuse the first few times. When we first ID'ed him as a suspect, we ran his name through the system, and he had no outstanding warrants. His only interaction with the law stemmed from the incident with the neighbor's pigs."

"So, the fact that he's a horrible person doesn't count? We have to find a crime he's committed?"

"That would work. We need an indication of illegal activity before we can search beyond what's in plain sight."

"It sucks. Majorly. I want to deck him, and I'm not a violent person."

"Drunk and disorderly conduct and domestic abuse aren't grounds for us to search his computers. Find us something useful, fast."

"Where should I start? With the computer mouse, doorknobs, sink handles, TV remote, the wife?"

"Start with the woman. You may not get another chance alone with her once the EMTs arrive. Find out her story."

"I'll do my best." I padded back to the bedroom and sat down on the floor beside Tip Dixon. Mayes watched from the doorway; Virg and Ronnie were talking in the kitchen. With a sense of time zipping through the hourglass, I gripped the unconscious woman's arm. Oliver leaned against my leg, chilling it.

Light bent and stretched out into a starburst. It coalesced into a Plexiglas window station, much like the visitation window we had at our Sinclair County Jail. The young woman's face reflected back at me was unrecognizable. When she smiled, I noticed that the tips of her front teeth overlapped.

"Not too much longer, babe. My lawyer said the release papers is goin' through the system," the young man who sat on the other side of the window said. He was beanpole-thin. Wiry even. It could be Dixon, but I wasn't sure.

"I've been getting stuff pulled together like you asked," the woman said.

"And my buddy. What'd he say?"

"Said we were good."

They were quiet for a moment, then the woman continued, "I wish we could take the kids."

"They're better off in the system. Livin' on the run ain't no life for a kid."

She smacked her palm on the counter. "Still. Missouri got no right to say I'm unfit for anything."

"The state's got every right. You can hang around here and pine for the runts, or we can start fresh. You don't wanna come, just say so."

"I wanna come."

The vision ended abruptly. Oliver and I were alone in the twilight. I knelt and said goodbye to my ghost dog. "Looks like I won't need you for this situation. Go and have a good romp." After a few more pets and licks, Oliver bounded off into the fog.

I dreamwalked back to reality. Two brown

eyes with wide pupils drilled into me. "Who the hell are you?" the woman said, wrenching her arm away. Her two front teeth overlapped at the bottom. "Why are you in my house?"

"I can explain, Mrs. Dixon," I began slowly. The overlapping teeth of my dreamwalk made sense now. Years ago, Tip and Ricky lived elsewhere and had a different life. He'd been in jail. To make a fresh start, they'd left their children behind. "My name is Baxley Powell, and I sometimes help the police. I'm here to keep you company."

The woman's guarded expression didn't change. "Name's Tip."

The rotten stench of her alcohol-laced breath hit me like a load of manure. I tried shallow breaths to keep from flinching. "Did your husband strike you in the face?"

She didn't respond. I tried another line of questioning. "Why'd you shoot the ceiling twice?"

"To punish that SOB, that's why."

"For what?"

Tip shook her head, her eyes widening as she stuffed part of a fist in her mouth. I could almost see gears whirring slowly in her head.

"You're safe now," I said. "He can't hurt you anymore."

She scooched up so that she was sitting on the floor and leaning against the frame of the bed. "You don't get it."

"Tell me."

"I got nobody else. Just him and me."

"The world's a big place, full of friendly people."

"People hate us."

"Why do you say that? Did someone else hurt you?"

"Yeah."

"Recently?"

"Nah. But I learned. I'm smart that way. You don't haveta beat the same lesson into me twice."

Looked like Dixon had been beating the same lesson into her for years. I needed another angle, some way to get her to open up. "What's your favorite food?"

"Vodka."

"I mean solid food, like bacon and eggs, salad, hamburgers."

"Vodka."

"Do you eat anything besides vodka?"

"Nope. And Dickhead won't go to the store. I need my vodka. You got any on ya?"

"Sorry. Fresh out."

Tip grumbled under her breath, wrung her hands together.

"Mrs. Dixon, you're going to the hospital

for a checkup. When's the last time you saw a doctor?"

"Dickhead!" Tip yelled. "Get in here."

Ricky Dixon wouldn't be coming. "A doctor will evaluate your condition."

She shrank away from me. "I ain't going nowhere. Dickhead! Where are you?"

Steeling my senses, I patted Tip's bony shoulder to offer her comfort. "Your husband has been detained, ma'am. He's under arrest. You're safe now. How long have you been with him?"

"Going on thirty years. What's it to ya?"

"Did you know your neighbor, Mandy Patterson?"

"Who?"

I repeated the name. Tip shook her head. "Other than the dogs, I haven't seen anyone since we moved here. I don't leave the house."

"He won't let you leave, or you don't want to go?"

"I'm not saying another word until I see Dickhead."

"He's not coming."

"He has to. I need him. I need my vodka."

Sheriff Wayne Thompson came to the door and caught my eye. "A word. Virg will keep an eye on Mrs. Dixon."

At the sight of Virg's Taser, Tip shrieked

and buried her face in her hands.

"Coming," I said. I scrambled up on all fours, then rose to my feet.

Wayne ushered me out the back door. The hunting dogs were locked nearby in a pen, barking nonstop. "You got something?"

I filled him in on my dreamwalk. Wayne nodded. "Good job. I'll run Dixon's prints through Missouri and find out who he really is. We'll lock this place down as soon as the fire people clear the flammables and the EMTs cart the woman away."

"Mayes and I might have a lead."

He raised a hand. "About the Patterson case?"

"Yeah. Not sure how it ties in," I said. "But it involves a recent dreamwalker client. We think the palm reader might be connected to the case. Mayes doesn't believe in the coincidental timing of her appointment with me."

"The Marsden woman can wait. I need Mayes to help me work this scene while Virg and Ronnie get Dixon processed. I'll run him home when we're done. Get Dixon's dogs out of here so I can think. Better that you keep them than they go to the shelter."

"But I didn't touch-test anything. Mayes thinks I should do that."

"Mayes isn't running this investigation. If

Dixon's got a criminal history, we'll have enough to hold him. Your assignment is to get the dogs out of here. Do you have a problem with that?"

Mayes' competence was a burr in Wayne's ego. "No problem. I'll take the dogs."

I had no kennel facilities at home, plus I already owned three dogs and a cat. Four additional dogs, which may or may not be house-trained, would wreak havoc in my household. Plus two groups of dogs equaled two dog packs. There would be a skirmish for pack leader of the combined group. One of my dogs might get injured.

"Nothing wrong with the shelter," I said.

"Your call. Just take the blasted dogs, Bax."

Minutes later, I hit the road with four healthy hounds in my truck. With no animal crates in my truck, I'd leashed them all and hooked the leads to my tie-down ring in the truck bed. To my surprise, the dogs seemed well mannered once they were released from confinement. This might not be a total disaster.

CHAPTER THIRTY-FIVE

I stopped off at the abandoned airfield to evaluate Dixon's hounds. I couldn't tell them apart just yet, since their appearance was nearly identical, but Dixon made it easy for me by engraving the names of the Fab Four on their dog collars.

John, Paul, George, and Ringo responded individually to the basic commands of heel, sit, stay, come, down, and quiet on leash and off. I turned them all loose in the field, and they romped and played together under sunny skies. They also responded to my basic commands off leash. Ringo appeared to be the alpha dog of the pack. I could remember that easily enough. Ringo was the ring leader.

They were nice dogs. As long as they integrated with my pets, they could stay with me.

The hounds chased tennis balls until their tongues hung low, and I felt I could easily introduce them to my pets now. My three dogs were over at my parents' place with my daughter. I couldn't leave these dogs unsupervised in my home on their first visit, and I couldn't fetch my animals and force them to get acquainted in the truck. We had to go to my parents' house. I loaded them in the truck again and was headed that way when Charlotte called.

"I know something is happening," Charlotte said. "Every emergency vehicle left town like they were chasing a tornado. Is this about the case?"

"Domestic violence in the county, but there may be a newsworthy twist soon."

"Dish."

"Can't. Ongoing investigation."

"That is spiteful and mean."

"Not necessarily. You'll have first dibs on the breaking news. Meanwhile, where are you and Duncan?"

"We were headed to your parents' place to commune with the pigs. Why?"

"I could use a few extra pairs of hands for some dog clients I unexpectedly acquired today. Turns out I'll be fostering them until their owner gets out of jail."

Charlotte giggled. "Poky puppies?"

"More like full-grown hounds. I recall Duncan has hunting dogs. It'd be great if he was there when I arrived."

"Seeing as how we just turned in the driveway, I'd say that's gonna happen. Bring 'em on."

Duncan and the hounds took to each other like sand to plastic wrap. These dogs were used to a male authority figure, and it showed. Duncan, Larissa, and I introduced them to our dogs. There was plenty of sniffing and tail wagging and romping. Duncan put on an obedience show for Larissa, urging Dixon's hounds through their paces. Mom and Dad decided to start a pot of soup, giving Charlotte and me a rare moment of privacy.

I stretched and yawned as I joined Charlotte on my father's favorite bench. He called it his thinking place because it was hard to be concerned about worldly matters with so much nature around you. These woods were special, exuding a peaceful, centered sense of well-being.

"Is your weekend everything you'd hoped?" I asked.

Charlotte beamed. "Couldn't be any better. We've got a homicide case about to bust open and at least one other promising big story on the horizon."

"I was talking about your, uh, personal life."

"That's great, but I'm half afraid Duncan will wake up and realize he can have any woman he wants."

"He doesn't appear to be asleep to me."

"Nah. He's full of energy and life."

"So are you. That's what makes you two well matched. You look happy together."

"I'm trying not to stress about the future, but I'm already behind the power curve. If I want a husband and children, I can't wait much longer. All the good eggs will be gone."

I wasn't sure if she was referring to men in general or the number of unfertilized eggs remaining in her ovaries. Better not to ask. "How was lunch? Did you introduce yourself to the new outlet-mall manager?"

"Sure did. Snapped a picture of her with Wayne that I already sent to my boss. Alicia wore this clingy red sheath and that popped really well in the photo. She wasn't available for a feature today, but she let it slip that she has a degree in marketing and intends to implement more universal good business practices in all the outlet stores."

"She sounds sharp. Wonder how long she'll last?"

"About five minutes after Dottie Thompson finds out Alicia had her hands all over the sheriff. Wayne was soaking up the personalized attention too. What's wrong with him? I thought he and Dottie were going strong again now that she decided to get out of her sick bed."

A few years back, Dottie decided everyone would wait on her, hand and foot. As time went on, she lost interest in getting up. Consequently, her weight soared and her health declined. I kept meaning to go over there and congratulate her return to wellness, but I didn't want to be Dottie's best friend.

"Wayne is . . ." I trailed off. I could get in trouble for gossiping about my boss. But this was Charlotte. I chewed my lip.

"I hate it when you do that," Charlotte said. "When you realize you can't tell me something because of our jobs. I resent being shut out of your world. I hate that crime fighting and newspaper reporting drives a wedge between us. You're my best friend. This isn't right."

Mourning doves cooed in the distance. A light breeze stirred the air enough to keep the heat from being unbearable. Even so, the natural environment didn't soothe Charlotte's distress.

"I'm used to telling you everything, so it's

hard on me as well," I added, my voice breaking as I spoke. "I won't comment specifically on Wayne, but it's my observation that people don't truly change. If their personality is one way, and they try to be something else for a while, they can maintain that alternate identity for only so long. Sooner or later, they show their true colors."

Like the sharp cookie she was, Charlotte pieced it together. "And Wayne Thompson has always been a tomcat."

I let the silence speak for itself.

"Anyway, Alicia wants to meet you," Charlotte said.

Charlotte sounded so energized, so excited about meeting this woman. I wasn't. Strangers who took an interest in me always wanted something. "How does she even know me? I barely know her name."

"She called you 'our resident psychic.' She knew about the cases you'd solved. Seems she'd read my articles in the *Marion Observer*."

Now that I was a police consultant, I was highly suspicious of everyone, especially people I didn't know. "I don't like it. Was Wayne talking about me?"

"Wayne was surprisingly mum about you."

Good. At least Wayne hadn't totally lost his mind. "Then how did my name enter into the conversation?"

"She knew we were best friends."

I shook my head. "How would she know that? I hope you didn't tell her anything about me. I don't trust strangers."

"I would never betray you, Baxley. I didn't talk about you at all," Charlotte said. "Alicia lives in Macon, but her business is in a town near there."

I drew in a long, contemplative breath. "Figures. Seems like the women we get from upstate all want a piece of me."

"What about you and Mayes? You two glow when you're near each other. Something happened, didn't it?"

That *something* was private and would remain so. "Mayes is a nice guy. Decent. Hardworking."

"You forgot that he's sexy as all get out and crazy about you."

I sighed. "It shows, doesn't it?"

"At least you'll never have to guess what he's thinking. When it comes to you, he's crystal clear."

"Which is something of a problem for me, but interestingly, a solution may be in sight."

Charlotte's grin vanished as her eyebrow raised. "Do tell."

"This stays between us. No Duncan. No newspaper. Right?"

My friend nodded. "Pinky swear."

Though we were alone in the yard, I leaned in close. "We know what it's like to be among the living, and lately I've become familiar with the dead. The problem is I can't find Roland in either world. Mayes suggested, and my parents think his idea is worth pursuing, that Roland is in yet another, alternate realm."

"Like the place where the Nunne'hi live?"

When we visited the Georgia mountains, the Nunne'hi had kidnapped Charlotte, Deputy Duncan, and the state archaeologist for a day. Their ploy forced me to produce Rose, my mentor on the Other Side. Rose worked out a deal which benefited her nicely, and we'd gotten our people back in the land of the living.

"Something along those lines," I said. "Am I a complete whack job for even considering this?"

"Your dreamwalking and our travels have broadened my horizons. I'm open to possibilities."

I snickered. "You're such a Renaissance woman."

"Ha. Good one." We both laughed and relaxed on the bench, the balance of our friendship restored. "So what's next, Bax?"

Though Wayne had told me to wait before

pursuing my next lead, I felt like I'd spent all day doing his bidding or waiting for him. I decided to follow up on a personal matter. "I was thinking about having my palm read. Wanna come?"

"Do I ever!"

CHAPTER THIRTY-SIX

Cipriona Marsden blocked her doorway as effectively as a linebacker. The statuesque palm reader wore spiky heels and an over-one-shoulder short dress that reminded me of a caveman's wife from the funnies. Her glossy black braids curtained her broad shoulders. Another bag of herbs graced her neckline, the dime anklet still clasped around her ankle. "What are you doing here?"

"Following up." I stood on the second riser of her steps, Charlotte below me on the ground, her trusty miniature tape recorder in hand. "You were concerned about your granny, remember?"

"Can't do nuttin' about Granny. I done tried everythin' I know to save her from a life behind bars."

I raised a plastic grocery bag in my other hand. "You left these suspenders at my house the other day. I'm returning them."

When I held out the bag, she shrank away and waved me inside. "Drop it on the coffee table," Cipriona said.

I edged past her into the small home. The pungent smell hit me first. Some form of incense, and a lot of it, had been burned in here. The place reeked to the point where my eyes watered. Deep-purple swaths of batik fabric edged the narrow windows. Fat squatty candles occupied almost every flat surface. One corner of the room seemed to be made of black fabric. Perhaps that curtained alcove was where she did her readings?

Not a single voodoo doll in sight. Drat. I'd hoped this would be easy.

After setting down my parcel, I turned to Cipriona and asked, "Why didn't you wait until I came out of the dreamwalk for my report?"

She shrugged. "Got spooked."

A big fat lie. I couldn't let it stand. "Are you sure? Because I thought you might've waited until I was otherwise engaged and then took what you really came there for. A hank of my white hair is missing. Did you think I wouldn't notice?"

She shook her head fast, and her tongue thrust forward through her teeth.

A negative response and a case of nerves.

I pressed my advantage, hoping she'd admit her misdeeds. "I know what you're about, Cipriona. I know what you are."

She retreated a step. "You know nothing about me."

I heard Charlotte's clothing rustle over by the doorway. It wouldn't do for her to interrupt, so I motioned with my hand for her to stop. "You tried to hurt me with voodoo. *Tried* being the operative word because I blocked you. Whatever you've been doing, it won't work. Wards are in place. Leave me alone."

Her brown eyes rounded as if she were truly afraid. "You have to stop."

"I don't have to stop anything, but humor me. What is it you think I should stop?"

"Everything. If you don't, he's going to kill me."

"He who? Did someone pay you to hurt me?"

Cipriona shook her head too fast, her long braids flailing, end beads clacking. "I done said too much already."

"Does this have anything to do with Mandy Patterson? Did you kill her?"

"I ain't killed nobody."

Another lie. A whopper by the dissonance in her tone. "I don't believe you."

"I don't give a flying flip what you believe.

Take your sorry hide and get out of my house."

"Did you know Mandy?"

"I said get out."

She muttered some words under her breath that I feared might be more mischief. "I can help you, if you'll tell me who you fear." I reached for her, hoping for a contact read, but she recoiled as if I carried the plague.

"You can't be here," Cipriona said, "and you danged sure can't touch me."

My tattoos heated. Rose. My spirit connection on the Other Side. What did she want? No way was I doing a dreamwalk in this place. Rose had to wait.

But since Rose wasn't good at waiting, I edged toward the door. "I'm not the enemy. If you change your mind about talking, you know where to find me."

Cipriona snorted in triumph. "Like that's gonna happen. Git yourself gone."

Charlotte and I hurried to the truck, and I saw the questions in her eyes. "Not now," I said.

Soon as I cranked the truck, Charlotte whipped out her notepad. "That was intense. She isn't what I expected. Are we going to arrest her? She killed Mandy, right?"

"Put the notepad away. You can't write

any of this down."

Charlotte huffed her displeasure and stuffed the notepad in her tote. "She's involved in the case. I knew it."

"Wrong. We don't know anything about her except she's a bad liar."

"And she's afraid of some guy. What guy would that be?"

"I don't know."

"You were trying to get the answer by touching her, weren't you?"

I smiled for a second. "Can't blame me for trying. She was too skittish."

"Yeah. I got that. Why'd you let her win?"

"I got another call."

"I didn't hear the phone ring."

I turned off and drove to a deserted riverside park. "Not that kind of call." I shut off the engine by the river. "Switch places with me. I shouldn't be out more than ten minutes. If the dreamwalk goes on any longer, call my parents. Don't move the truck, okay?"

"You sure got bossy all of a sudden, and you welched on our deal. I was supposed to get my palm read."

"Got a news flash for you. If I delay this dreamwalk any longer, both of us will have short lifelines."

CHAPTER THIRTY-SEVEN

"Took you long enough," Rose said. She was biker-girl casual in her leathers and tats. The steady tapping of her booted toe caused the murk of the Other Side to roil and billow. Even a blind woman would know Rose was in a foul mood.

"I came as quickly as I could. I had to extract myself from a conversation and drive to a safe place before I could make the transition to meet you. What's going on?"

"Why haven't you closed this case? I need you for something else."

"Sorry. Didn't know there was a wait list for my services. What do you need?"

Rose growled and looked away. "I can't tell you until you discover Mandy Patterson's killer. You are doing it all wrong because you should've collared your suspects by now."

"I'm doing the best I can. A voodoo priestess attacked me, and thanks to you,

I've got a man who thinks he's my boy-friend."

Rose's lips turned up the slightest bit, like a grinning cat. "We need him."

"*We* don't need him. I'll decide who I sleep with and when."

"Don't trifle with me. You're more powerful with him around, which means I have access to his power now that you're emotionally bound."

"Is that why you had us become intimate? To get your hooks in him too? Here's a news flash. He doesn't think much of you."

"Doesn't matter. Long as he's in lust with you, he'll do my bidding."

"My sex life is off the table. Anything else I can do for you?"

"I wish," Rose snarled, "but the boss is watching me. I gotta abide by his rules. Strictly a hands-off policy on Earthly matters. For now."

Rose had been reprimanded? Wonders never ceased. "May I talk to Mandy? Will you take me to her?"

"Can't."

"But she's a spirit. On your turf. She's not in the human realm any longer."

"Your problem is in the human world. You're the go-between, Dreamwalker. You have to find ways to reach her on your own."

"I was at her place this morning, but I came up empty. Dreamwalks there didn't yield strong leads."

"You're making excuses."

My patience boiled away. "Look, we've got a greedy sister, a mixed-up son, a controlling boyfriend, a neighbor who isn't who he says he is, and the voodoo woman."

"And . . . ?"

"And what?"

"Do I have to spell it out for you in toe taps? Who else is new in town and taking up your time?"

"You can't mean Mayes and Duncan. They never met Mandy Patterson."

"Someone else."

"Who? Why can't you come out and say the name?"

"Discovery. You've discovered her. You haven't connected her to the case." Rose started to fade.

"Wait. I don't have any idea who you're talking about."

"Do your job, and make it snappy. I despise waiting."

I hurtled through the veil and awakened in the truck. The sun still shone, the trees and the river still looked the same color, but something had changed. Charlotte was nowhere in sight.

Not again. If she'd been kidnapped by Other World entities again, I'd never forgive myself. I craned my neck to look for her. Heard a giggle and released the breath I'd been holding. She'd stepped out to take a call. Same as me. Only hers sounded a lot more fun.

A part of me didn't know what to make of a Rose-in-trouble. My Other World mentor had always acted like she had complete autonomy, but now she had strict guidelines to follow. Made me wonder if her journey as an angel in disguise was as fraught with trial and error as my dreamwalker journey. Made me wonder if her assignment was a punishment for something else.

Seemed like there had to be a better way to facilitate supernatural communication than all this fumbling around in the dark.

The door clicked open, and Charlotte joined me. "That was quick."

"But not very helpful," I said. "My contact thinks we should've solved this case already. We don't know who killed Mandy or which recent events are connected and which are trivial."

"I'm willing to act as a suspect sounding board," Charlotte said.

"I nearly had a heart attack when I awakened and you weren't here. I can't put your life in jeopardy again. We had a close enough call at Stony Creek Lake."

Charlotte pointed at the big branch I'd parked beneath. "That water oak limb could shear off and crush your truck, killing us both. That would not be your fault, same as my abduction wasn't your fault. We were on vacation in the Georgia mountains when I got kidnapped, but that event was the best thing that ever happened in my life. I got a boyfriend out of that incident. The way I figure it, I'm disaster-proofed now."

"Not funny. You're my best friend. The sister I never had. There's a killer running around in our neck of the woods. You don't own a gun, and your house is a firetrap. Those aren't strong points in your favor, Char."

"Bah. I accept the risk."

"No. I can't do it. I just can't. What happened before was beyond our control. But a flesh and blood person set the fire that killed Mandy. That person is walking around Sinclair County free and clear because we don't know who he or she is."

"You've gotta be looking at the sister," Charlotte gabbed, as if I hadn't just dismissed the idea of her becoming my confidante. "June's looking to be the new Mandy in Meth World. And that scuzzy boyfriend really gets around. I can't believe he's sleeping with Mandy's sister. What a sleaze. I heard about Ricky Dixon and his wife on the police scanner. Dixon is a miserable human being. He wouldn't need a reason to kill anyone. He'd just do it. And the kid. He's a teen. They categorically hate their parents for ruining their lives. How'm I doing?"

"Pretty good. That's about where we are."

"And now we know Cipriona is after you at someone else's behest."

"True. . . ."

My friend poked me with her finger. "Your voice trailed off. You know something else. Something your contact confided. Tell me."

Charlotte was better at puzzling things out than most cops. No point in denying it. Maybe she'd deduce whoever Rose had been talking about. "Rose said there's someone else involved. Someone who's new in town."

"Not my Duncan."

"Not Mayes either."

"Then who?" Charlotte asked.

I shrugged. "We'll figure it out in due time. What did Duncan have to say just now on the phone?"

Charlotte grinned and cranked the truck. "Said he and Mayes were waiting for us at the ice cream parlor."

My hankering for ice cream was immediate and profound. "Why didn't you say so?"

CHAPTER THIRTY-EIGHT

At the ice cream shop, I chose a hot fudge sundae, Mayes got a banana split, and Charlotte and Duncan split a milkshake concoction full of candy. Since it was mid-afternoon, there were only two other patrons seated in the dining area. Neither of them so much as looked our way, which was a relief because I was dying to ask Mayes the news about Ricky Dixon. But then there was the Charlotte problem.

She was a member of the press. Even though I trusted her not to share privileged information before it was time, her coworker had swiped and published her notes on another occasion. The sheriff wasn't likely to forget that leak anytime soon.

So we listened to Duncan rave about his visit with the hounds. Duncan was in high cotton.

"I grew up on a farm," Duncan said. "I've always dreamed of having acreage and livestock of my own."

"Really?" Charlotte asked. "And I'm just hearing about this now?"

Duncan's face glowed with a dreamy, goofy expression. "It's no big deal. I've been saving for the right piece of land, and it doesn't matter where it is."

"You aren't going to live near your mother?"

"I could, or I could live anywhere. Out West even."

Charlotte's freckled face turned all blotchy and red. "Whoa. Just whoa. I never agreed to live *any*where. We talked about in-state options. North Georgia is far enough away from home, thank you very much."

Duncan's face fell. "It's all right. We'd be together."

Their conversation made my thoughts bounce all over the place. Duncan and Charlotte had been talking about a future together. Charlotte sounded like she'd agreed to leave the coast to live with him. I silently cheered for her because finding the right guy and starting a family were on her bucket list. That and writing for a power-house daily.

I exchanged a glance with Mayes across the table, but his tight expression hinted at disapproval. Was he upset with Charlotte?

How could she be held at fault for something she knew nothing about?

"It's okay," I soothed. "Y'all have plenty of time to talk about future plans. Nothing has to be decided right this moment."

Charlotte glared at Duncan, tears in her eyes. "I can't believe you put me in this position. I thought my opinion mattered, that we were a team."

When she stormed out the door, Duncan ran after her. I rose, hoping to mediate, but Mayes shackled my wrist with his hand. "Let them work it out."

"But Charlotte —"

"If they are to have any chance at a future, they have to learn how to communicate. Will you be there every time they have an argument?"

"No."

"Duncan is a good guy. Your friend is the kind of woman he's been searching for — someone who is grounded, who values tradition."

"I've never thought of Charlotte in those terms, but those are two of her best qualities. She's also smart as a whip. She fleshed out our entire suspect list for Mandy's murder without me saying a word. I've often told her she'd make a great detective."

"Dunc needs someone to keep him on his

toes. I hope this one works out for him."

I didn't like the sound of that. I plopped down beside Mayes. "This one?"

"Like I said, he's been ready to settle down for a while, but none of the women he dated have been a good fit. I wouldn't have guessed Charlotte as a possibility, but there's good synergy between them. Just like there is with us."

He hadn't let go of my arm yet, so I gently pulled away. "Energy isn't the only consideration. Relationships are more complex than that."

"Our relationship is coming along fine, if you ask me."

"Mayes."

"I know. I'm pushing it. Just thought I'd work it into the conversation since we were talking about the future."

He knew how to push my buttons, only I wasn't ready to touch the future button. "Sometimes the future seems very far away. I take life one day at a time, one case at a time. Speaking of which, what's the news on Ricky Dixon? Is he an ax murderer?"

"His prints are in the system, as are his wife's."

"Oh?"

"Turns out Ricky Dixon's been living a lie. His real name is Reggie Dobosh and his

wife's name is isn't Tip Dixon. Terry Tipin-
ski. Turns out Reggie has another wife living in Phoenix, and Tip's parents died
under suspicious circumstances forty-
something years ago."

"So they're bad guys?"

"We don't know what they are. Dixon's
being held in jail overnight. We tried questioning him, but he's issuing threats and
not making much sense. Tip had such a
high blood alcohol level, they sent her to
the hospital for detox."

"Any tie-ins with their former neighbor,
Mandy Patterson?"

"Nothing's turned up. What'd you and
Charlotte do this afternoon?"

"We decided to have our palms read."

Mayes' expression shuttered. "We were
planning to interview the palm reading
woman together."

"You wouldn't have gotten into her place.
She wasn't happy to see me, and I was only
allowed inside because she was afraid I'd
touch her. She didn't want anything to do
with me or Charlotte. We did learn something."

"Go on."

"She's deathly afraid of some man."

"Which man?"

"The man who's telling her what to do.

293

Once I told her the voodoo crap wouldn't work anymore, her demeanor changed." I was beginning to sense that Mayes wasn't a fan of drawn-out revelations, so I hurried to finish. "She went from proud and secure to being a nervous wreck. She ordered us to leave."

"Name?"

"She wouldn't say his name. I tried to comfort her with a light pat. That's when she threw me out."

"The reason cops interview suspects at the station is that we're in control of when the interview ends. We need that name."

I didn't care for his lecturing tone. "I would've pushed harder to get it, but Rose called. I had to get out of there because I don't feel safe dreamwalking around Cipriona. Been there, done the voodoo-victim part."

Our ice cream was melting quickly. I scooped up another mouthful of mostly fudge sauce and sighed at the sweet pleasure. Why wasn't fudge sauce packed with nutrition? That would sure make meal time easier.

"You saw Rose?"

"I did." I quickly filled him in on the exchange. "She's unhappy with me, says she needs both of us for a job."

"Like that's going to happen." He looked away briefly as a young family entered the shop, the mom carrying an infant, the dad holding hands with a toddler and a boy. "Did Rose give you any other indication about this outsider who's involved with Mandy's murder?"

"No. She was especially closemouthed. Seems she's still in trouble for interfering in my life."

"You realize you turned up two potential leads this afternoon, but we can't check them out because we don't have any names."

When Mayes spoke through clenched teeth, his face tightened into a bad-cop mask, giving me a hint of what he'd be like in an interrogation. I was thankful I wasn't a suspect. But I'd had experience with difficult people my whole life. He couldn't intimidate me.

"Watch it," I warned. "We're on the same team. This is how I work a case, with bits and pieces of information. If you can't handle that, you need to reconsider your presence here."

He reached for me, his hand surprisingly gentle on mine. With the contact, I received another dose of his attraction to me. I got a lot more emotion too. Fear. Frustration. Irritation. A tinge of desperation.

And the desperation changed everything. I couldn't stand for him to be hurting. "Mayes, it's okay. I know how to handle myself."

"You make me weak. I can handle what life brings me, but I need to keep you safe. I want us to spend the day together. Just us. No cases, no family or tribal concerns. I want to spend time with you."

"Do you trust me?"

"I do."

I blushed at the intensity of his words, knowing full well they were part of a marriage ceremony. "I trust you as well. But for us to be friends and partners, you have to accept that we work in a dangerous profession, in this life and on the Other Side. My dad survived, and I will too."

He gentled his voice. "Do you worry about my safety, Walks with Ghosts?"

He hadn't used his pet name for me since he'd arrived. My heart softened. This man had come a long way to see me, and I'd been glad to see him. Still was. "If something happened to you. . . ."

Mayes squeezed my hand as my voice cracked. "Feeling's mutual." We sat in silence for a few moments as the young family got situated near us. With our privacy limited, Mayes nodded toward the door, and I followed him outside, my emotions all roiled up. I couldn't lie to myself. My feelings for Mayes were intensifying, and the biggest obstacle to our being together, my presumed dead husband, might be resolved soon. Could I handle a green light when it came to Mayes?

Not right this minute I couldn't. Practicalities came first. This was Sunday afternoon, and Larissa would be in school tomorrow. I wanted to spend time with her. But first, there was my friend to consider. Duncan and Charlotte were gone, as was her car. They must've left to find somewhere to talk in private. I envied them that clear-cut freedom to do as they pleased.

I fished out my truck keys and headed toward my parents' place. "Let's use the drive home to regroup on the case."

Mayes nodded. The conversational void felt fertile instead of awkward. I liked that silent encouragement.

Another turn and we were on the highway out of town. "I've been thinking about this. The reason the leads don't connect is because we assume there's one killer. What if two or more people were involved? I believe the GBI is right, in that Mandy died because of her drug lab. Someone put her out of business on purpose and eliminated their competition.

"The meth lab sailed under the radar as far as the cops were concerned until the fire. In truth, if another lab was set up in the deep woods, and there were no local sales, it would float under the radar again. The business model is golden in a rural, wooded community like ours."

My words seemed to swim around the truck cab. Mayes made no comment. I reached over and poked him. "Say something."

"I don't disagree," he said, "but your multiple killer theory adds a layer of complexity. The simplest answer is usually the best. Mandy was murdered because someone wanted her job. That's what I believe."

I continued to mull everything over as I slowed to travel through an S-curve in the road. Some of the vines in the adjacent woods were already starting to turn burnished gold and orange. Fall was here, even if the temperature still made it feel like summer.

"Well?" Mayes asked.

"Well what?"

"Give and take. Isn't that what we were doing with our case review? Your turn."

I bit back a smile. It was nice having

someone to brainstorm with. "The GBI is stalled on the drug case, but here's what I know. A man with a mobile occupation like Todd Derenne is the logical connection between Mandy's meth lab and the greater Macon drug market. We don't know if the trucker operates independently or if he's a cog in a bigger drug machine. Cipriona is afraid of a man, and the only two men we know of in the case so far are the whack-job neighbor and Mandy's control-freak boy-friend. I saw nothing at Dixon's place to indicate drug income. No personal luxuries like big-screen TVs or butter-soft leather recliners. But then Derenne doesn't flash a lot of cash either. He has no home address, sponges off defenseless women, and hits them to keep them under his control."

"You're forgetting Mandy's son. He's a male."

As much as the thought appalled me that a kid might kill his parent, I had to consider it. "I didn't forget Doodle, but he's a kid."

"In calendar years he's a juvenile, but he's seen a lot in his short life. He's no innocent. Don't feel sorry for him. We don't know who he really is."

Made sense. "That leaves Aunt June, who wants to open her own meth lab. And now Cipriona is frightened of her male boss."

"You think the palm reader's involved?"

I smiled wanly, aware of the answer he expected. "I changed my mind after meeting her. My gut says yes, and sneaky is her MO. She lied to me multiple times."

To his credit, Mayes didn't blink, but his heavy sigh spoke volumes. "If this is a conspiracy, the seams are tight. We haven't found any evidence to point in that direction."

"But we will."

My phone rang. My dad. He rarely used the phone unless mom got a feeling about something. I took the call. "Dad? Everything all right with Larissa?"

"She's fine, but she's very upset."

"What's wrong?"

Mayes placed a comforting hand on my thigh as tears welled in my eyes. I punched the accelerator on the straightaway.

"It's the pigs. Someone killed them," Dad said, his voice quavering.

"Did you hear the gunfire?"

"Arrows. My guess is they were felled by an accomplished bow hunter."

"Why?"

"Only one arrow in each of them. Seems highly precise if you ask me. Oh. There's something else. Their harnesses are missing."

300

"Secure the area and call the sheriff's office," I said.

"Will do. I already put your dogs in Larissa's room and the hounds in our bedroom."

"Great. I'll be there in seven minutes."

CHAPTER THIRTY-NINE

"They weren't hurting anybody," Larissa sobbed in my arms. "Why kill them? I don't understand how someone could be so mean. They're gonna pay for this, right, Mom?"

I hugged my precious daughter close. Mayes and my parents faded from view as I gave her my full attention. Her labored gasps for breath between sobs broke my heart. "I hope we catch whoever killed them, Rissa-roo. It doesn't make sense to me either. Like you say, the pigs weren't bothering anyone. Nothing for them to get into out here."

"You can touch Petunia and Patches and see who did it, right?" she managed, dashing the moisture from her cheeks, a flash of fire in her emerald-green eyes. "Then the sheriff can arrest them."

"I'll see what the pigs tell me, but even if I learn who did this, my touch reading won't be evidence for an arrest warrant."

"It should be. The person who did this should get punished. Someone should shoot them with a bow and arrow and let them see how it feels."

"Sweetheart, it doesn't work that way. But we'll figure it out. I have every confidence of that."

"If they wanted the pig harnesses, why didn't they just take them?"

Good question. I remembered how edgy the pigs were around Mayes. "Maybe they tried, but the pigs wouldn't let them get close."

"That's mean. I hate them."

"We can talk about it later." I glanced at the crowd of people around us. "Maybe you'd like to have a cup of tea in Mama Lacey's kitchen?"

Her chin jutted defiantly. "I want to go with you. I want to dreamwalk with you."

Whoa! Where'd that come from? "Not today. We've talked about this before."

"The pigs were my friends." Her voice broke, and she looked down to blink away fresh tears. "I'm not a kid, Mom. I can handle it."

Pretty strong words for a ten-year-old. I stroked her head and ponytail. "I know you have special talents, Larissa. Here's the thing. I don't want you dealing with death and spirits at your age. I want you to grow up and enjoy hanging out with the living. There'll be plenty of time for dreamwalks later on. I've got this."

Larissa wailed a little more, then pulled it together. "What about the dogs? Can they track down the killer?"

"Good idea, but we can't use them until the police examine the scene. That's why Pap put them up for now."

"In that case, you need Oliver, Mom. Get him to track the bad person. He won't leave any prints."

Oliver, my Great Dane ghost dog, had helped me in other cases. "Good idea. I'll see what the pigs tell me first, okay? Please stay with Mama Lacey for a bit longer, Mayes and I will go with Pap to examine the pigs."

Larissa touched my arm. "We can bury them, right? They deserve a proper funeral."

"We'll check with Doodle. Technically, they are his property."

"But he gave them to us. He didn't want them anymore. They're ours."

"He didn't have a place to keep them, which is different."

I gave my mom a look of "What now?" and she stepped forward to herd Larissa toward the kitchen. Larissa gave me a last look that spoke volumes. If I didn't get justice for the pigs, she would.

My father gestured toward the garden as we walked there. "I can't believe this happened," Dad said. "Like Larissa, I want justice for these animals. This place has always been a sanctuary. I feel . . . violated." He halted and fixed me with a stare. "I'm counting on you to make this right."

"I'll do my best, Dad. Did you hear anything? How did you realize something happened?"

"That's just it. I didn't, and your mother didn't either. I headed out to work in the garden a little while ago and found them. Larissa was right behind me. We saw them at the same time. I'm sorry. I wouldn't have taken her with me if I'd known something had happened out there."

"Not your fault," I said. "This case is circling around on itself. That means we're getting close."

"Someone's nervous about our investigation," Mayes added, unlatching the gate and striding into the fenced garden area. He stepped aside, waited for us to pass, and latched the gate behind us. "I wish we had a better handle on the suspect."

"Or suspects," I said. We walked beside

305

lush rows of potatoes, greens, and late-blooming tomatoes. My father had fenced the garden years ago after he got tired of sharing with the deer. That was why the pigs couldn't get into trouble out here. They couldn't get to the veggies. The latch was too high for Petunia to reach. For them to be in the garden, someone had to open the gate and give them entry.

"You think we have another killing team on our hands?" Dad asked.

"We're not sure of anything," Mayes said, with a quelling look at me. "Each case is different, and it limits us to jump to conclusions without evidence to support that leap."

I didn't agree with him over whether it was one person or two who did this, but it was pointless to argue theories when we had no proof. Time would tell how many suspects were involved.

As we walked, I noted the tidy rows of the dark-green kale and the bushy plants laden with green peppers. My father had one heck of a green thumb, but then, so did I. The plants in my landscaping business flourished, unless my clients neglected to care for them.

Directing my gaze over the tops of the plants, I could see where the pigs lay. Each had an arrow to the heart. My breath hitched in my throat. Not what most mothers wanted their elementary-school kids to see. But if Larissa had nightmares, I could help her deal with them. Years of suppressing my talent had yielded many strategies for making dreams go away.

Waves of anger radiated from my father. I touched his arm. "Dad, it's okay. Mayes and I have this. You don't need to be out here with us."

"I took responsibility for those animals. They should've been safe here." He wrung his hands. "I feel so helpless, so upset. The energy here is wrong now. The plants. Every living thing in the garden will suffer because of the violence wrought here."

"You and Running Bear can cleanse it." I gentled my voice. "Truly, Dad, it would be best if you went back to your place and helped Mom with Larissa. A cup of Mom's herbal tea would do you a world of good."

"You sure? Because I can help. I can dreamwalk with you, share energy, or whatever you need."

His negative energy made me anxious. "Please don't take this the wrong way, but what I need is for you to give us room to do our jobs. Allow us to take the first step toward cleansing your sanctuary by listening to the spirits of the dead."

He didn't look convinced. He stood his ground. "Just because I retired from being the Dreamwalker doesn't mean I'm useless."

"You're absolutely right." I led him back toward the gate. "I'll have plenty for you to do later. Help me now by talking with Running Bear and planning a cleansing ceremony for your property."

He nodded, but his agreement was slow in coming. "How'd I get so lucky to have a beautiful daughter like you?"

Despite the tragedy nearby, a smile wiggled its way out. "Same way I got lucky with the best parents in the world. Now scoot."

Minutes later, Mayes and I stood alone over the pigs. Flies buzzed aimlessly, landing and then taking off. They seemed as confused as we were.

So senseless. These animals were pets. For tame animals to be hunted was so wrong. I dreaded breaking the news to Doodle. These pigs were all he had left of his mom.

The areas where the harnesses had rested on their torsos were lighter, a grim outline of what was missing. Were the harnesses trophies? I'd seen them, and I didn't recall anything other than faded leather.

With my eye on a protruding arrow, I dropped to my knees. "Guess I should get started."

Mayes squared his stance and scanned the area. "Go right ahead. I'll keep watch."

Steeling my jumpy nerves, I touched Petunia and Patches. Nothing. Not even a glimmer of something. I tried the arrows. Same negative result. *Drat.* I wanted to have an answer for Larissa.

"Nothing here," I said, standing. "But you knew that already."

"I've hunted plenty of pigs over the years. I've field-dressed the animals. Not once have I gotten anything from an arrow or a dead hog."

"You could've said something."

"You would've checked anyway."

He had a point. Not wanting to look like a total dweeb, I studied the ground near the dead pigs. "This is the tidiest crime scene I've ever seen. Everything is where it should be except for the pigs."

"Good observation. These pigs would've bolted after being shot," Mayes said. "No way would they have died side by side in a locked garden. None of the bushes are trampled, none of the produce seems ruined or missing. Their location is significant."

"They were placed here? How? And why?" I searched the adjacent tree line for danger. I'd assumed the killer was long gone with the harnesses. Was he or she watching us right now? "Wasn't killing them enough of a statement?"

"Placing these carcasses here, inside your dad's garden, is a warning."

A cold chill flashed down my spine. "They're coming after my family?"

Mayes studied the area, leaning over some bent grass. "Not necessarily. That's a big leap from hunting game animals to hunting humans."

The pigs were several hundred pounds each. "No woman could move this much dead weight, and I don't know how a guy carried them either, not for any distance. So we're dealing with a guy who knows how to hunt. The obvious answer is Todd Derenne. He's a bow hunter."

"I'd like to question him again, that's for sure, but right now, we need Oliver's services."

"You've got a lead?"

He pointed to the grassy tracks leading away from the pigs. "I do."

CHAPTER FORTY

He did it again. Said "I do." Was Mayes taunting me with matrimonial words on purpose? Was he encouraging me to be his girlfriend or his wife? Was he even aware he was doing it? I stole a glance at him, but he wasn't looking at me to gauge my reaction. From outward appearances, he was focused on the case of the murdered pigs.

That's what I should focus on as well. The pigs. I summoned my ghost dog, Oliver. The large Great Dane licked me all over. After I explained what I wanted from him, Oliver went right to work tracking the pig killer. We followed Oliver and the drag marks out the back gate and down the swale for nearly half a mile, then Oliver veered off into the woods. He settled on a spot not too far from a drainage swale.

I pointed out the dark patch of sand to Mayes. "Oliver says right here."

Mayes examined the setting from every

angle before nodding his approval. "This is where they came to rest. They would've been shot nearby, run off together, and bled out here. Tire tracks come back this way. Given all the underbrush along the narrow trail, we're most likely looking at a small utility truck with four-wheel-drive capability."

I noted the narrow wheel base impressions in the sand. "Or one of those truck-shaped golf carts. I've seen several of those around the county."

"Yeah, one of those haulers would have four-wheel drive and enough horsepower to drag this much weight." He glanced around. "How far are we from the highway?"

"A couple of miles still."

"The main track we were following connects to the highway?"

"It does. Some people still come to my parents' house the back way. They've had all kinds of folks over the years visit them in secret. You wouldn't believe the domestic situations some of our community leaders have been in. When they reach their wit's end, they come out and stay with my mom and dad. By the time they leave, their heads are on straight."

"Is the back access marked at the county road?"

"No. It looks like every other logging trail — merely a grassy bump-out on the highway's shoulder."

"Unless the killer has local ties, the odds are in favor of a local person who ambushed the pigs."

A protest boiled out of my mouth. "No way was this a random event. My parents have loads of 'No Hunting' signs up along the lane."

"Never said it was random. Let me check a few things. If you want to read the blood spots, I'll narrow down the kill zone and search for the hunter's blind."

"Copy that." While Mayes followed pig tracks through the underbrush, I knelt again by the largest blood stain. Opening my senses, I expected a vision to flood my thoughts, but I got nothing. Nada. Zip. I removed my hand and tried again. Same result. I scooted over to the other dried blood pool. Nothing.

Oliver returned from romping with Mayes. I gave him my thanks and a hug and sent him on his way into the between-worlds fog. While it was nice to have access to Oliver, there were times I wished for his sake that he'd glom onto someone in the spirit world so that he could have company all the time. He'd had plenty of offers, but he'd elected to stay with me.

Mayes helped me up and gave my hand a squeeze. "Find anything?"

His cocksure tone ruffled my feathers. "Nothing, but I'm sure you knew that already."

His smile was slow and sure. "Yes, ma'am, I did."

"Sneaky way to keep me occupied." I set aside my pride to do my job. "You find anything?"

"I didn't, which is puzzling. There should've been an area nearby where the grass was trampled or broken small branches at eye level for increased visibility. I didn't see any signs indicating someone had lain in wait."

"Weird. I wish the arrows had told us something."

"As I understand it, your psychometry gift works when the person is in the grip of a strong emotion. You can detect an energy signature when it's been laced with fear, anger, rage, and the like."

"True, but psychometry isn't helping with this crime scene. Someone killed those pigs in a premeditated manner. What kind of person kills without emotion?"

"Psychopaths are wired differently," Mayes said.

Despite the afternoon heat, I shivered. "That's what we're dealing with?"

"Too soon to make a call, but yeah, someone in this case is a major liar. They've fooled us because they are very good at concealing their true nature. They are living a lie."

Psychopaths and liars. People who naturally lived by a different set of rules, people who were on a killing spree in Sinclair County. They'd murdered Mandy in her home. They'd killed her pigs on my dad's property. We had to stop them. We had to figure this out fast before someone else got hurt.

"Anyone could've killed Mandy," I began slowly. "That fiery explosion didn't take brute strength, merely an ignition source in her lab. For instance, a decent bow hunter could've shot a flaming arrow through the window, and we'd never know. That points to Todd Derenne."

Mayes nodded. "A Molotov cocktail would've had the same effect. I saw bottles, rags, and gas on Dixon's back porch. He had all the makings of a Molotov cocktail at his disposal."

"Yeah, but June had better motives for killing her sister. Greed and romantic love. June inherited her sister's kid, her boyfriend, and possibly her meth business. I'm sure June has the makings for those incendiary devices around her place, but is she an archer?"

"That is a very good question," Mayes said. "We could search online for her name in archery-contest results for the last twenty or so years."

I didn't want to mention the last name on the list. But there was no getting around his having the opportunity to enact this. "Then there's Doodle."

"You buying into my mindset with the kid?"

"I don't know what to think." Pines sighed overhead, mirroring my mixed feelings. "The kid's got street smarts and book smarts. I've always thought he knew more than he was telling. I agree he could've snuck over to the neighbors' porch and helped himself to the Molotov cocktail ingredients. A kid like Doodle would've had lots of unsupervised time."

I chewed on those thoughts for a minute. We didn't know who'd killed the pigs. Chances were good this investigation was a dead end. All our suspects had the means and motive to kill Mandy. At least one of them, possibly more, was a skilled archer.

"Someone could've used the arrows to

throw suspicion on the boyfriend," I said.

"If the arrows are a red herring, then our most likely suspect for the pigs' murder is the person who could get closest to them."

The pigs followed Doodle around like dogs. If he was the baddie, he could have walked them into the garden — they'd have trotted after him — and killed them there. But that wasn't what happened, according to the evidence. "Doodle cared for those pigs. It has to be someone else. Someone might have drugged the pigs to get close. I wouldn't put that past June, Dixon, or the trucker boyfriend."

"We need answers."

"Not getting much in the way of those from this scene."

"I wonder. . . ."

I tugged on his arm, sure of two things. He had an idea, and I was fresh out. "What?"

"Animals have spirits. We know that, or you wouldn't have Oliver trailing after you. And you have an affinity for animals, so if there's information to be gained from this site, you are the most likely person to detect it. What if the signal strength is too low for you to detect? If that's the case, we may still have a chance to read this scene."

"I don't understand."

"We boost the detector."

He seemed happy about his conclusion, but I remained confused. How could I do any more than I already had? My dream-walking battery was fully charged, but I'd gotten zilch on two attempts here.

Guess my blank expression tipped him off to my cluelessness. "We dreamwalk together," Mayes said.

The smug arrogance on his face irritated me. Even when I'd dreamwalked on another case with my medium friend Stinger, I hadn't felt like I had amped powers. The difference with Stinger had come after the dreamwalk, with recovery time almost nil. Stinger had recharged my energy loss quicker than crystals, restorative broth, and bed rest did.

"I'm willing to try it," I said, "though I've dreamwalked previously with my dad, his friend Bubba Paxton, and once accidentally with the sheriff, but the end result was not a surge of energy, more like two toddlers engaging in parallel play."

"The difference will be me," Mayes said.

CHAPTER FORTY-ONE

Thin clouds sailed overhead in a blue sky. Wind whispered through the pines, while crickets and frogs warmed up for the nightly sundown concert. Normal, everyday things, but normal wasn't on my dreamwalking agenda this afternoon, it seemed.

I wasn't going anywhere in this world or the next until I had answers. "Have you been holding out on me? Because nothing you said makes sense otherwise. If you can effect an aggregation of our power, why haven't you mentioned it before?"

"The merging of power has drawbacks, but it also has benefits," Mayes said, his fingers warm around mine. "As the holder of the focus when we transferred energy to another person in the mountains, I burned substantially more power than everyone else, but I had control of the flow. By aligning our energy into a tighter focus, the raw

319

energy available to the seeker will be multiplied."

So much about dreamwalking was still a mystery to me, but Mayes took the strangeness in stride. My brain sputtered like a car out of gas. Clarity wouldn't come as long as I was touching Mayes. His touch gave a rosy glow to everything, and I definitely needed my wits about me before I tried amplified dreamwalking.

I tugged my hand free under the guise of removing my ponytail band, finger-combing my hair back into another ponytail, and securing my hair again. The economical motions allowed me time to blow the dust off my little-used knowledge of basic science. His statements didn't compute.

"I know a little physics," I said. "Energy can't be created or destroyed. What you're saying is impossible."

Mayes nodded. "Like you, I tried to explain the idea through science. Quantum energy teleportation comes the closest to what I believe happens. But now this. Dreamwalking can't be explained through what we currently know about science. My grandfather said it was possible; therefore I believe it's possible."

"You've done this before?"

"I haven't tried it yet."

"Why not?"

"Hadn't found anyone I trusted with my life." His dark eyes glittered with emotion. "Until now."

His *life*? Was he kidding me? I stepped back. "We haven't known each other that long, and I lost control during that energy transfer to your sheriff. Are you certain we should experiment with something neither of us has tried before?"

"There are few guarantees in life. For instance, there is a risk every time you cross over to the Other Side. As many times as you've done this, you've had occasional problems. Extended return times, disorientation, misdirection, even."

He wasn't in my mind, and yet he knew the things I'd experienced. "You too?"

His grim nod let me know he'd been lost in the void before, and he'd also faced the certainty he'd never see the light of day again. Oddly, that shared misfortune cheered me. "I thought I'd screwed up."

"Nothing in this life or the next is free. Between the resident tricksters and so-called guides, between exhaustion or distraction on our part, and sometimes a ripple in the continuum, we have various ways to become trapped in the drift."

I warmed to the conversation. Dad had

always been so cagey about everything to do with the Other Side, and now Mayes was giving me the Cliffs Notes version. " 'The drift'? Is that what it's called?"

"Yeah. It's a fragmented place, not here and not there. Few people emerge from extended stays in the drift alive. Only the strong ones survive."

I accepted the backhanded compliment, then my brain circled around. Was he inferring he was also strong? Was I supposed to intuit a deeper meaning in what he said? I didn't like the sudden confusion I felt.

"Let's keep this on an elementary level," I said. "I don't analyze conversations for symbols or hidden context. Thanks for telling me you've been caught in the drift as well. There are many aspects of my dreamwalker job I can't explain, that I take on faith. Now we're going to amplify our probe of this evidence. A year ago, I would've denied any of this was possible. Now I know how possible the impossible is. I do it every day."

"That's the spirit," Mayes said. "You ready?"

I was. I no longer dreaded trying something new. In his way, Mayes had assured me that we had this. His experience and solid presence gave me newfound confidence. "Sure."

"We're going for expediency, right?"

I shrugged. "Seems best. That way we have some afternoon left if we need to follow another angle."

He studied the area, then his intense gaze caught me. "You need to be touching the blood pool. I need to be touching you. The most *expedient* way is the personal-energy-transfer position."

Heat waves seared my neck and cheeks. The position he suggested was extremely personal and intimate. "And the less expedient way?"

"We could try one point of contact, but to concentrate my energy in you will take much longer. Think of it this way. Would you rather drip water through an eye dropper or turn on the fire hose?"

He had me there. We had places to go, people to see, murders to solve. The pig killer might be important to solving Mandy's murder, but it might be unrelated. I couldn't afford to tie us up here all day because I was squeamish. "All right."

Seconds later, I was lying on the ground beside the bloodstain. Mayes straddled me. "We must join hands."

His voice sounded huskier than usual. Was the contact as powerful for him as it was for me? Nerve endings were going haywire from the brush of his thighs against mine. I was hot and cold, nervous and giddy.

I lifted my hands, matching my palms to his, allowing our fingers to intertwine. The buzz of his energy field glided along my skin, as if he was enveloping me. He moved forward, leaning on his elbows to keep most of his weight from me. With clear purpose, he positioned our joined hands above the stain. My heart thudded against my ribs.

"Let me in, Dreamwalker," he commanded. "Let me be in you, and you in me."

A niggle of panic surged, and I quashed it. This was Mayes. He trusted me with his life force. I lowered my guard completely. He surged into my thoughts, into my very blood. He kissed me, tenderly, reverently, and I felt less and less of myself and more of us.

"You set me on fire, Dreamwalker," he muttered.

I couldn't talk because it was happening. The floodgates of him had opened, and the part deep inside my soul, the part that was just me, became something else. I was still conscious of my body, mind, and spirit, but I had twice the awareness. Impossible, and yet, we'd done it. We'd merged our everything.

Ready?

He'd spoken in my head, but the tone and resonance of his voice was as if he'd said it beside me. Though I wanted to explore all of what I'd become, expediency was our goal. We were probably burning twice the usual amount of energy.

Ready, I answered.

I lowered our clasped hands onto the bloodstain.

CHAPTER FORTY-TWO

We flashed through the void like a laser beam. The usual sensations of bitter cold and tumbling randomly through space were gone. Instead, I felt like Superman vectoring in a straight, powerful line. We didn't experience the sensation of stopping either; we just weren't moving anymore. There was no lightening of the curtain of gloom.

All around us in the darkness were feelings of bitterness. Of anger. Of revenge. Were these emotions there all the time, or were they related to the case?

Mayes? Are we there yet?

We are on the Other Side, he replied in my thoughts. *Not sure if we're where we need to be. This is a first for me too. You still dialed in to the pigs?*

Far as I know.

Getting anything else besides the emotional resonance?

A distant sound wafted over. Weeping. A

woman's crying.

Find her.

There was a sense of rapid movement, but it was smooth, as if we'd entered an express elevator. The mist thinned, and I saw a woman hugging her tummy. I recognized the floral sofa from previous visions and the woman. Mandy. We'd found her. Maybe this time we'd get something useful.

It was weird talking to Mayes in my thoughts with him also inside me. His spirit and mine were joined, so I had no physical sense of him. Just the pulse of him in my mind.

About time, he said softly. *See if she can hear you.*

I hoped like anything that this would be an interactive dreamwalk. Most spirit quests were reruns of prior events, but every now and then, a spirit would have something to say.

"Mandy?"

She kept crying. I didn't know if she heard me because she didn't acknowledge my presence. I listened to her cry for several long moments, then I figured, what the hay. If she can't hear me, it won't matter if I talk. But if she can hear me, maybe she'll react to something I say.

"Mandy, I'm sorry about your pigs," I said

matter-of-factly. "Petunia and Patches were good pets. I can't believe someone shot them. They were in a safe place at my father's cottage in the woods. No one should've harmed them there. It was pre-meditated because there's no hunting on my dad's property. We found them in the vegetable garden, in a fenced area where they weren't allowed.

"The guy who's helping me investigate showed me how their bodies were moved and placed inside the garden where they'd be found right away."

Mandy's weeping continued. Still no sign that she heard me. Maybe she needed more information.

"The means of death for both pigs was an arrow to the heart," I continued. "Someone had to be a good shot to get both pigs that way. We figure the pigs might have eaten drugged food first. Far as we know, Todd Derenne is the only hunter in our suspect pool."

Nothing. I needed to reach her, but how? What could I offer her? "Your son moved in with your sister. He seems to be a fine young man. You did a good job of raising him. I can only hope someone will say the same about me and my daughter one day."

The weeping subsided. Maybe she was

hungry for news from home. "Todd moved in with your sister too. He seemed pretty upset about your death."

Mandy muttered something.

"Excuse me?" I asked. "I didn't get that."

"I said, *right.*" She lifted her head from her hands and glared at me. "There are rules over here, but I've already broken them, so I'll pay the consequences either way. I lived in a snake pit on Bartow Road. Any of them could've killed me. I made something of myself, and my sister couldn't stand it. Todd used me. I saw it, and I used him back. But killing my pigs goes beyond belief. You want answers? Find Ava Leigh. And as for my son —"

A loud noise sounded in the distance. Mandy stiffened as though jolted by electricity. One moment she was there before me, and the next she was gone.

"Wait. Who's Ava Leigh?" I asked, but no one was there to hear my words.

Let's go home, Mayes said in my head. *We're done here.*

He spoke the truth. There was no one around, not even any bad-boy ghosts giving me crap. Joining forces with Mayes had dialed my locational director in so precisely that I'd bypassed the usual dangers up here. I wasn't the least bit tired, whereas knowing

I had to endure a bumpy ride to get home would've had me heading back already.

We could look for Roland while we're here, I suggested. *With such specificity, I could find him.*

He's not here, Mayes said. *You said so yourself. He's in another realm altogether, and we need more help to get there.*

Oh. Seemed like there was nothing to do but go home. So I did. The ride back was another superhero vector straight through the void. I awakened with Mayes on top of me, our hands still entwined. He was staring at me oddly.

You want him back, don't you? Mayes said in my head. *You want him. Not me.*

CHAPTER FORTY-THREE

I had enough presence of mind to recognize the suffering in his mind-voice. Mayes wasn't the type to get all weepy when his emotions were engaged. Instead, he got cop serious. Like now. I'd hurt him, and that hadn't been my intent at all.

My limbs weren't numb or tingling. I'd come to expect physical-recovery time after dreamwalks, but that needles-and-pins sensation wasn't there. Instead, warmth flowed from Mayes to me and back through our joined hands. I wasn't exhausted or the least bit tired. I could get used to Mayes joining me on dreamwalks. But I was hot, steaming hot, and not all the heat came from me. It radiated from Mayes like July asphalt.

I shut off the mindlink on purpose and butted him gently with my head. "This isn't about you. Get off me so I can sit up."

"I'm not moving until I get an answer.

Which is it, him or me?"

I pushed him harder and squirmed, but there was no budging this man. Anger welled up inside me, mean and heartless. "Neither of you. Are you satisfied?"

His face froze into an even sterner mask. "I don't understand."

"Look. We shared an amazing dreamwalking experience. I can't believe you're not as excited and upbeat as I am about it. I feel like I could conquer the world."

He didn't say a word. But I studied him with an objective eye. He didn't radiate much of anything except constancy and heat. Now that I looked at him, *really* looked at him, I saw the ashy tone of his skin, felt the slight tremble of his hands against mine. Realization dawned. All that juice to get there and back. It came from Mayes. Horror struck me. Once again, I'd blundered into an area where I didn't understand the cost of things.

I'd held Mayes' life in my hands quite literally. He'd freighted the energy burn for both of us, and I'd been clueless. If I'd taken off and started looking for Roland again on the Other Side, I would've killed Mayes. I would've been worse than the psychic vampire we encountered in the mountains. I was better than that, so I immediately began restoring his strength.

"I need an answer," Mayes said.

I owed him more than an answer. I struggled to find the right words. "I like you. Maybe a lot more than like you, but I can't move forward with my life until I can put Roland behind me. I need to know what happened to him, to find him and tell him I'm okay so he can have peace of mind. Tell him Larissa's okay. Until then, I'm unwilling to move ahead with any personal relationship." I drew in a deep breath for courage. "Over there, it seemed like it would be so easy to visit any corner of the universe. I've never felt so . . . empowered before. I was going for expediency, needing to tie up that loose end. Believe me, there's nothing I want more than to get out of this limbo I've been living in. I've proven to myself and my family that I can make it without Roland. I don't need a man to complete me. Or provide for me. I can do it myself."

Mayes was silent. Then he murmured a soft word I didn't recognize. "You complete me. When we are joined, I am home. I don't like being without you, and I want you to know that I desire you. I won't settle for a friendship with you. I want you in my life, and I want to wake up beside you every morning."

My eyes misted at his heartfelt declaration. This man, this wonderful, special man, understood my challenges. He'd done more than trust me with his heart. He'd sacrificed his very life force to help me.

He mattered to me in ways I couldn't begin to articulate, and he was waiting for my response. Honor and loyalty crowded in, squashing spontaneity and passion. I had responsibilities. I couldn't live in the moment.

"Even if we resolved Roland's fate, obstacles stand in our way," I reminded him. Every contact point between us hummed as I willed my life essence into him.

"We've danced around this topic before. If you truly believe in us, it will happen."

"I want to believe there could be an *us*, but I can't be objective from this position."

His appreciative gaze raked over me. "This is the position I like best."

"You would. Is sex all you think about?"

His answer was slow in coming. "What we share transcends words and physicality. I think of you. That's what I think about. *You*, Walks with Ghosts."

My irritation increased. He'd promised to give me personal space. "You're crowding me, Mayes. When I agreed to your visit, it was under the guise of sharing information about dreamwalking."

"I've fully delivered on that account."

His voice and his gaze had softened. When he gave me that look, both strong and vulnerable, something inside me responded, whether I liked it or not. "That dreamwalk was amazing. You were amazing," I said. "How did it go so smoothly? How did we avoid the side effects of traversing the drift? Did you do something different?"

"Everything we did was different. I had heard my grandfather speak of such a melding of spirits, but I'd never experienced it before today."

Just a little more energy would go a long way toward him regaining his equilibrium. Things always seemed darkest when you were exhausted. Once he recharged, surely he'd be less emotionally needy. "Did you experience the same sensations as I did? The trip over and back was so brief, so event-free. It felt like I'd finally dialed in the right coordinates. Instead of freewheeling though the darkness in a hamster ball, it felt like I had a jet engine strapped on my back."

"I experienced the drift through your senses, so yes, I experienced the same things. The vector was straight and true, like a beam of light in the darkness."

"Can we do that individually now that we

know what it feels like?"

"Anything is possible." He leaned in until his lips were inches above mine. "You didn't have to do that, you know."

I could pretend I didn't know he was talking about the energy transfer, but what was the point? We both knew our current position optimized energy sharing. With so many contact points, I'd pushed a lot of energy his way. "I did. You should've told me we were burning your energy only. I nearly made a costly mistake. I don't want anything to happen to you."

"A kiss of forgiveness?"

I nodded, but before I could add conditions, his lips touched mine. Instead of the passion I expected, the kiss was surprisingly chaste. Worse, it left me unsettled. I wanted the other kind of kiss from him. The burning, yearning kind.

He pulled away, releasing my hands and moving off my body. He sat beside me on the sandy ground. I sat as well, but the chill of separation throbbed deep in my soul. I'd been something more, and now I was less. Maybe it was the energy drain, but at that moment, there was nothing I would've loved more than to nestle close to Mayes.

A yawn slipped out. I needed a nap and my mother's restorative broth, but the day was still young. We had pigs to bury, and no answers for my distraught daughter.

"The case. We didn't learn much. Our top suspects are still the boyfriend, the neighbor, the sister, and the kid. Two of them could've teamed up, which may be why we've been unable to narrow the field."

"I'm still thinking single suspect," Mayes said. "A team would indicate a dominant partner and a submissive one. I'm not seeing anyone in that group who is submissive. There's a reason for that 'keep it simple' phrase. Once you complicate a situation, mistakes happen. We haven't seen any evidence of a partnership or a failing partnership. One suspect, and I like the son for it."

His arrogant summation aggravated me. "Doodle's a kid, not that much older than Larissa. I can't believe he would be so violent. He doesn't have a police record. Don't bad seeds escalate? Isn't there a trail of violence to property or animals first?"

"Oftentimes there is a progression of violence, but Doodle lived an isolated life," Mayes said. "Not many neighbors. No one would've known if he hurt strays or wild animals, for instance."

"But he volunteers at the animal shelter. You said yourself the pigs didn't like you

337

because you were a hunter and have a warrior spirit. Wouldn't the pigs have had the same reaction to Doodle? I think you're on the wrong track. June benefited the most from her sister's death. She's my top suspect."

Mayes rose to his feet, and I followed him. We trekked to the garden, the late afternoon sun warm on my head and shoulders. When the trail widened and we could walk side by side, Mayes brushed against me and took my hand. At once, my step felt lighter; the tension within me eased.

Was there something else to this melding of spirits? How connected were we now? His touch centered me in a new way, a necessary way. Should I have been more cautious about trying something new? Why were there always consequences connected to anything on the Other Side?

And why hadn't my alleged guide and mentor on the Other Side noticed our joint foray into her realm? According to Rose, she knew my every action. She had her hooks in me. Another thought occurred to me as we walked. Had Rose known all along what Mayes and I were capable of? Is that why she took over my body and cavorted with him? Had she dangled me in front of him so that she could snare herself another

Dreamwalker?

"You're deep in thought," Mayes said.

Rose wasn't a safe topic, so I veered to a more neutral one. "I'm trying to understand how everything fits together. It's maddening to have bits and pieces of the jigsaw puzzle coming together, only there's no box with the picture on it to follow. We're putting this puzzle together blind."

"You're forgetting we have a new lead from our dreamwalk: Ava Leigh. Who is she?"

"Mandy's mention of her was the first time I've heard the name. Far as I know she isn't local. I'll call the sheriff and ask him to run Ava Leigh's name."

"No need to call him," Mayes predicted. "He'll be at the garden when we reach it."

"You have long-range Spidey senses?"

"Nope. Masculine intuition. Once word reached him about an incident at your parents' place, he'll drop everything to hotfoot it over here."

I snorted. "For pigs? On a Sunday? I don't believe you."

"Believe what you like. That guy considers you family, and not in a sisterly way."

"Jealous?"

"Should I be?"

My heels dug into the grassy path. "Wayne

339

and I aren't dating and never will. Aside from the fact he's married and I wouldn't date a married man, I've never been interested in him. One day he'll realize that."

"You're wrong. You'll always be the one who got away. The lure is irresistible."

"You have a woman like that in your past?"

"In my present." He tightened his grip on my fingers. "Only I'm not letting her get away."

We both laughed, but underneath his laughter was something else. It flashed fiery and ruthless, just long enough for me to see it. And worry.

CHAPTER FORTY-FOUR

"Sheriff. Sorry we pulled you away from Sunday dinner," I said as we entered the garden. Once I'd heard voices as we approached my father's garden, I knew Mayes had guessed correctly. Sheriff Wayne Thompson was missing Sunday dinner with his family because of two dead pigs. Burnell Escoe, the GBI guy, stood to the left of him, hands on his hips.

Great. Mr. GBI was back in town, and he didn't look thrilled about covering a double pig homicide. Given his lack of faith in psychics, I wished his business had kept him in Savannah for a few more days.

The black flies were louder now, buzzing around the dead animals. Sure, it was the circle of life, but I wasn't in the mood for a biology lesson or a confrontation with either man. I yearned for some of Mom's restorative broth.

"What you got, Powell?" the sheriff asked.

"Mostly nothing." I filled him in on the kill site and transport. "Touching the pigs and the arrows wasn't helpful. Mayes thinks the person we're looking for is a psychopath. That would explain the lack of emotional residue on the carcasses and arrows."

Wayne swore. Escoe shook his head. "It's one thing to kill a drug kingpin, but killing pets is beyond the pale. We need to put an end to this."

I tugged on my ear. Surely, I'd misheard him. No, I hadn't. He valued these pigs over Mandy. Whatever miniscule respect I had for his authority vanished.

"Drug kingpins are people too," I said.

"Tell yourself that when you see kids so strung out they don't know what they're doing," Escoe said, fervent and indignant, his eyes ablaze. "You bleeding-heart people are all alike. What is it about the meth cook that makes you think she's a person? Is it a mom-connection? What mother raises a child in a toxic wasteland? Tell me that."

I had plenty to tell him, and I couldn't swallow them one more time. I puffed up with anger, brushing off Mayes' cautionary hand on my arm.

"Do you know what it's like to have nothing?" I asked, rounding on him. "To have bills and no way to pay them? To make one mistake and have it hound you the rest of your life? Mandy may not win Mother of the Year, but she cared about her kid. Everything she did was for him. She wanted Doodle to have a college education and rise above the life she'd made. She did what she had to do to survive."

"Even if your suppositions had merit, and there's no evidence to support such liberal claptrap, it doesn't matter," Escoe said. "In the eyes of the law, Mandy Patterson was a criminal. She consorted with felons and produced illegal drugs."

I glared at him and was about to launch into him for being an insensitive asshole when Mayes gripped my arm.

"Escoe, rein it in," Mayes said. "Mrs. Powell's ten-year-old found the pigs going on two hours ago. Instead of comforting her child, Mrs. Powell worked this scene because she's a professional. You are way off base, and I will report your unprofessional conduct to my superior. Trust me, you do not want to make my boss mad, because she plans to be the next governor of Georgia. Meanwhile, I'm taking Powell to see her daughter. Don't come near her again unless you can be objective and courteous."

"You can't talk to me like that," Escoe shouted. "I'll have your badge."

Mayes stepped up to him, nose to nose. "Try it. I'm not afraid of you, and I won't let you bully people who are helping you do your job."

Wayne put his hand between the men, his palm against Mayes' chest. "Gentlemen. Step back. We're guests on private property and making a bad impression on my number one consultant." Wayne guided Mayes my way. "You two, go on up to the house. I'll stop in there as soon as I finish here."

Escoe looked like he wanted to spit bullets. I snickered inside, careful to keep my expression bland. He should've known better than to keep poking the bear. My bear had sharp claws.

Once we'd walked out of hearing range, Mayes spoke softly. "I notice you left the new lead out of your report."

"I'll tell Wayne later, but Escoe can suck wind far as I'm concerned."

"You're not being a team player."

"News flash, Mayes. Escoe isn't on my team."

"But I am?"

"Most definitely."

Doodle and his aunt occupied the sofa in my parents' living room when we arrived. The TV was tuned to the weather station, as always, though someone had mercifully muted the volume. Mom took one look at my face and nodded to Larissa. Moments later, Larissa carried a tray with two steaming mugs to Mayes and me.

As I sipped the restorative broth, Mom offered some to Doodle and June, who refused. I edged toward Mayes. He took that as a green light and drew me close with a hand around my hip. I was too tired to be alarmed by his show of possessiveness and reveled in the comfort of being held.

The broth worked its usual magic. Someday, I'd have to ask my mom what she put in here. I felt calmer and lighter, as if sunshine was cleansing the darkness from the dreamwalk dregs. The net effect was a lift of my spirits.

"I'm as upset as you are," my father said to Doodle. "Nothing like this has ever happened before. My place is a sanctuary for people and wildlife. For someone to do this, I'm . . . it's awful."

"They would've been safer turned out at his old place," June said in a nasty tone. "You're a terrible person to let this boy's pets die on your watch."

Doodle fiercely blinked back tears. When he spoke, his voice cracked. "I can't believe they're gone. I grew up with those pigs.

They were the last thing I had of my mom's. Now I've got nothing. You stole that from me. I ought to sue you or something."

I couldn't let him attack my father like that. I cleared my throat. "The police are out there right now, investigating. They'll get to the bottom of this."

"Just like they're investigating my mom's death?" Doodle sneered. "I know all about the need to catch the killer in the first forty-eight hours. We've passed that time limit, and you haven't caught anyone yet. I've lost everything, and no one's going to pay. In what world is that fair?"

"Doodle's right. We ought to sue you people," June said with a decisive clap of her hands. "You can't take everything from a boy like that."

Mayes stiffened beside me, but I wouldn't let them cow me. "My parents had nothing to do with Mandy's murder or what happened to the pigs last night."

"Doodle relinquished the right to his animals when he left them here," Mayes said. "I am an eyewitness, a very credible one, who heard every word spoken. You'd better think twice about bringing a lawsuit against these nice people."

June's eyes widened, then narrowed. "Ain't that just always the way. Crap hap-

346

pens to us poor folks and no one gives a darn. Something happens to friends of the po-lice and the world stops spinning. It ain't right. I'm going up to that newspaper and giving them an earful about law and order in Sinclair County. Nope, not law and order. Law and disorder. Come on, Doodle."

Doodle didn't move as fast as his aunt, but he paused in the doorway when I said, "Wait."

"What?" he said, without turning.

"You ever heard the name Ava Leigh?"

His head jerked back. He whirled, fire in his eyes. "How do you know about that?"

"I'm following up on a lead in the case," I said.

"No one's supposed to know. Ava Leigh's a secret."

"Does your aunt know?"

"She better not find out. I gotta go."

June and Doodle scratched out of there, but not before turning a tight, lawn-ripping donut in the side yard.

"I can write them a ticket for property damage," Mayes said.

"Not worth it," Dad said. "I don't want anything to do with those people. The woman's mean as a snake, and the kid . . . I thought the kid had gumption. The way he let his aunt parade him in here with his grief. The way she kept harping about hunters out here, when there aren't any. And the kid, he looked me straight in the eye and asked me if I was a bow hunter."

"You're not," I said. When his expression didn't change, I asked, "Are you?"

"I'm not. I don't own a gun or a crossbow. That's the point."

"What point?" I asked.

"When I called to tell them about the pigs, and when they arrived, I never told them how the pigs were killed."

Chapter Forty-Five

Sheriff Wayne Thompson stopped in at the house once he and Escoe finished with the pig crime scene. "I apologize for Burnell Escoe. He's under a lot of pressure to solve this case quickly. He was certain he could sweep in here and figure out what's going on in five minutes and get a huge promotion out of it. Ain't gonna happen."

"I don't like him," I said with a yawn. Mayes, Larissa, and I had piled on the sofa. Graphics from the weather channel flashed on the TV screen across the room. I thought about sending Larissa outside, but she'd already heard so much and seen so much today. A few case details wouldn't matter. "I'm tired of the suspicious way Escoe looks at me like I'm from outer space, and it's impossible to work with him. It's amazing he got anywhere in a law enforcement career. He has no people skills."

"Got news for you, Powell. People skills

aren't always important at solving cases. He trusts old-fashioned police work and nothing else. But when he left town, stuff started breaking on the case. He's gotta think we're withholding evidence."

"We are."

"Spill." Wayne's gaze turned to steel. "Right now."

"You can tell him if you like, but I'm not helping that man get a promotion. Mayes and I did another reading of the bloodstain at the kill site."

"And you didn't mention it before?"

"Because of how we did the reading," I said. "We don't want it getting out that we can amp the sensitivity by doing this together. We found Mandy. She was distraught about her pigs. She ran through the suspect list and chastised us for not seeing what's going on. Then she mentioned Ava Leigh."

"Who's she?" Wayne asked.

"We don't know," Mayes said. "But she may be an it."

"Explain."

Mayes looked at me, and I got the hint. He wanted me to do the report, so I did. "When we got back to my parents' place, Doodle and his aunt were being their nasty selves and threatening to sue Mom and Dad. June stormed out first and I asked

Doodle privately if he recognized the name Mandy mentioned during our dreamwalk. He liked to have burst an artery. And the way he talked made us believe Ava Leigh wasn't a person."

"What else could she be?" Wayne asked, leaning against the doorframe. "Another pig?"

"I was thinking about that after Doodle left. He doesn't want his aunt to know anything about Ava Leigh."

"He doesn't control what we do with our leads."

"Even so, that got me to wondering." I sat up and leaned forward, intent on making my point. "What if Ava Leigh is a code name for something, or even an ID for the account where all the drug money is stashed?"

"We haven't found any large stash of money. That's as good a guess as any."

"But here's the thing. If we find the cache and seize the money, Mandy's wish for Doodle to have a better life will vanish. That money was supposed to buy him a college education and a fresh start." Everyone in the room stared at me, but I didn't care. Someone had to be this boy's advocate. "Even if we locate the money, can we leave it there? For Doodle?"

"You don't know what you're asking," Wayne said. "I can't set aside evidence. And Doodle might be our killer."

I watched weather graphics flash across the screen of the muted television. Forest fires dominated in the West. The entire Midwest was too hot and too dry. "It wouldn't be hiding evidence if our inquiry into that name isn't part of the official record. Besides, my dad learned something else."

"What's that, Tab?" Wayne asked.

My dad spoke up from the corner of the room. "The boy, Doodle. I called him about the pigs, and he and his aunt drove straight out here. The people that know about the dead pigs are right here in the room. Anyway, I never mentioned how the pigs were killed. And yet, he asked me if I was a bow hunter."

"With the arrowhead found in the meth lab and now arrows through the pigs, I'd say our killer is a bow hunter." Wayne stretched. "That leaves us with Doodle, his aunt, and Mandy's trucker boyfriend for suspects."

"The voodoo woman should be on that list," I said. "She's working with or for someone in regard to this case. She flat out lied to me this morning."

"I'll run them all in tomorrow when I'm fresh. Dottie and the boys weren't happy I left, so I should get home. Tab and Lacey, thanks for your hospitality. The pigs are yours to bury or dispose of as you see fit." He turned his attention to where Mayes and I sat, side by side. "I'll expect you two at the office at oh-eight-hundred tomorrow morning."

"We're close to having answers," I said.

Wayne nodded. "So close I can taste it. We'll have our man, or woman, tomorrow."

Another vehicle pulled up in the yard. Over Wayne's shoulder, I recognized the car and its occupants. Charlotte and Duncan.

Wayne noticed too. He flushed. "Not talking to reporters today either. Handle it, Powell."

With that, he dashed from the house, hopped in his Jeep, which he'd left idling this whole time, and drove off.

Charlotte bounded in. "Is there a fire? The sheriff nearly ran us over trying to zip out of here."

"No fire." I rose to give her a hug. "All better?" I asked in a whisper only she could hear.

She nodded and mouthed "Later" to me before she pulled back and spoke to everyone. "I shouldn't take Wayne's dislike personally. He never liked talking to me in school or anytime afterward. He gets along fine with my competition, Bernard Rivers, but I'm toxic to him."

"Not toxic, per se, but a force of nature he'd rather sidestep," I said. "He accords you the same respect he gives Dottie."

"Avoidance and cheating on me by hanging out with my rival? That describes his personality to a T."

I laughed. "You and Duncan grab a seat. We're thinking about what to make for dinner."

"I fix a mean barbecue," Duncan said. "I'd be happy to cook."

"Mom!" Larissa flung her arms around me. "We can't eat the pigs."

"No one's eating the pigs." I gave her a reassuring squeeze. "They don't know."

"Know what?" Charlotte asked.

"The pigs. They're dead. Someone took them out last night or this morning. We discovered them an hour ago."

Charlotte did a double-take. "No!"

Duncan's face fell and then a fierce expression tightened his lips. He gripped Charlotte around the waist, drawing her close as he quartered the room for threats.

His concern for my friend melted my heart. "It's true," I said. "And because it's related to the investigation, I can't tell you anything more about the incident. None of us can. However, Wayne is optimistic that he'll have an arrest tomorrow."

"Excellent. I can scoop Bernard with the story before I hand in my two weeks notice."

"You're quitting?"

"Yes. Duncan and I had a long talk today. We want a life together. He wants to stay on the force where he is right now while we look for land. We're both planning to start over wherever we settle. Between his savings and mine, we'll be sitting pretty financially while we get established." Charlotte paused to glance up at Duncan. He nodded and his hands moved to her shoulders. "There's more," she said.

"Tell us."

Charlotte reached for Duncan's hand and held it. "Duncan asked me to marry him, and I said yes. We're buying the rings tomorrow after I finish proofing at the paper, and we'll have a civil ceremony before we leave town."

I jumped up first, ran over and hugged her. My best friend was engaged. "Wow. Congratulations. Looks like we're celebrating tonight."

CHAPTER FORTY-SIX

It was past Larissa's bedtime by the time we got home. The dogs unloaded from the back of the truck with a few happy barks and much sniffing of the grass.

Mayes carried my sleeping daughter to the door for me. I unlocked the house and stepped inside, but the dogs didn't come in and settle down. They charged ahead, barking as if a horde of invaders were in the house.

My feet stopped of their own accord. "Something's wrong."

"Outside," Mayes said softly. "Switch places with me so I can clear the house."

"You think they're still here?" I took my sleeping child from him.

"I don't know what to think until I look. Wait here."

I wanted to flip on the porch light, but standing in the dark made us less of a target if an intruder was watching. With that thought, I huddled into the deepest shadows on the back porch. Unlike Mayes, I didn't wear a gun. Roland's Glock was in my bedside table, and my Beretta was in the glove box of my truck. Should I risk going back to the truck?

No. Too much moonlight. I should do a perimeter scan instead of guessing if a shooter had a bead on us. Leaning into the wall, I closed my eyes, opened my senses, and searched for lifeforms. I quested over a mile out from the house in all directions, but no one lurked in the woods or across the street. I shut down my extrasensory perception with a sigh of relief.

I picked up only one heat signature inside my house, so I believed Mayes would report the house was clear. Why would someone break into my house? I owned little of value, unless you were crazy about my grandmother's antiques. I'd inherited the house from her and left it as she'd furnished it.

The dogs quieted.

Every now and then I heard the creak of a door opening as Mayes cleared each room. Larissa lay like a dead weight in my arms. She'd barely made it to the truck before falling asleep. Between the emotional upheaval of the pig deaths and Charlotte's engagement announcement, we were all exhausted.

Seemed like it'd been hours since Mayes told me to wait outside. What was taking so long?

Then he appeared before me and opened his arms to take Larissa. "All clear."

I transferred her over to him. "Good. Let's get her to bed and then I can see if anything is missing."

"You cleared the outside?" he asked.

"I did. Whoever was here is long gone."

"I closed all the drapes anyway. We can turn lights on once you two are inside."

"Most of those drapes haven't been moved in twenty years. I'm surprised you're not sneezing."

"Almost lost it in the living room, but I managed to hold on."

"Good going."

Once he put Larissa in her bed, he stepped out and I got my baby tucked under the covers. She roused enough to ask about her black lab. "Where's Maddy?"

"I'll bring her in later. You're my top priority."

" 'Night, Mom."

I closed her door behind me, turned on every light in the house, and began my search. The kitchen was as I'd left it, with my water glass by the sink and all the counters tidy. The stove was off. The fridge contents looked okay, though Sulay the cat and little Ziggy hissed at me from their high perch atop the appliance. I quickly scanned the drawers and cabinets. Everything seemed fine.

Mayes searched the dining room, living room, and laundry room while I hustled back upstairs to check my bedroom and the guest room. Nothing was missing. Should we risk another joint dreamwalk on the doorknob? If that was the access point. How'd the person get in here anyway? The back door had been locked when I arrived, and it opened with my key.

We met up in the living room. "I found nothing missing. Did you?"

"I don't think anything is missing, but in truth, I'm not as familiar with the keepsakes in the rooms. None of the furniture seems to have been moved. I did find one thing that struck me as odd."

"What's that?"

"There was a pink throw draped over the arm of the sofa, and it was touching the space heater."

My blood iced. "What space heater?"

He stepped around the coffee table and pointed to a compact heater. I gulped. "That's not my heater. I don't own a space heater. They're fire traps, and besides, it's too hot to need a heater right now."

"No kidding."

"Why would someone break in here and add a space heater?"

The answer dawned on me as soon as I posed the question. Someone wanted me dead. They wanted it bad enough to set my house on fire despite the collateral damage: my daughter, Mayes, Dixon's four hounds, and our five pets.

CHAPTER FORTY-SEVEN

We phoned in the housebreaking and attempted arson. Dispatch sent Deputies Harper and McConnell, who took photos of the heater and throw, and then took the heater into evidence. As for point of entry, the downstairs bathroom window now had a ladder outside that hadn't been there before. Though I'd locked the house before leaving, I'd left that window open this morning, to vent the room.

Wayne called my cell. "You need anything else tonight?"

"No. I'm headed to bed," I said. "It's been a very long day."

"Put Mayes on the line."

I yawned and handed the phone to Mayes. After a few exchanges about the break-in, Mayes turned all cop-steely. "Will do," he said. He clicked to end the call and returned the phone.

"What'd he say?"

"He said I'm to stay in the house tonight. As your bodyguard."

Given the men's animosity toward each other, I laughed out loud. "He ordered you to sleep with me?"

"Nope. He told me to sleep in the hall outside your door."

"Wayne's an idiot. You're not sleeping on the floor."

Hope lit his eyes. "I'm not?"

"Don't be silly. You're welcome to use my guest room."

Mayes took a moment to digest this news. "What about the bathroom windowsill? Should we try a dreamwalk?"

"Yes." Both of us squeezed into the bathroom, laid our joined hands on the sill, let our senses drift. I felt a jolt of rage. Feminine rage. But nothing else. We vectored back to reality.

"That narrows the burglar field to either June or Cipriona," I said. "Let's hit the hay. Tomorrow will come soon enough."

Despite my need for rest, sleep evaded me. Sheets tangled around my limbs as I tossed and turned. Bits of the case cartwheeled in my mind, along with the names of my two top suspects, the victim's sister and the voodoo woman. I'd nearly nod off, then I'd startle awake and stare at the shadows in my room to see if they were moving.

Unrelated case facts seemed important. The missing pig harnesses could be a clue or a false lead. And that trail cam on the victim's property we'd raided for the memory card . . . what happened to that? I'd ask Mayes in the morning. I wanted to make a chart of all the suspects and the evidence. Seems like we were missing something. Or someone. Or Ava Leigh.

I could get up and do it now, except Mayes would hear me. He'd been so hopeful about staying in here with me, and I couldn't let him do that. Not until I figured out how to let Roland know he didn't have to hold on for me anymore. I counted the four corners of an imaginary square inside my eyelids, a usual sleep remedy, but that failed miserably.

Just too keyed up to sleep. *Relief is right down the hall,* my thoughts whispered. *Not happening with Larissa two doors down,* I whispered back.

Bored, overtired, and jittery, I reached out to my Watcher. To locate him, I lowered my guard and quested outward from the house, searching for that faint ping of nothingness. For the longest time, I let my thoughts cast out and wind back as I trolled for a bite, like a fishing line. When I couldn't locate him, aggravation leaked into my thoughts. They broadcast through the extrasensory pulses I emitted, and like a gathering storm, I found a spot of nothing that might be something after all.

Are you there, my Watcher? I called. *I need to talk to you.*

The bit of nothing began a slow spiral of energy. Ah, he'd heard my call. Good. I began talking to him through mindspeak. *I know you're listening because I can feel your presence in the woods now. During a recent dreamwalk recovery, my father had access to my thoughts, and he knows about you. We've talked about who and what you are, neither living nor dead. Am I right so far?*

The bit of nothing grew larger, but still no response.

Roland, I know it has to be you. No one else would feel the need to watch over me. This is hard for me to say, but you don't have to stand guard anymore. I'm doing okay on my own. And there's a Dreamwalker I've met. He's helping me learn the nuances of the profession. I don't know what it costs you to cross realms to get here, but I want you to move on with your life. I'm okay. I've got friends and family who care for me. I want you to have that again, wherever you are now. I hate for you to be stuck neither here nor there.

I listened as hard as I could, alert to every micro-sound. Finally, I heard a faint brush of something. *Bring the other Dreamwalker next time.*

CHAPTER FORTY-EIGHT

Monday morning dawned clear and bright. As I stacked the dirty cereal bowls in the dishwasher, I realized how stiff my shoulders were. Too much weekend and not enough rest. Still, I was happy for my best friend. Marriage topped Charlotte's bucket list. She'd found a guy who'd totally flipped over her, and they'd already survived a conflict that might have led another couple to call it quits.

Charlotte was in good hands with Duncan. I didn't want to lose her as a friend and confidante, but thanks to computers and cellphones, we'd stay in touch. And, with Mayes poised to become a fixture in my life, I'd be visiting north Georgia again in the near future.

Mayes sauntered downstairs, freshly showered, and looking completely at ease in my house. In his slacks and uniform polo from the Junction County Sheriff's Office, he radiated integrity and professionalism. And he smelled great, to boot.

"Ready?" he asked.

With Larissa already on the bus for school, the breakfast dishes done, and the dogs walked, my morning chores were done. Time to go to town and solve Mandy's case. "Let me double-check the locks, and I'll be ready."

"Good idea," Mayes said, heading straight for the bathroom window I'd left unlocked before. He'd find it locked. I wasn't always street-smart, but I never made the same mistake twice. I tried the first-floor windows, then went upstairs to check the rest. Larissa's window was cracked open.

I pulled it down, locked it, and joined Mayes in the kitchen. He held little Elvis in his arms. Elvis looked very content. "Good to go," I said.

"You carrying?" he asked, setting the little Chihuahua gently on the floor.

Did he expect a shootout on the way to town? My pulse skittered as I reached for my purse and grabbed my keys. "Do I need a gun?"

"You never need a gun until you don't have it."

"That sounds like a Yogi Berra-ism."

"Nope. It's experience talking."

"I keep a Glock upstairs, but my Beretta is in the truck. I can bring them both and my grandmother's shotgun, if you like."

He choked out a laugh. "The Beretta should suffice. Loaded?"

"Yes, but before you scold me, Larissa knows about gun safety. I've had her target shooting too. She would never touch a gun without my permission."

Mayes snagged the keys from my hand and gave me a quick peck on the cheek. "You're my kind of woman, Powell. It pays to make personal protection a priority."

I locked the door behind us and tromped down the stairs. Since Mayes was here, I'd upgraded my jeans and T-shirt office attire for navy slacks and a butter-yellow blouse. I'd even left my sneakers and work boots in the closet. There was a chance the sheriff wouldn't call me on my wardrobe upgrade, but now that I was putting in more hours as a consultant, I needed to look more professional.

"Six months ago, I would've insisted guns had no place in my truck or on me. But, between dreamwalking and consulting, I've bumped into folks who don't have a kind bone in their bodies. I'm a quick study."

His smile spoke volumes. "That you are."

I held onto that appreciative glow all the

way to the Sinclair County Law Enforcement Center. Larissa and I had tried to make an acronym out of the first letters, but there wasn't a lot you could do with SCLEC. It sounded so harsh. Easier to just say the mouthful of words.

We rolled in a few minutes before eight. The sheriff waved us into his office right away and closed the door. "You're late."

I never arrived this early, but shift change was at seven. If he'd expected us here for that, he should've said so. I specifically remembered him telling us to be here at eight. But he was the boss. Best not to smart off at him. "What would you like us to do?"

"I want answers before these people start yelling 'lawyer.' Virg and Ronnie are rounding our suspects up."

"June, Doodle, and Todd Derenne?"

"Yeah. They're probably all stone-cold killers," Wayne said. "I've only got two interview rooms, so I want you two to babysit the aunt for me while we grill the males. Escoe informed me he'll be conducting all the interviews, but I'll be in there with him. June will be in here with you two."

"You could split us up," Mayes said. "You'd move the process along faster if one of us questioned the other witness."

"Nope. Escoe'd have my head. His show.

His rules."

Escoe needed to take a chill pill. "You want us to talk to June or keep her from bolting?"

"Keep talking to a minimum. Escoe wants all the glory, and I'm past ready for him to be gone." Wayne cleared his throat. "I've got a search warrant coming for June's place and Derenne's semi. Once you're no longer needed here, I want you two out there with the search party, doing whatever you do to get answers. We need tangible evidence to close this case."

"Speaking of evidence, any thoughts about the pig harnesses?" I asked. "Why would someone take them?"

"I won't know that until we find them."

"And the video from the trail cam?" I asked. "Any leads?"

"There's a picture of a dark car coming in the yard, sitting, and turning around, but it was too grainy for any details. I sent it to a friend of mine yesterday. He said he'd clean it up and email it back. I'll shoot it to you via text message if it comes in during the interviews. Maybe one of us will recognize the car if we can't read the plate."

"Gotcha."

At the sound of a commotion in the hall, we headed for the door, with Wayne leading the charge. Escoe stood, pressed and tidy, in the doorway of Interview One. Derenne went in there. Meanwhile, Doodle cooled his heels in Interview Two. Virg and Ronnie herded June in Wayne's office.

"Have a seat," I said to our charge. "We're keeping you company."

"This isn't right," June insisted. "I haven't even had a cup of coffee or any of my medicine. What gives those redneck deputies the right to come into my house and roust all of us? Huh? I outta slap a lawsuit on everyone in this place."

Lawsuits cost money, but I was trying not to get chatty with June as per Wayne's orders. June paced the room twice, then collapsed in one of the visitor chairs. I took the other one beside her, so Mayes settled behind Wayne's desk.

"Well?" June asked. "Can I get a cup of coffee?"

"I've had the coffee here, and you'd be better off with a soda from the machine," I said.

"Coffee. I want strong, black coffee." She pointed at me. "And you can fetch it for me. I want to talk to this handsome young man."

Wayne hadn't said I couldn't give her coffee, so I left to grab a cup. On the way to the break room, I slid into the observation room for Interview One. Escoe was leaning forward, poking the table with his finger like a jackhammer. Todd Derenne didn't look impressed. The smirk never left his face.

He probably thought he was in the clear. I flipped on the audio switch and heard Wayne informing Derenne about the search warrant. He visibly paled. "We'll also be checking out your financial transactions," Escoe added. "You're the consistent link between the supply and the demand for the meth lab. If there's even one receipt that links to purchase of raw ingredients, you're going down."

And Escoe would take the credit for catching him. Based on Derenne's expression, I felt confident he was hiding something. Wayne was a good cop. I was sure he'd seen the same thing I saw.

Back in the office with the coffee, June wouldn't take the cup from me. "Put it on the desk," she said. "I don't want you to touch me."

"I won't hurt you." Miffed, I followed her request and sat near her. Not a single word of thanks from her.

"Bah. The dead should stay buried." June gulped her coffee. "You got no business going anywhere to talk to the dead."

"You've got nothing to clear up with your sister?" I asked, ignoring the sharp look from Mayes.

June's face took on a pinched look as if dill pickles seasoned her coffee. I hoped it was the bitter black coffee.

She gave a theatrical wave of her hand. "Good riddance. The world's a better place without her."

That was harsh. I wonder what else June had up her sleeve.

CHAPTER FORTY-NINE

"What on earth is taking so long?" June asked. "I've been cooped up in this tiny little office for going on thirty minutes. I need breakfast, and I need to go to the bathroom. You people can't treat me like this. I have legal rights."

"Guess again. You're a murder suspect," Mayes explained. "You can be detained for questioning."

June huffed out a tragic blast of air. "I'm a murder suspect? You can't believe I'd kill my sister. That's unbelievable. Barbaric. What kind of people are you?" She quieted for a minute. "You think Doodle killed his mom? No way in hell. Derenne is who you want. He's capable of killing. He told me about a mark that crossed him once. The guy didn't live to tell the tale."

My eyebrows rose at how quickly she threw Derenne under the bus. So much for our assumption she wanted everything from

Mandy's life.

"Where was this?" Mayes asked.

"Somewhere up Warner Robbins way. The guy owed Derenne money and wouldn't deliver. He was bragging about the take-down right after the Fourth of July."

"What was the man's name?"

"I don't remember. It was a regular name. Like Bob or John or Mike. Mike! That's it. The guy's name was Mike."

Mayes nodded at me. I left the office again and knocked on the door of Interview One. When Wayne stepped out in the hall with me, I relayed the information we'd gathered. "Ask Derenne about Mike, the man he allegedly killed in Warner Robbins," I said.

"You weren't supposed to question her," Wayne said. "But I'll take it. We aren't getting anywhere in here."

"June won't shut up," I said. "We tried ignoring her, but she won't stop talking. By the way, she wants breakfast and a bathroom break."

"Take her to the bathroom but return her to my office afterward. I'll be down there soon."

Marching orders in my head, I escorted June to the bathroom. While she was washing her hands, I stood where I could read her expression in the mirror. "You know

375

anyone named Ava?" I asked.

"No. Ava sounds pretentious." June paused. "Funny thing about that name. My sister always said if she had a girl she'd name her Ava, but she had Doodle instead. Doodle's about as far away from Ava on the hoity-toity scale as you can get, don't you think?"

I mentally flipped back to what I knew about Mandy. She'd only had one child, a son. But she might have used the name for something else. Doodle had recognized it, after all.

June gazed into the mirror and reapplied her lipstick. "You know, there was one time I thought old Mandy was filling out. Baby in the bun and all that. Nothing ever came of it. You would think she'd tell me if she was pregnant, but Mandy never shared a blamed thing with me. I could be starving on the roadside, and she wouldn't toss me a heel of bread. She was so mean to me."

Jackpot. I sent a mental invitation to Mayes. *Join us in the ladies' room.* I hid my satisfaction by relaying something I'd heard. "Is that right? According to both Mandy and Doodle, she loaned you thousands of dollars, which you never repaid."

June gasped. "You have no right to say that."

I practiced my stink-eye, cop face. As the seconds ticked by, June lost her brassy composure. Finally, she raised her eyes to glare at me. "I got into some trouble, all right? Mandy bailed me out, but she owed me."

"Seems to me like you owe her."

"What do you know about anything? Huh? You don't know what it's like to have nothing. To have people look at you like you're dirt. You've got everything. Maddy had everything. It was my turn, dammit."

She knew nothing about me and was dead wrong on all counts, but this wasn't about me. "Is that why you killed her, June? You wanted her life? Tell me the truth. Derenne start using you as a punching bag yet?"

I wished I had a camera. A storm of emotions crossed her face, but her lips remained sealed. Behind me, the door opened and closed softly. I felt Mayes' presence behind me.

"Doesn't feel so good, does it? Did he break your ribs?" I asked. "He always hit Mandy where no one else could see. You know what else? Derenne was the least of her problems. The drug people don't let you go once you get sucked into that life. You work for them or you die. Mandy was trapped, and they kept expecting more and more from her. She wanted out of that life. She wanted her son to go to college, to have a chance at making a decent living. She wanted her sister to have a second chance. That's why she loaned you the money. To give you the fresh start she never had."

Her trembling hand rose to cover her mouth. Then she gagged and puked coffee in the sink. I stepped back into Mayes. "Good thing we were in the bathroom," I said.

June ran some water, rinsed her mouth. Slowly she lifted the edge of her blouse. Purple and yellow bruises marred her pale torso. "He did this to me. He said he loved me, but he beat me. Nothing's broke, but I hurt all over."

Mayes stirred as if to speak, and I placed my hand on his arm. "Will you press assault charges?" I asked. "He won't stop, you know."

"I hate him. I thought I loved him, but I hate him. Yes, I'll press charges. I can't live like this. Mandy should've killed him a long time ago."

"Why didn't she?" I asked, holding my breath.

"He was her supplier. Without him trucking in the raw materials, she couldn't cook. Too many flags would raise if she bought the stuff locally. Besides, she didn't have time to shop for anything."

"How do you know that?"

"Because I tried to get her to make me a partner," June said, her voice quavering. "But I couldn't stand cooking. I'm claustrophobic, and you can't do it without wearing a mask. The one time I tried, I ripped my mask off and ran out of there. Mandy liked to have had a fit. Said I contaminated her home. She lived in a meth lab. That was no home."

I'd screwed up. We weren't supposed to be interrogating June. Worse, we didn't have any record of what she was saying. The sheriff would have my head on a platter. Mayes stroked my back. *Keep going,* he said with mindspeak. *She feels safe in here. I'm taping this on my phone.*

I met his gaze in the bathroom mirror. *Thanks for saving the day.*

Keep her talking. This is the break we need on this case. Wayne told you to bring her in here, so you've done nothing wrong.

But is it evidence? Was she Mirandized?

Yes, she was, when they picked her up. Keep her talking.

Heartened, I continued, "It was her home. She had nowhere else to go."

"She must've had money," June said.

379

"They paid her good for the work."

"Did they now? How do you know?"

"I heard things. And Todd would come over and brag about how rich they would be. It wasn't fair that they'd get rich. That's why I encouraged Todd to come around. I wanted my slice of the money pie."

"How long have you two been together?"

"Going on a year now. Mandy never knew we were sleeping together. But he never hit me, not until she was gone."

"Because he got his jollies hitting her. You sure you want to step into her shoes? From where I'm standing, it doesn't look so hot."

"I never wanted her job. But I wanted Todd's complete attention, the money, and the kid. Now I find Todd's no prize at all, the money isn't in her bank account, and the kid won't do what I tell him. He hates me."

"He probably thinks you killed Mandy."

"He's wrong. I didn't kill Mandy."

Truth rang in her words. I believed her. Still, I needed to push a little more. "Maybe not directly, but you didn't help her either. By considering her loans to you a gift, you forced her to be a slave to those people."

June wept. Then she got the heaves again. Intuition hit me like a flash. "You're pregnant. With Todd's baby."

"Thought it would make him happy." June grimaced. "Know what he said? If he wanted to be around rug rats, he'd go home to his wife in Warner Robbins. Said he'd never marry me. That me and Mandy were his property. That he could do whatever he liked with his side girls, and no one would stop him."

"You can stop him, June. You can put him in jail for a very long time. Did he ever mention names of people he worked with?"

"Maybe. But I ain't giving up any names until you put him away."

"Doesn't work that way. If you don't cooperate, the domestic-violence charges won't keep him in jail long. We need names in the drug-supply chain."

"I need a deal, and I know you can't make one with me. If you can't assure my safety, I'm not talking."

"One name," I pleaded. "One name could make a difference between a lifetime of living at the beach or getting Todd's heavy-handed version of love for you and your child. Give me the man's name."

Her nose tilted in the air. "It ain't a man, and I'm done talking to you."

CHAPTER FIFTY

"Good work," Wayne said, later that morning. Mayes and I had waited until the suspect interviews were completed to talk with the sheriff in his office. "Escoe and I got enough from Todd Derenne about his part in the supply chain to keep him out of circulation for a long time. He's not giving up anyone else in the organization, though. Escoe wants the whole thing exposed. I'm afraid he may be in our hair awhile yet."

"And June?" I asked. "What'll happen to her?"

"Far as I can tell, she's guilty of greed and stupidity," Wayne said. "If she didn't act on those charges, I can't hold her."

Greed and stupidity. Much as I hated to admit it, those words aptly described June Hendrix.

"And Doodle? What will happen to him?"

"I know you like the kid, but I've got my doubts about him. Something's off about the boy. He must've known Derenne was whaling on his mom, but he told no one? He knew about the drug lab in his home, too. No way was it a secret."

"Wait. You saying he killed his mom?"

"We don't know who killed her. The drug case is pulling together, but not much else." His computer chimed. Wayne busied himself for a moment, then waved us around his desk. "We might as well look at this together."

"What is it?" Mayes asked.

"The trail-cam video. My guy says this is the best he can clean it up." Mayes and I stood behind Wayne's chair and watched the snowy image. I couldn't tell a thing.

"I got nothing," I said. "Anyone else?"

Wayne grunted. Mayes said, "Run it again."

A dark blob pulled up in the yard. Sat there for a few minutes, then turned around and drove off. My second impression was no better than the first. So much for our finding the trail cam in the tree house. The image resolution was terrible. Perhaps that was a car that had come to Mandy's trailer, but I wasn't even sure of that much.

"You see that?" Mayes said. "Shark-bite grill. And the taillights."

Wayne leaned forward, squinting, as the

video ran again. "You may be onto something. Good catch."

"What?"

"Mustang," Wayne and Mayes said in unison.

"A recent model," Mayes said. "They brought back the retro grill, but the taillight design is new. Should be easy to find out who has a dark-colored, late-model Mustang around here."

"Won't be a problem," Wayne said, firing off a quick text to the GBI man. "Nobody around here drives a muscle car like that. However, I've recently made the acquaintance of a businesswoman from mid-Georgia who drives that very model of car."

The puzzle pieces clicked into place. There was one more new person in our community. "Alicia Waite? The manager for the outlet mall? How's that possible?"

"Anything's possible. Escoe will spearhead the search for her and the ongoing drug investigation. If she's the brains of this meth outfit — and after meeting her, I believe it's highly likely — Escoe will get the collar."

The GBI man barged in, his expression expectant. "You've got something?"

Wayne waved Escoe forward. "Thanks for responding so quickly to my text. We have a vehicle ID from the video."

"I saw the video and couldn't get anything from it," Escoe said. "How could you make a positive ID from such poor-quality footage?"

"Mayes pointed the shapes out to me, and now I can't stop seeing them. Check out the car front. See the shape of the grill? Look at those three parallel taillights when it turns around. Mustang all the way."

"Did you run it?"

"Don't need to. Alicia Waite, the new outlet-mall manager, drives a car like this. She comes from the Warner Robbins area. I've met with her several times, for, ah, business purposes, and she has the savvy to pull this off. We need proof of her involvement, but if you check her out, you'll find something. No matter how good they are at hiding in plain sight, there's always something that brings the mighty down to our level."

"We got her," Escoe crowed and headed for the door. "We're finally shutting this drug ring down."

"We don't have her yet," Wayne said. "There's still plenty of evidence-gathering to do before we tie her to the drug case."

"What about your homicide?" Escoe asked from the doorway.

"Still open, but I'm confident we'll wrap it up soon."

"You want to question Waite?"

"I've sent a text to my deputies to bring her and her car in."

"Virg got his Taser?" I asked. Having been on the wrong end of that device before, I was quite content for Virgil to use his quick-draw weapon of choice on criminals.

"You're electroshocking our suspect?" Escoe's face turned blotchy and red. "Stand down."

"My men will bring her in by whatever means necessary. Grab some lunch, everyone. We'll be busy this afternoon."

Charlotte and Duncan met us for lunch at the sandwich shop. Charlotte was dancing on air. "I've been fired."

I'd never seen her so excited. Her happiness infected me. "Get out! Kip fired you? He can't run that paper without you."

"Ya think?" Charlotte grinned. "When I handed him my letter of resignation this morning, he asked if this was what he thought it was. When I said yes, he said I was fired, effective immediately. I wasn't even allowed to box the stuff at my desk."

"Why are you happy about that?"

"Because Kip let pride get in the way of common sense. If I resigned, I wouldn't be eligible for unemployment. Now I am, because he fired me. That's more money to put in our house fund."

"Wow. I didn't see that coming."

"Me either, and the best thing is, we don't have to wait until this evening to get the rings."

"Congratulations," Mayes said, shaking Duncan's hand and hugging Charlotte. "You two deserve a chance at happiness."

A perky blonde waitress named Karen came to take our orders, so we made our selections. Steak sandwiches for the guys, grilled shrimp salads for the gals.

"And the case?" Duncan asked when we were alone again.

"Wrapping up," Mayes said.

Charlotte's eyes grew round. "You arrested Mandy's killer?"

"Not yet, but we're close," I said, hoping it was true.

"Dang. Another big story, and I can't cover it. Bernard is probably crowing about his good fortune from the Marion Bridge."

"Bernard is probably elbow deep in all the routine tasks you did to keep the paper running. Those guys won't know what hit them."

"Not my problem. I planned to work another two weeks and show them the ropes. But now I'm free as a bird. They can figure it out themselves."

"Your parents?"

"They want to meet Duncan. We decided to drive down to Florida before we head to the mountains. Maybe even this week while you wrap up the case." She glanced shyly at Duncan. "We've also been talking about emptying my place. I won't need it, and there's no point to keep paying rent on it."

I'd seen the inside of Charlotte's place. It might take a year to clear out the treasures she'd squirreled away in there. "Larissa and I can help you in the evenings."

"Great!"

Lunch passed in a busy blur of planning and well wishes. As people at nearby tables realized Charlotte was engaged, they stopped to congratulate her. I was relieved when Wayne texted me to return to the office ASAP.

While Mayes drove, I aired my fondest wish. "Must be a break in the case. You think they located Alicia Waite?"

He shrugged. "Could be."

"If it's not Alicia, do you think June, Doodle, or Todd Derenne confessed to the murder?"

"It doesn't feel settled."

To my annoyance, he didn't continue. "Go on."

"When a case winds down, all the pieces connect. My gut says this one isn't there yet."

"Hmm. I thought once we located Alicia Waite, everything would fall into place. We'd have the chain of command for her entire operation."

"Drug dealers are slippery, but the king-pins rarely have any direct link to the action. The ones who are sloppy don't last long in the business."

"Their own people kill them?"

"That's right," Mayes said. "All we have is a grainy video of someone in Ms. Waite's car turning around at Mandy's place. We can't ID the driver, and a good lawyer will have her out on personal recognizance so fast it'll make your head spin. I've seen it time and time again."

I hadn't considered that aspect. If Alicia was good at the drug business, she'd skate scot free. Conversely, if she'd burned bridges with her connections, we might not catch her, but they certainly would. "We may never know who killed Mandy?"

"Could be."

My jaw clenched. He seemed so pragmatic about the whole thing. "Not good enough. I want justice for Mandy, the kind that comes with prison time."

"Every cop gets a case like this, one that won't hang together right. They become fixated on the case, but no matter what they try or how many times they go over the evidence, the leads don't materialize."

I needed someone to pay for the childhood Doodle never had. I wanted to catch the bad guy or gal. My hand itched, so I rubbed it. "I don't accept that. Every case I've ever worked has closed."

"Good for you, but open cases happen. You should prepare yourself for that eventuality."

"I won't quit on the case."

"Not saying you will, but other cases will take priority. Mandy isn't the only victim out there. She didn't deserve what happened to her — no one deserves that — but the world is full of people who have to be stopped. Will you choose to work Mandy's case over putting ten other criminals behind bars?"

"I'll do both."

He parked my truck, switched it off, and looked at me. "Cops who get tunnel vision don't make it. They put in too many hours, neglect their families, and make a fatal mistake. All I'm suggesting is that you program flexibility into your mindset. I don't want anything to happen to you."

"Agreed." I quit scratching my hand. Glancing down, I saw that I'd been rubbing the tattoo Rose applied to show our connection. I didn't have the sense she wanted to meet, but the ink seemed different. "Look at that. The lines are blurring, from the inside. How's that even possible?"

Mayes lifted my hand to his lips. "A kiss to make it all better."

His touch lit me up inside. "Definitely better."

"Let's go catch some bad guys."

Chapter Fifty-One

The brisk vibe in the cop shop was gone. Instead of the pre-lunch optimism infusing these walls, a dark presence had settled on the place. Goose bumps prickled everywhere on my body as soon as we unlocked the employee door. I lowered my guard to shoot a telepathic message to Mayes. *Something's wrong.*

He pulled his gun, held it by his right leg. *I feel it. Keep the link open, okay? We've got to stay sharp and work as a team.*

My gun is in the truck.

You don't need it, Mayes said in my head. *What's happening here won't be solved by guns.*

I'm scared.

You should be.

We crept down the deserted corridor, our footsteps echoing, and the hairs on the back of my neck at full attention. Something was horribly, undeniably wrong here.

The door to Wayne's office was closed. I knocked. "Wayne?"

No answer. I tried the knob. Locked. "Where are they?" I asked aloud.

"Something happened here."

We checked each office, interview room, and even reception. Not a soul in sight. "Should I summon Oliver to track them?"

"No need. By process of elimination, they're not on the admin side. Must be on the jail side."

I thought about the double doors you had to go through to enter that side of the house. This place was set up like air locks to keep anyone from getting away. Only one door could open at a time, and someone from the centralized security area had to buzz you through. I had nightmares about getting trapped between the doors.

"Let's go outside and enter through Receiving and Booking," Mayes suggested as if reading my fear.

I swallowed my anxiety. "Security could buzz us through, and it would be faster."

"If everyone's over there, Security has been compromised."

"Right." Heat rose to my cheeks as we retreated. Mayes had to think I was a complete dolt.

Outside, with the sunshine warm on my

face, I felt worlds better. "Let's call for backup. Virg and Ronnie are on shift today. I have Virg's cell."

"Call him."

I dialed Virg's number. "No answer. They must be tied up."

Mayes looked at me. "Yes. Tied up. That makes sense. We need Oliver after all. Summon him, and let's head to the jail."

"I'm getting my gun while we're out here."

"Suit yourself."

I grabbed my gun, connected with my ghost dog, and nodded to Mayes. "Ready. What's the plan?"

He motioned me around the building, scanning the area with each step. "Rescue our people. Stop the bad guys."

I trailed him closely. Oliver beside me. "Duh. Get serious. Besides that, how will we proceed?"

"You've got Rose on speed dial, right?"

"Rose can't help."

"She'll help," Mayes said. "Our problem comes from her world."

"And you know this how?"

"I've felt this disturbance before."

"Something from the Other Side is here? In our jail?"

He shot me a scary grin. "Not for long. We're sending it back where it belongs."

My feet stopped, and my heart raced. Mayes looked like he'd been handed the best Christmas present ever. I wanted to run and hide. Except this was my job, and I had two supernatural helpers by my side and another one on call. My grip tightened on my gun, and I trailed Mayes through the door.

CHAPTER FIFTY-TWO

"Took you long enough, Dreamwalker. Come join the party."

The eerie gender-neutral voice came from Sister Cipriona, the palm reader. She wore another animal-print dress, but she'd left her hair down. Braid upon braid spilled over her shoulders and back. For a moment, I thought I saw the braids move independently.

I blinked at the distraction and looked away. Like Mayes, I quartered the room and stepped over the three flashlights lined up side by side on the floor. A cluster of people stood in the drunk tank, the sheriff included. He was yelling something I couldn't make out.

Doodle knelt on the floor behind Cipriona, his hands in a prayerful pose. Escoe was flat on his back beside Doodle, only Escoe's leg flared at an unnatural angle. I watched Escoe until I saw the slight rise and fall of his chest. Good. At least no one was dead, yet.

Patchouli-scented candles burned on the reception desk, and a light dusting of powder made a path along the floor. Whatever was happening here wasn't regulation. I was too scared to think, but I'd long since discovered courage was possible even in the midst of stark terror.

"Put your hands in the air where I can see them," Mayes shouted. "Now."

"I do not submit to your laws. Put your guns down," the palm reader said, shaking a finger at Mayes. In that moment, Mayes struggled with an invisible force for his gun. He staggered a few steps and stepped in the powder. Then he froze.

She'd done something to him. Not wanting to end up like a statue, I placed my gun on the floor. "What do you want?"

Cipriona laughed. She seemed to grow taller and more statuesque than she already was. Her hair was definitely moving, and the swaying braids were mesmerizing. I closed my eyes and counted to three while I pinged Mayes telepathically. No response. I gazed at the floor by Cipriona's glossy high heels and waited. She still wore that anklet with a dime on it, and if I could stand to look at her face, I'd bet she still had a mini-sack of herbs around her neck. Oliver leaned against my leg, grounding me with his chilly presence. My fingers automatically went to the rose tattoo on my hand, and I sent up a silent SOS signal to my mentor on the Other Side. *Rose! Help!*

"Are you praying?" Cipriona asked. "That won't do." She clapped her hands. The noise jolted me as if she'd fired a gun. "Minion, fetch the weapons."

Fabric rustled. I glanced Doodle's way, and sure enough, he was rising. His eyes looked feverish. Was he possessed? This was beyond my paygrade, and I was on my own.

I had to think. I had to neutralize this threat. If only I knew how or why she'd gathered this group of people together. Mandy's son, sister, and boyfriend — they were all present. And Alicia Waite, the mall manager who'd cruised Mandy's yard — she was locked in the drunk tank too. Since Doodle was the only person in earshot, I started with him.

I waited until he was beside Mayes and yelled, "Why'd you do it, Doodle? Why'd you kill your mom? Why shoot the pigs?

The loud noise startled him, and he jostled Mayes enough to knock him over. Both of Mayes' feet ended up outside the powder trail. Progress. *Oliver, bark at Mayes and keep barking until he wakes up.*

"The boy can't answer you, Dream-walker," Cipriona gloated. "I own him body and soul."

"You don't own anyone," I shot back. "You may have taken advantage of a young man's unhappiness, but he isn't yours. He's Mandy's son."

"Not anymore. He removed her from the picture. These clowns don't realize what they had, but I did. Secret meth labs are the wave of the future. I've got three ready to come online as soon as my adopted son trains more cooks."

I reeled from the news, so angry I wanted to throttle Cipriona, but knowing I needed to keep my distance and find a chink in her resolve. On the psychic plane, Oliver danced around Mayes, barking and nosing him. I sent Mayes another telepathic ping. *Wake up. Mayes, I need your help. Wake up.*

Mayes remained mute and immobile. I could only hope he was fighting his way through the thrall to return to me. Meanwhile, I had to improvise. "What good is money to someone as powerful as you?"

"In your world, money buys power. I've got a lock on the Warner Robbins market and I'll take Macon next. If I feel like it, I'll take on the Mexican drug cartel in Atlanta."

"They'll kill you."

"They can't get close to me." Cipriona laughed, a horrible sound. "Thanks to you, I have an entire police force and a GBI agent who'll do my bidding."

"They won't."

"Sure they will. Everyone has a weak point. You, for instance. You'd do anything for your daughter. You'd make sure she wasn't sold into sexual slavery and kept drugged for the year or so she'd live."

My marrow iced. "Stay away from my kid. I'll kill you if you touch her."

"See, we understand each other quite well. You do my bidding, and your daughter won't come to harm from my hands."

I didn't trust her not to kill us all right here. The people in the drunk tank were shouting again. The sounds filled my ears until I couldn't think. It wasn't normal. Cipriona was doing this to me. I pushed the sounds from my head, from my ears.

Cipriona laughed as Doodle crouched at her side with the guns and knelt. She reached down to pat him like a dog. Anger churned inside me. If I could shoot fire out of my fingertips like Rose, I would. I'd scorch that woman without a second thought.

"Who are you?" I asked. "What are you?"

Cipriona uttered an evil monster laugh that curled my toes. "You may call me Bezzy, slave. I will become your closest friend, your only friend."

I was no one's slave, not in this world or the next. Bad enough that Rose had her hooks in me. At the thought of Rose's name, my tattoos heated on my hand and on my back. Finally, she was paying attention. Since she hadn't made an appearance, I must have more work to do. But what? Cipriona had originally come to me because her Granny was in prison for life for killing her father, who had killed her mother. When I visited the father on the Other Side, he said Cipriona wasn't what she seemed.

No kidding. Okay. If she was more than a person and bad to the bone, my next thought was demonic possession. Crap. Not another demon. The last one nearly killed me. Couldn't dwell on that now. How long had Cipriona been possessed? Time to ruffle a few demon feathers.

"You let your Granny take the hit for your father's death," I said. "That was you, wasn't it?"

Cipriona strutted around the room, careful to avoid the trail of powder. "Yes. You're the first to figure it out. Dear old dad didn't toe the line. He wouldn't serve his daughter.

Imagine that."

"Before your dad, you killed your mother."

"I did. Sucked the life right out of her. She wouldn't serve me either."

I shuddered. "How'd you go so long between murders?"

"Who said I showed restraint?" The air bristled with Cipriona's boasts. "My Granny brought me souls to steal until I reached my full potential. There are always drifters coming through town, people no one misses. Think of me as a Bermuda Triangle for disposable people."

I wanted to throw up. "You enslaved your grandmother?"

"She summoned me through a portal she stumbled across. But the damn thing closed before I could bring my associates through. I've been biding my time, waiting to make my move. The time has come for me to rule. You're the real deal, easily crossing between worlds. Your task is to open the gates of hell."

And let destruction rain down on the Earth? No, thanks. "Visiting your father on the Other Side was a test of my abilities? You didn't stick around for an answer."

"Couldn't. Had to get over to Mandy's place and watch the firemen go nuts over my handiwork. I knew you'd left this realm.

I felt the emptiness of your human vessel. I could've taken possession of you right then and there, but this way is much more fun. Look at the prizes I collected, all these souls to torment."

Everyone in this room faced a hellish existence if I obeyed Cipriona's command. We would be powerless to stop the atrocities we committed. "You're a monster."

"That's right, and don't you forget it. Open the portal or die."

CHAPTER FIFTY-THREE

If I did her bidding, civilization as we knew it would end. Cipriona, or Bezzy as she wanted to be called, would summon her closest buddies from the afterlife and wreak havoc everywhere. It wouldn't be a slow death of drug addiction for humanity. It would be much, much worse.

"No. I won't do it," I said.

"You will." Bezzy kicked Doodle, knocking him over. He cried out in pain. "Shoot her in the leg."

Doodle scrambled to comply. He put one gun down and aimed the other one at me. "Wait," I said, making it up as I went along. "I meant I can't do it with so much noise in the room. I can't concentrate."

Bezzy raised her arms and pointed at the drunk tank. Every person in there dropped like dead weight to the floor. The immediate silence was worse than the noise.

I gulped. All my work friends were in that

404

room. What had I done? "Are they dead?"

She marched over to me, and I crabbed away from her pointy-toed shoes. "Not yet. Open the portal, slave."

Mayes was almost within my reach. Oliver trotted to my side, standing between me and the demon, barking. I cowered on the floor as if too terrified to move. My tattoos heated to the point of discomfort. I shot my mentor an urgent summons across worlds. *Come on, Rose, what more do you need?*

"Sit up," Bezzy ordered in her creepy gender-neutral voice. "Sit up, or I'll kill your friend."

I sat, scooching back until I was between her and Mayes. He was so close, I could touch him.

"Don't go getting any ideas," Bezzy said. "How do I look? I haven't seen my friends in ages."

I glanced up. Too late, I realized my mistake. The writhing hair ensnared me. And what was with the curled horns on her temples? I mentally recoiled. I would've physically recoiled, except I couldn't move a muscle.

"Open the portal," Bezzy commanded.

When I did nothing, she stepped on my hand. Terrible pain lanced my arm, wrecking my will, shattering my thoughts.

She snatched my ponytail and yanked it hard. The contact burned and throbbed, and my will to resist waned. Her evilness coated me with a heavy layer of revulsion. Dark emotions stirred in my soul. Every slight I'd ever felt, every argument I'd ever lost, they all came racing into my head.

"Obey me now, or feel the terror of eternal possession."

"Yes, master." I quested through the drift, spinning and turning. I reached the gloom on the Other Side and awaited my next orders.

"Yes," Bezzy said from my side. "This will do nicely. Don't move."

As she stalked away, Mayes joined me. "Shh. Don't let her know I'm here. Oliver's here too. Where's your contact?"

"Master!" I called.

But Bezzy was too far away to hear me.

"Snap out of it," Mayes said. He worked my rigid arms, but they wouldn't move on their own.

"I know you're in there, Baxley," Mayes said. "I won't let go of you."

"Master!" I called again.

Rose popped before me in her biker duds, grinning. "You did it."

"You're too late," Mayes said. "The demon has her."

"Not anymore." Rose placed both hands on my head and spoke words I didn't understand. The darkness consuming me ebbed and vanished. She let go, and I sagged into Mayes. He snugged me in close, his belly pressed to my back.

I tried to parse what happened. Couldn't. Somehow, I was on the Other Side with Mayes and Rose. Was this a dream? Why did my entire being ache like I had the flu?

"Congratulations," Rose said. "You did it."

I hugged my belly. "I did what? Wiped out humanity?"

"You lured Bezzy into our trap. High Five. Mission accomplished."

"I didn't lure her anywhere," I said. "She's got her own agenda."

Lightning flashed. Thunder rolled. Three times.

"See? She won't bother you again. The boss has Bezzy."

I shuddered. My knees felt weak. "Can't be."

"But it is."

I glanced at Mayes, and he grinned like a court jester. Rose was telling the truth. I was safe. My family was safe. My friends were safe.

Another emotion smacked me in the gut.

Bitterness. I reached over and tried to slap Rose. She didn't budge.

Her laughter iced my anger cake. "Why didn't you help me?"

"Now that you know your way around, I can't help in the same way as before. Take your mate home and celebrate your victory."

Victory. I didn't feel like a champion. I felt hollow. Exhausted. My thoughts cleared. Bile rose in my throat with remembrance. Bezzy had taken over my body. She'd forced me to bring her to the Other Side. Not a soul had been standing when we left the jail. "I can't leave without answers. Bezzy knocked everyone out before she left. How will we revive them?"

"In her absence, they'll revive on their own," Rose said.

"What about Cipriona's body? If you trap Bezzy here, won't Cipriona die?"

"She will."

"That's a problem."

"You've got two heads between you. Make the problem go away."

"You could fix it. You could give Cipriona back her soul."

"You're misguided if you think I'd do that. After a lifetime of exposure to Bezzy, that woman's soul is black. It's better this way. A mercy killing, if you will."

Mercy. Did Rose believe in it? She seemed so hard at times. Did she love her undercover persona too much? Because it seemed to me she clearly relished her bad-girl role. Or at least that's the side of her I always saw.

"Did Doodle really kill his mom?" I asked.

Rose tapped her foot. "He did."

"The pigs too?"

"Bezzy ordered him to kill the pigs so he had nothing left to love."

"Will he remember his crimes?"

"Do you want him to remember?"

Another shudder ripped through my virtual body. "I want justice for Mandy."

"You got it. Bezzy used the kid to be the instrument of her death. Case closed."

"We don't have any evidence against him or Bezzy, I mean Cipriona."

"Have you searched her place?"

"No."

"You should. Now run along, children."

I glanced up at Mayes. He nodded. "Thanks," I said. "For everything."

Clinging to Mayes, I imagined us back in Receiving and Booking. We vectored through the drift in a mostly straight line. Still, the light seemed over-bright when I opened my eyes.

"Baxley," the sheriff spat out, his angry

face an inch from mine. "You've got some explaining to do."

CHAPTER FIFTY-FOUR

As Rose predicted, the folks in the drunk tank had awakened once Bezzy was no more. Doodle had as well, and the first thing he'd done was release them. Burnell Escoe had been transported to the Emergency Room with a broken leg. Cipriona Marsden took a one-way ride to the morgue.

"I don't have all the answers," I admitted, sipping my Coke and glad to be back on solid ground in Wayne's familiar office. Mayes had gone with Virg and Ronnie to search Cipriona's home. I'd had my throbbing, stepped-on hand examined by the EMTs, and nothing was broken. "Cipriona Marsden was in the middle of everything, and that's why my contact suggested we search her home."

"How'd she get us in the drunk tank?" the sheriff asked.

"You're not going to like the answer, and I can't prove a word of it."

"Tell it to me straight."

"She was possessed by a demon named Bezzy. She killed her dad and her mom too, and let Granny take the rap. Over the years, Granny fed the demon souls, so I imagine there might be several bodies on or around Granny's former property."

To his credit, Wayne didn't bat an eyelash. I continued, "She put the root on Doodle and his family, intending to build a bigger and better drug empire. She made Doodle kill his mom and the pigs. She was grooming the teen for management, but at least she won't hurt him again. What will happen to him?"

"It will depend on Doodle."

"You won't arrest him?"

"I can't arrest anyone without evidence," Wayne said. "I already asked him what he remembers of the last few weeks, and he said it's all a blur."

"I can't prove this either, but I believe Cipriona had her hooks in everyone in this case. She made June more jealous and spiteful. She made Todd Derenne meaner and more ham-fisted. She made Alicia Waite more opportunistic."

"How will we spin this?" Mayes said. "Escoe's going to be spitting bullets when he gets back here on those crutches."

I wasn't looking forward to dealing with Burnell Escoe either. "Too bad for the GBI guy. We've got the answers for the murder and the drug case but no evidence to speak of. At least with the investigation winding down, he'll be leaving soon, and unless a miracle occurs, he won't be solving the drug case or getting a big promotion."

"I'm thinking we say Cipriona Marsden burst in here with Tamika after lunch, which is true. She took Tamika hostage with a gun and made us put down our phones and guns and march over to the drunk tank. But there were too many of us for a small room, so we passed out from oxygen deprivation."

"Sounds good."

"Always stick as close to the truth as possible when lying." Wayne grinned. "Escoe came running in to save the day and with super-human strength, she knocked him in the air. His leg broke when he fell, also true. Once he was down, she conked him on the head with the gun, rendering him unconscious. You and Mayes arrived next, and she knocked Mayes out and forced you to contact someone from the Other Side for her. But the effort from stopping Escoe cost her. She had a heart attack and died instantly."

"You forgot to account for Doodle in your story."

"Doodle was also unconscious in the room, but before she knocked him out, she ordered him to cosh Mayes on the head with an empty gun."

I thought of Ava Leigh, the phrase that made Doodle so nervous about his aunt. If it was related to his inheritance, I wouldn't make any waves about it. The kid deserved to have a chance in this world. I hoped his choices were better than his mother's. I hoped he knew where the money was hidden, because we had no idea.

"How do you explain the candles and the powder on the floor?"

The sheriff chewed his lip before answering. "What candles and powder?"

Hmm. Did Rose help out after all? "Nothing. Just testing your memory."

"My memory's fine, I think."

"Will there be any leads at Cipriona's place?"

"It would be nice, but I'm all for telling the other suspects that Cipriona was responsible for Mandy's murder, even if we don't have evidence to prove it. They need closure."

So did I.

"Will Mayes play ball?" the sheriff asked.

Translation: would Mayes go along with the story? "Ask him."

The sheriff's cell rang. "There he is now." He answered, a broad grin taking over his face as the conversation progressed. He hung up. "Everything we need to close this case is at Cipriona's place. The bow, the arrows, the pig harnesses, the Molotov cocktail ingredients, and the raw ingredients for cooking meth. Even a rain barrel of money with the name Ava Leigh painted on the outside. Case closed."

Cipriona had seized the kid's college fund? That figured. "Can Doodle get the money back?"

"No way, no how. It's drug money. But I'll make a deal with you," the sheriff said.

I steeled myself. Wayne always came out on top when he made a deal. "What do you have in mind?"

"If the kid applies himself and keeps his nose clean, the department can help him with college money. Not all of it by any means, but enough to get him started."

"Your budget is under county jurisdiction. How can you pull it off? Won't everyone demand a scholarship for their kids if word gets out?"

"Word will not get out, because only two people in the world, me and you, know about this generous offer. The kid caught some bad breaks. He can make something of himself, but I've seen kids like him give up. He has to earn my respect. Then I'll help him out with some of our miscellaneous income from seizure sales."

In other words, Wayne's offer was totally off the books. No one would hear of it except Doodle, and he'd never know about it unless he stuck to the honor roll and did his mother proud. It wasn't the best bargain in the world, but Wayne didn't have to do anything. He made the offer because the boy mattered to me.

"Thank you," I said, knowing in my heart that I'd tutor Doodle if need be. I would do my best to make sure he didn't lose hope or get dragged into the drug world. Together, the sheriff and I would become Doodle's Ava Leigh, his safety net.

The case might be closed, but I had unfinished business in my personal life. Charlotte and Duncan had borrowed Mayes' truck and camper to go down to see her folks, taking Dixon's hounds with them. Mayes moved into my guest room, and we spent a few days walking, biking, and boating. It was nice. Very nice.

But Mayes had to return to his life in

Stony Creek Lake. Even if he wanted more. No, even if *I* wanted more. I could finally admit the truth. It was past time for me to let Roland go. Time for me to do more than go through the motions of life.

After Larissa went to bed one evening, Mayes and I sat on the porch swing, listening to the frogs and crickets chirp in the thick twilight. We hadn't talked about parting ways, but it loomed like a supertanker on the horizon.

"It's peaceful here," Mayes said. "You've done all right for yourself, Baxley."

"I was a mess when I first came home. No money, no proof Roland was dead, and too much pride to move in with my folks. But I learned a lot about life. I used to think accepting help from others was a sign of weakness. Now, I understand everything better."

Shadows crossed his face with each pulse of the swing, but even in the waning light, I noticed him trying hard not to smile. "You understand because you've been cast in the role of helper?" he asked.

"Partly. The real truth is I've learned to face my fears. I won't always know the answers, and parts of dreamwalking still scare the bejeebers out of me, but I know I won't collapse into a puddle of goo when things go wrong. And they always seem to go wrong. My point is some people are born to help and refusing their offer hurts them and you. Not to say I mooch off anyone, but I see the bigger picture now. Sometimes I help a person; sometimes that person helps me or someone else. It's a never-ending caring bank. Does that make sense to you?"

"You make complete sense to me. In my spiritual journey, I've uncovered many basic truths and adjusted my thinking accordingly. You are young to be so wise."

"Not much younger than you."

"Still. Your perspective is much like that of an elder from my tribe."

His tribe. His people. I'd gotten so used to having him around, to hearing his voice in my house, to absorbing the rock-solid nature of this man. I let out a shaky breath.

He noticed and cupped my chin. "We'll figure this out, Walks with Ghosts. You and I are two halves of a whole. In your heart, you know I speak the truth, but first we have unfinished business."

Roland. He was talking about my alleg-edly deceased husband. "You want to do that now?" I hated that my voice grew shrill.

"Delaying won't make it easier. You had an easy day today with no dreamwalks, and you've had time to recover from the encounter with your demon-infested voodoo priestess."

I couldn't hold my hands still. An icy dread filled my heart at the mere mention of that creature. "I'll never forget Bezzy."

"You shouldn't. Meanwhile, you need closure with Roland. The world has already written him off, but you haven't. Somehow he's managed to connect with you. If you let him go, he can continue his spirit quest. As we've seen, death has many doors. His strength of will has kept him in the hallway for quite some time."

His words whirled through my thoughts. I'd taken my Watcher for granted for months now. Not once had I dreamed I might be keeping Roland from his eternal fate. Not once had I realized that my unrelenting search for him had broadcast across this world, the next, and quite possibly everything in between.

"So much for my universal understanding. It appears I've been quite selfish in refusing to let him go."

"Roland obviously cares a great deal for you. He doesn't want you to be alone and afraid. He wants to protect you."

The silence settled around us. Mayes wasn't asking me to choose him or Roland.

He was asking me if I loved Roland enough to let him go.

Everything he said made perfect sense, but I'd never viewed my situation objectively. I'd expected to share my life with Roland. He'd expected to spend his with me. He'd managed to cheat the afterlife by lingering between worlds — for my sake.

Tears filled my eyes. I'd made sacrifices and adjustments while Roland held steady, waiting and hoping and helping me. I loved him, and I always would, but it was time to let him go.

"Okay," I said. "We'll do it tonight."

The screen door creaked open and Larissa dashed into my arms, followed by the entire pet parade. "Me too," she said. "I want to say goodbye to Daddy."

"Oh, Larissa, honey, this is an adult situation —"

"She should be allowed," Mayes said. "He's her family too."

"This goes against everything I've done to protect her," I said. "Larissa should have a normal childhood."

"You are an extraordinary family," Mayes said. "Accept that she has needs too, and she needs this closure as much as you do."

Larissa nodded, her eyes luminescent in the moonlight. My arms tightened around her. I could put my foot down, but what was the point? Mayes was right. We all needed this. "Okay. She can join us, but if it gets scary for her, we shut down the link."

"Got it," Mayes said, his arm tightening around my shoulder. "Let's maintain physical contact. I'll hold the mind link and Baxley will contact Roland. We'll follow her lead." He gave Larissa instructions on how to reach us on the immediate spiritual plane. When she was prepped, he nodded at me. "We're ready."

Larissa was waiting with Mayes when I transitioned. *Relax and float in the thought plane,* I told them. *It often takes a while for him to respond.* I began questing out in my thoughts as I normally did, pulsing beyond the confines of my property, reaching as far as I could with thought energy. The signal was out here, somewhere, I knew it.

You're all over the place, Mayes said in mindspeak. *Focus on what you need to do. Keep the parameters the same as the last time you met him.*

Last time . . . I'd been upset. Worried and anxious. I pushed those emotions into the search. I was worried and anxious about Roland's well-being. A glimmer of energy coalesced on the plane. I amped up my need to talk with him, adding all the grief I'd held

close for years. The energy field strength-
ened.

*Roland, I'm here. The other Dreamwalker,
Mayes, is here too. And Larissa.*

Within the energy field, the fog quickened
and turned in on itself. Larissa glommed on
to my thoughts, and I reassured her this was
normal.

We came to say goodbye, I continued. *I'm
sorry if I kept you from moving on. I want you
to be free of earthly concerns. Larissa and I
are fine. Mayes is a friend, a good friend, and
we came to meet you. He asked me if I loved
you enough to let you go. And I do. Love you
that much. I've been selfish reaching out to
you like this.*

The swirl that was Roland spun into high
gear on the spiritual plane. I listened and
listened but there were no words. An out-
pouring of emotion bathed us. Supercharged and full of love. I understood. He'd
heard my thoughts and approved.

Mayes' thoughts commandeered the
mindlink, his mind-words blazing across
time and space. *Mighty warrior, the battle is
done. Your reward is near. Hold onto what is
good, to what you believe, and accept your
new beginning, noble one. Respect wisdom,
innocence, and trust. Look within for illumination and let your spirit soar. Ascend the Great*

Divide, opening your heart and soul to the Great Spirit. We salute the light within you, wherein all creation dwells. For when you are there, and we are at our centers of light, we are one. We raise you up and welcome your return to the circle of life, brother. Hear the voices of the wind. Listen and let go.

His prayer touched my spirit with bittersweet emotion. He must know what to do because he'd guided other warriors through death. My husband had fought all odds to watch over me. It was time for his spirit to rest.

Mayes chanted something in Cherokee. The melody soothed me and quieted the energy blitz before us. When Mayes ended the song, we waited, listening and hoping for Roland's spiritual release. When he finally spoke, his words were very faint.

Thank you, spirit guide, for nurturing my family, Roland said.

I will care for them as my own, Mayes said. *You may travel on to your resting place.*

Daddy! I love you, Larissa cried out.

Love you more and your mom too.

Journey on, Roland. Our love goes with you. My spiritual voice trembled and shook its way through my goodbye.

The energy didn't fade away gradually as it normally did. Instead, the color brightened from Other World murk to white and then flashed to golden. Simultaneously, the shape changed to a compact, translucent sphere. It hovered nearby for one last, shining moment, and then streamed above until it was no more.

Mayes, Larissa, and I returned to our bodies, holding each other and reflecting on what we'd experienced.

He'd gone. I felt the Roland-void in my heart and soul. I was truly a widow in every sense of the word. But I wasn't alone, not now, not ever. Mayes had healed the rift in our world and in my heart. He'd taught me how to live.

ABOUT THE AUTHOR

Formerly a contract scientist for the U.S. Army and a freelance reporter, mystery and suspense author **Maggie Toussaint** has nineteen published books, sixteen as Maggie Toussaint and three as **Rigel Carson.** Her previous mysteries include *Gone and Done it, Bubba Done It, Doggone It, Dadgummit, Death, Island Style,* the Lindsey & Ike Mysteries, and three titles in her Cleopatra Jones series: *In For A Penny, On the Nickel,* and *Dime If I Know.* Her latest mystery, *Confound It,* is Book Five in her Dreamwalker series about a psychic sleuth. Maggie won the Silver Falchion Award for Best Cozy/Traditional mystery in 2014. Additionally, she won a National Readers Choice Award and an EPIC award for Best Romantic Suspense. She lives in coastal Georgia, where secrets, heritage, and ancient oaks cast long shadows.

Visit her at www.maggietoussaint.com.

The employees of Thorndike Press hope you have enjoyed this Large Print book. All our Thorndike, Wheeler, and Kennebec Large Print titles are designed for easy reading, and all our books are made to last. Other Thorndike Press Large Print books are available at your library, through selected bookstores, or directly from us.

For information about titles, please call:
(800) 223-1244

or visit our website at:
gale.com/thorndike

To share your comments, please write:
Publisher
Thorndike Press
10 Water St., Suite 310
Waterville, ME 04901